Books by Phoebe Atwood Taylor available from Foul Play Press

Asey Mayo Cape Cod Mysteries

THE ANNULET OF GILT
ASEY MAYO TRIO
BANBURY BOG
THE CAPE COD MYSTERY
THE CRIMINAL C.O.D.
THE CRIMSON PATCH
THE DEADLY SUNSHADE
DEATH LIGHTS A CANDLE
DIPLOMATIC CORPSE
FIGURE AWAY
GOING, GOING, GONE
THE MYSTERY OF THE CAPE COD PLAYERS
THE MYSTERY OF THE CAPE COD TAVERN
OCTAGON HOUSE
OUT OF ORDER
THE PERENNIAL BOARDER
PROOF OF THE PUDDING
SANDBAR SINISTER
SPRING HARROWING

THREE PLOTS FOR ASEY MAYO

Writing as Alice Tilton

BEGINNING WITH A BASH
FILE FOR RECORD
THE HOLLOW CHEST
THE LEFT LEG

PHOEBE ATWOOD TAYLOR

FIGURE AWAY

An Asey Mayo Cape Cod Mystery

A Foul Play Press Book

THE COUNTRYMAN PRESS
Woodstock, Vermont

Copyright © 1937, 1964 by Phoebe Atwood Taylor

This edition first published in 1991 by Foul Play Press, an imprint of The Countryman Press, Inc., Woodstock, VT 05091.

ISBN 0-88150-206-5

All rights reserved

Printed in the United States of America
10 9 8 7 6 5 4 3 2 1

FOR KAY

The island of Billingsgate has for many years rested beneath the waves of Cape Cod bay. No town of Billingsgate exists outside this book, no characters mentioned or described are other than purely imaginary.

CHAPTER 1.

"YOU listen to me, Asey!" Between each word Weston Mayhew paused and banged the top of his desk. "You listen, Asey Mayo! This is important! You've got to—"

The rest of his sentence dissolved into the vast miscellany of noises which for days had been enveloping the Town Hall of Billingsgate.

Listening impartially to the sum total of din, Asey found it difficult to dissect the individual elements. But in a general way, it all began in front of the Hall's viciously Colonial entrance, where a score of men pounded professionally at a nearly completed grandstand. It gained somewhat down in the Women's Club Parlor, whose walls were gradually disappearing under miles of bunting and crepe paper and carpet tacks. Real volume came from the assembly hall, where the moans of vacuum cleaners and floor-waxing machines competed with the practice swings of Upjohn's Merrymakers, hacking away at a popular tune. Everything came to a head outside the selectmen's office. There the dauntless soprano, imported especially from Boston, rehearsed "Billingsgate Beautiful" with forty members of the Grange chorus.

There were of course other noises, but Asey lacked the spirit to delve into them.

"Will you stop making faces and covering up your ears, and listen!" Weston shouted. "You got to, see? You *got*—"

Asey Mayo rose from the window seat, tilted his yachting cap to the back of his head, and grinned at his cousin.

"I *got* to cover 'em up, if that's what you mean," he said gently, during a sudden lull, "or split my ear drums to shreds, I never heard nothin' like this hullabaloo. No wonder you're rampin' around like a wild man. Come off somewheres quiet, where you can start all over at the general b'ginnin' of what's ailin' you. Come on," he took Weston by the arm, "an'—"

Weston drew back. "But I can't! That's just it. I can't go off, Asey, don't you see?"

"Why not? You got the use of your legs, ain't you?" Asey demanded. "Stop bein' so temp'ramental, Weston. This rampin' an' roarin' ain't like you. Come on, now—"

"I can't." Weston sat down at his desk. "I don't dare. That's why I locked the office door. They're after me, the whole bunch. The less time there gets to be, the more they—why, they mobbed me so this morning, they tore my shirt! They all want—"

The noises started up again.

Asey winced as the soprano outside clambered to the high note in the fourth bar and clung there, while the disorganized choristers played vocal tag about her.

"That song, that damn song!" The ordinarily undemonstrative Weston clutched at his forehead and proceeded to unburden himself in a series of shrill yelps, like a man bitten by a number of bees at once. "That cussed song! Banners! Ice cream! That radio guy—blah, blah, blah, Mr. Mayhew! Blah,

FIGURE AWAY

blah, blah! What about the parade torches? And the flagpole? And the fireworks? And the judges. And the exposition. And who's going to meet the governor, the fat hunk of gurry! Who's— Asey, what're you doing, Asey? You—"

Ignoring Weston's protests, Asey folded his pocket handkerchief lengthwise and forcibly bandaged his cousin's head. When a member of his own family took to near-hysterics, something had to be done.

"What're you tying me up for?" Weston yelled. "What— don't unlock that office door! Don't—oh, you gone and done it, now! Now they'll all—"

The second the door opened, people began to surge in. Weston closed his eyes as the questions began to pop.

"Wes, them banners ain't—"

"Weston, who's got the programs? Jeff says you, and Brinley says—"

"Mr. Mayhew," the golden voice of Vincent Tripp arose above the others, "the microphones are not yet—"

After glancing at Weston, Asey cleared his throat, pointed to the improvised bandage, and summoned up his best quarter-deck bellow. Vincent Tripp gasped in admiration as Upjohn's Merrymakers, a floor away, halted abruptly.

"Accident!" Asey roared. "Let us through, please! He'll be back. Gangway—gangway, here!"

He hauled Weston through the crowds of solicitous men, and anxious women who brandished smelling salts and spirits of ammonia. Passing by the Women's Parlor, he caught sight of eighty-year-old Sara Leach, honorary aunt to half the town; her knowing wink heartened him to push through the corridor mobs and out to his car.

Ten minutes later and fifteen miles from the Town Hall,

Asey drew his long blue streamlined roadster to a stop, and pulled out his pipe.

"Now, cousin," he said, "what seems to be your difficulty?"

"Old Home Week," Weston said bitterly, twisting his tie back in place. "Old Home Week."

Asey sighed. Sometimes he wished that the Billingsgate branch of the family were not quite so obtuse. The town's forthcoming celebration was not news. Not, at least, to anyone on the Cape who possessed even a rudimentary use of ears or eyes. Billingsgate Old Home Week posters were tacked on practically every scrub pine. Old Home Week news blared from radios and loud speaker trucks, and everyone had been talking about it constantly for at least eight months.

"Uh-huh," Asey said. "I know. I sort of heard about it. Three hundred years of Billingsgate, an' how it grew. With frostin', an' early settlers—say, I hear you got ole Winslow Billings washed an' scrubbed an' sobered up. I'd be kind of wary about displayin' the last Billings. They're a slow but hard rilin' family."

"Brinley's idea," Weston said. "Asey, listen to me. I called in state cops. The town's full of'em. I got extra constables to handle traffic and crowds and all. I got extra fire wardens, and fire volunteers, and extra coast guards and life guards. I got the Boy Scouts and the Legion all lined up, and then I got a dozen good solid men I know, all armed and posted and ready. I s'pose," he added thoughtfully, "I could get that destroyer up from P-town, if I pulled enough wires. I'd like—"

"Specifically," Asey inquired with a chuckle, "what are you expectin', cousin? Fires, or riots, or just war?"

"You see," Weston went on seriously, "that fool Brinley—J. Arthur Brinley, he thought this Old Home Week up, and

FIGURE AWAY

Uncle Jeff Leach and me, we thought it seemed a good idea. The three of us selectmen, we pushed it through. It was good, and it still is. Only it's got too big. It's got beyond us. That's why I called you over, Asey. Mostly I'm mad, but I'm scared, too." He hesitated. "I—I guess, I'm pretty scared."

Asey looked at his cousin, then took his pipe out of his mouth and transferred his attention to the bowl.

When one of his family, his own family, confessed to being afraid of something, there was no sense to oh-ing and ah-ing and dallying around with useless questions. Weston Mayhew and the rest of the Billingsgate relatives might spell their name the old way, but they were none the less Mayos. They had all the physical hallmarks. Even sitting at a selectman's desk for fifteen years hadn't hurt Weston's waistline. He was tall and lean like the rest. There were mental likenesses, too. The Mayos thought quickly and to the point. None of them were easily moved, but once moved, they went into action. To the best of Asey's knowledge, there were few cowards in the lot, and Weston was not among them. His jugful of war medals and his record in France proved that.

Yet here was Weston, ramping and yelling. Aroused, but dithering. And not just dithering, but admittedly afraid!

"And the trouble," Weston said plaintively, "is that I haven't the time to be scared in. This Old Home Week's got to go over with a bang. Now, Asey, your name means a lot. People know all about you, and the cases you've solved and detected and all, and the chances are that your just being here'll stop this mess. It won't take even a week, either. Just from tomorrow, Tuesday, until next Sunday night. I'll pay you myself, and make you honorary chief of police, or something—"

"Let's get this straight," Asey interrupted. "I got it as far's your bein' scared. N'en I kind of lost track. Where do I come in?"

"As chief of police, or something," Weston said, "you can handle everything. There!" he leaned back against the blue leather seat cushion. "Whew! Am I glad to get that settled! Now, hustle back to the Town Hall. Now this's off my mind, I can cope with that bunch. I can cope with anything, as long as I know what it is I'm coping. Get along, Asey. I got fifty million things to do before tomorrow morning."

Asey laughed, and continued to laugh.

"This isn't funny!" Weston was highly indignant. "And don't you think it is, either! It's no joke!"

"Maybe not, but what's this all about, Wes? What're you scared of? Why'm I supposed to turn into a police chief for? What is this, anyway?"

"Didn't you hear anything I said to you, back there in the office, when I explained?" Weston demanded.

Asey shook his head. "I tried to tell you that the boiler factory had you licked from the start. Oh, I knew you was all het up. You got that much over."

"You mean, you didn't hear about how they tried to set the Town Hall on fire? Or—"

"Who tried to set the Town Hall on fire?"

"I don't know. Or about cutting the grandstands, so's they'd smash down? Or about stealing the town keys, every last one of 'em? Or—"

"Wes, don't you think," Asey began, and then broke off. A look at his cousin's face convinced him that the man was entirely in earnest.

"Or about the shotguns disappearing, or any of the rest?"

"What," Asey asked with great restraint, "what rest?"

FIGURE AWAY

"About someone trying to kill me, and all?"

"'And all'?" Asey repeated. "You mean, there's anything else to add to that?"

"Well," Weston said, "they've tried to get the other two selectmen. Brinley and Uncle Jeff. Only those two are too dumb to catch on. There. There's the whole story. You can take care of it. It'll be a cinch for you. Now, hustle this roadster back off to town."

"You're quite sure," Asey made no attempt to veil the irony in his voice, "you're quite sure that's all there is, are you, Wes?"

"It's all I know, anyway. Start up, Asey. I got to get things going. While I'm busy, you just fix up this mess."

"Wouldn't want me to throw in a solution of the farm problem, would you?" Asey drawled. "Or the labor problem? Or the fiscal problem, or decentral'zation, or somethin'? Wes, be sensible! If one tenth of what you said is true, you need help, an' you need p'fessional help, an' quick. Call in the state cops."

"And get this into the papers?" Weston's eyes narrowed. "Let everyone know? Huh! Asey, what I told you is true. And what's more, you're going to settle the whole business yourself, see? Now you listen. We're a town of around a thousand. We got more'n five thousand coming here to stay for the whole week. We got thousands more tourists coming by the day. We're going to be paid by Philbrick's for broadcasting every day. Quaint old-time town, see?"

"I see, but—"

"And we're going to be a quaint old-time town, see? Nothing's going to spoil it! We're going to make enough out of this coming week to pay up all the town debts, and have a surplus left big enough to pay up roads, and the Town Hall, and the new wharf, and everything. No more relief and unemployment problems for us, see? We're going to wipe out the red ink and start out fresh, and—"

"But Weston, you—"

"And furthermore," Weston's fist was pounding the car door, "furthermore, we've gone and spent so much that if this doesn't go over, we're licked for good! Whatever's going on has got to be stopped, quiet and quick. Nothing's going to keep this Old Home Week from being a success! And whatever's trying to, you got to settle it! See?"

"I got the point," Asey told him, "about five minutes ago. In a nutshell, the fair name of Billingsgate's got to shine till the coffers get filled. It's a patriotic point, cousin, an' well taken. Half a column of sabotage tidin's, an' pop goes the budget. Only I ain't—"

"I never," Weston spoke deliberately, "put any stock in all the chatter about your always being willing to solve cases for rich summer folks, but nobody else. Of course, as a matter of fact, all the problems you took on have been for rich people. I suppose knowing the Porters so well, and all their rich friends, and helping Bill Porter with these cars, you've kind of lost touch with the Cape. I hear you get thousands and thousands of dollars, just finding lost cats and things, and of course I see where you wouldn't be interested in helping out here, for, say, fifty dollars the week. I got some bonus bonds," he added thoughtfully, "and I suppose I could always mortgage the house. It's never been mortgaged in all the two hundred years we had it, but—"

"Now see here, Wes," Asey's tone made Weston feel that perhaps he had gone a little too far. "I don't mind your layin' it on with a trowel, but I do r'sent your bringin' in a steam shovel! You're usin' good Cape tactics—family tactics, 'cause I know'em. But you're headin' the wrong way—"

"I just wanted to—"

"I know. But first off, you know right well the only reason I never took on anything for the folks around here is that they don't get themselves into trouble like summer people an' city people always do. No one hereabouts ever asked me for help, except like for fixin' cars, or boats, or pumps, or houses, or such. An' you know I never took a cent for helpin' anyone in all my life. I don't need money. I got all I want. The only thing I'm tryin' to bring out is this, that if things is as serious as you say, you don't want me. You want real help. You got to put your Week across, an' you can't risk any slips. But if you explain things to the p'lice, they'll keep mum. I'd be glad to help, but—"

"You will?" Weston said happily. "Then you'll settle things? You won't need the cops. Not you, Asey. All you got to do is to see that nothing bad gets out, or happens, until next Sunday. You will, won't you?"

Asey hesitated. He had visions of all the family landing on him if he didn't, and landing with both feet.

"Well," he said at last, "I'll see what I can do. But mind you, if I get bogged with your mal'factors, or tourists, an' microphones, an' if your bonanza dries up on you, don't you go to blame me!"

"I won't, I won't!" Weston said. "You can have anything or anyone you want to help, but it mustn't get into the papers. Nothing must get into the papers, that is," he amended, "but good things."

"Huh. An' furthermore," Asey said, "if I need p'lice help, I'll call for it. And—"

"No, you won't! You can do it all—"

"If I do, I will! Get that, cousin? It's the chance you're takin'. It's your r'sponsibility. I'll see what I can see, but if it's somethin' serious that sticks its head out, well, from then on, I do as I see fit. Golly!" he stopped short and whistled.

"What's the matter?"

"Bluefish," Asey said. "Syl said this morning they was runnin' lickety split out in the bay. We was goin' to take my big boat an' spend the week out there. Oh, well—"

"What do you care?" Weston said as the roadster turned back towards town. "Anyone can catch bluefish, Asey."

CHAPTER 2.

SHORTLY after five o'clock that same afternoon, Asey strolled into the Town Hall by the rear entrance.

Except for occasional thumpings from the basement, the noises had stopped and the crowds dwindled to handfuls. The vacuum cleaners and the waxing machines had done their duty nobly; everything was spick and span, gleaming with an anticipatory polish. Weston had got back onto his job, too. The bulletin boards were covered with schedules in his neat writing, listing every angle of every committee assignment for the entire week.

Grinning, Asey paused to read through the orders of the Welcoming Committee, for whom there was apparently to be never a dull moment. Upjohn's Merrymakers, instruments under their arms, jostled past him to their bus. The captain of the coast guard station called out a greeting as he herded a detachment of Boy Scouts into his big-tired beach truck.

Asey waved and strolled on down the hall to the Women's Club Parlor. Years of experience with the decorations of church fairs, suppers, and similar entertainments told him that the room was Done. He tried to make his survey impartial, but the results still left him with an intense dislike for crepe paper in quantity, and still wishing that Billingsgate had chosen for its official colors some other shades of blue and yellow.

Only a few women lingered in the parlor, and they were too busy packing up tack hammers and aprons, and trying on huge blue and yellow rosettes in front of the mirror, to notice his presence.

He was about to speak to one of them when a girl, a stranger to him, approached him in the corridor. She was a tall girl, good-looking in a dark way, and probably a summer person, he decided from her smartly cut blue overalls and jacket. Bill Porter's wife Betsey had some like those, and he and Bill had howled at New York's prices for faded denim.

"Mr. Mayo? Aunt Sara Leach sent me to—"

"I was huntin' her," Asey said. "Has she gone?"

"Yes. She said she thought you might want her, and I told her I'd wait and take you over to Briar Path."

"Thanks, but my roadster's here. I can—"

"But she said I was to be sure to take you," the girl persisted. "She said that you were to leave your roadster at the garage."

Asey nodded. Aunt Sara Leach had some information for him, and she didn't want everyone to spot that famous roadster at her door.

"Okay. Thanks— God A'mighty, what're those women doin' over there? They just got them quilts up on the wall, an' now they're yankin'em down an' cartin'em off!"

The girl smiled. "They've got the effect," she explained, "and now they're needed. There's a tremendous blanket and quilt shortage, what with the tourist trade, and all the old settlers coming back in droves."

"You mean to tell me," Asey said, "they're goin' to hang

them old quilts up to show'em off by day, an' then rip'em off to take home at night?"

"That's their solution. Half the antiques for the exposition are in a state of flux. And no watchmen to look after all that valuable stuff, either. Why, anyone could come in and twitch a quilt off the wall, or make off with a lustre pitcher. Mary's nearly insane. She thinks it's crazy."

"Mary?" Asey asked.

"Oh, I forgot. I'm Jane Warren. I'm staying with Mrs. Larkin Randall. Mary, that is. My godmother. And her daughter Eloise. Look, take your car to the garage, and I'll pick you up there."

After issuing firm orders at the garage that nothing was to be touched on the Porter roadster, Asey climbed into the girl's battered beach wagon.

"Newcomers to town, huh?" he asked as they rattled along.

"I am, more or less, but Mary and Eloise have lived here a couple of years. They run the antique shop, in Pleasant Valley. You know."

Asey nodded. He had never even heard of the place, but probably the town was re-naming itself for Old Home Week.

"Like antiquin'?" he asked conversationally.

"Filthy business," the girl said bitterly. "All work and no pay. Antiques are all right, if you can afford'em, but I can't be convinced that wormholes make a thing of beauty out of a broken-down kitchen chair. Mary says," she braked to avoid hitting a car and trailer that shot out of a side road, and Asey never learned what Mary said. "Damn the tourists, everything's overrun with them already! I say, isn't Aunt Sara a grand old girl? She may be eighty, but she's a dynamo. Was she born here? I always wondered."

"She don't talk it," Asey said, "on account of goin' to school in Boston. Her father was a senator, an' she kind of caught the dynamo business from him."

"She seems to be a power here."

"Unbeknownst to the general populace," Asey informed her drily, "Aunt Sara has run this town for forty years, since Jeff decided to be a politician."

"Run it?" the girl turned and looked at him. "Oh, I don't think she— I mean, she's not the least bit officious, like that Mrs. Brinley. There's a pain in the neck!"

"That's the beauty of Sara," Asey said. "But she keeps swingin' Jeff to the majority she wants. If Aunt Sara hadn't been for this celebration, there wouldn't of been any. A great postmaster general was lost to the world in her. Tell me, is this week goin' to be a success?"

"It ought to go over." Jane hesitated. "Everyone's worked like a slave, and Weston Mayhew's planned things like a time table. Mobs are coming. The radio'll boom it—oh, what an awful pun!"

Asey wanted to know why.

"Where've you been? Don't you know about General Philbrick, the sponsor?"

"That old ramrod on the point, in the house with all the porches, an' iron deer, an' fountains? That one?"

Jane giggled. "The house that fireworks built. He's the sponsor, didn't you know? Every program begins and ends with fireworks. The town is lousy with fireworks."

Asey laughed. "I can hear old Smoothie announcin' it. 'Billingsgate's Old Home Week, ladies and gentlemen of the radio audience,'" he mimicked the golden voice of Vincent Tripp, "'coming to you through the courtesy of Philbrick's

Fireworks. BOOM!' An' then that town song. Well, it may balance the budget, an' I s'pose you can always r'tire to a hillside an' fill your ears with cotton wool. Huh. So you don't think the week's goin' to work out?"

"I didn't say that. But you can't ever prophesy results, can you, when you cram a lot of humanity into one spot? I mean, there'll be cases of ptomaine, or someone'll steal some of the antique exhibits—they're crying for it. Or cars will smash up. And what with the fireworks, the carron oil business ought to flourish. Maybe it'll go over, though. I'm no seer. Well, Mr. Mayo, here you are. Want me to call for you, or anything?"

"Thanks, but I'll manage," Asey said. "Much obliged for the lift. 'Night, or should I say, 'Boom-boom'?"

The girl laughed, and the beach wagon bounced away.

As he started up the walk to the Leaches' white salt-box house, he caught sight of a slim erect figure in the garden beyond the elm trees. Aunt Sara waved at him.

"It's about time for you to show up, Asey Mayo! I expected you a week ago!"

"Am I a crystal gazer?" Asey demanded. "How should I—"

"You're like your father," Sara said, "and he had an extra sense for spotting trouble, usually a month before it happened. Asey, it's indecent, the way you stay young. How old *are* you?"

"Speak for yourself," Asey told her, with a chuckle. "I'm old again as half, as the sayin' goes. Sara, how do you know about these goin's on? Wes said he was the only one that had caught on."

"Weston Mayhew," Sara observed, "made a fine quartermaster, and he still does. Where did he think it began?"

"Oily rags in the Town Hall basement. That might have been some careless workman."

"But oily rags in the Women's Club Parlor closet, tucked into the best linen, does not mean two careless workmen," Sara said. "That means business."

Asey nodded slowly. "This grandstand sawin'—is that news to you? Well, it didn't amount to a row of pins. I lay it to that dumb relief help. Them fellers don't know a saw from a nail, an' they might well have used half-sawed boards. On the other hand, maybe not. But when you get to the key stealin', an' shotgun stealin', an' someone poppin' at Weston with both barrels of a shotgun, that sort of r'moves it from the ha-ha-boys-will-be-boys class, don't it?"

"When Jeff and I were popped at Saturday night," Sara snapped off two dead zinnias, "Jeff decided it was someone shooting skunks. Brinley laid his to boys, or muskrat shooters, I can't imagine why."

"Wes, he thought of raccoons," Asey said. "Then he took to broodin', an' called me. Know any more? Neither do I. An' my only guess was Weesit, an' that petered out. I find the town of Weesit ain't a bit jealous, it's singin' like a lark over the tourist trade that's spilled their way."

"All profit and no output," Sara said. "I know. My guess petered, too. It wasn't much of a guess, more of a vague wondering. I thought of Slade, the artist—"

"The communist that started the relief rumpus here a year ago? An' all? But say, Sara, I'm sure I saw his name on the Welcomin' Committee. That's why I—"

"He's a welcomer, with white flannels and a blue coat, and a hair cut." A smile played around Aunt Sara's mouth. "He's subsided since I had Jeff make him permanent head of the Planning Board, on a salary. He's a little flighty on sewage, but sound on housing. I rather think he'll die a Republican."

"Givin' him an outlet, huh?" Asey suggested.

"In a way, but I always rather liked the fellow. He has so much spirit, it seemed a pity to waste it. I've had him made the town art committee, too. Did you notice our new planting, and decorations?"

"All I noticed," Asey said, "was the Women's Club Parlor. If he did that—"

"He didn't. That was our Mrs. Brinley. We had to toss her a sop. Anyway, I didn't think anything about Slade, under the circumstances, but I wondered if some of our artist colony, or some of the workmen imported for the county power plant, might have been at work. I called Slade over here Sunday, and talked with him."

"What did he have to say?"

"At first he was so mad he couldn't talk," Sara said, "and then he got so mad he couldn't stop talking. Finally he sat down and made a list of all the mental and moral incompetents we both could think of, and then he investigated."

Asey wanted to know how.

"It was quite simple. All the shootings happened on Saturday night, between eight-fifteen and eight-forty-five. Practically everyone on the list was either seeing Greta Garbo at the movies, or fire fighting at one of the bluff cottages. Slade accounted for the rest. He simply stormed about it. So did Zeb Chase—Zeb's living with us this summer. He— Asey, I hear the car coming up the lane, so I've got to talk fast. Don't let Jeff know. He's got enough to worry him. Whatever's going on we've got to stop. Somehow."

"Wes's made me police head, or somethin'," Asey said. "Honorary, for the week."

"Fine. I needn't have bothered about your car if I'd known

that. Asey, tonight you stroll uptown and make yourself very conspicuous. Let everyone know who you are, and that you're spending the week here, and perhaps—"

"You mean, put on an act?"

"Exactly." Sara gathered up her flowers and started toward the house. "I know you don't want to, but if this is just boys being boys, your presence will put a stop to it. If it's serious, things won't stop. I suppose," she added, "you're quite accustomed to being shot at?"

Asey grinned. "While we're on the subject, Sara, just you stick to crowds for a while, will you, until we get somethin' ironed out? An' don't roam around by yourself, or putter out here in your garden—"

"Oh, I'm armed," Sara told him. "I've a nice cloverleaf Colt under the flowers in that basket you're so gallantly carrying. I've had it since the year Jim Fisk was shot with one just like it. I feel very safe indeed."

Asey looked down at the erect white-haired figure beside him. "I s'pose you know how to use it?"

"Dear me, after all the years I spent traipsing around with father, you ask me things like that! I'm perfectly capable of taking care of myself—after eighty years, I find I'm getting awfully tenacious about life, anyway. Wait— Asey, please do be careful not to let him suspect things—"

She pointed to her husband, just getting out of his car by the front steps. Jeff, Asey thought, grew even more regal as the years passed. He always had looked like the Portrait of a Statesman, in McGuffey's Fourth Reader, and his side whiskers—Asey shook his head. You could only say about them that they resembled a gull in full flight.

"Who's the young feller in the grocer's apron?" Asey asked.

"With Jeff? Why, I told you. Zeb Chase. He's here for the summer."

"I thought you meant old Zeb, of course—what'n time's the son an' heir of Chase's Baked Beans doin' in that outfit? I always heard he was just ornamental."

"He came down this spring, to fish, and it seems," Sara said, "that he got Business. Like getting religion. That's his story. I think myself that it's Jane Warren and not baked beans that spur him on. He's clerking at Matt's. No one expects it to last. Now mind, don't let Jeff suspect!"

Swinging his gold-knobbed cane, Jeff walked over to them. He was obviously delighted to see Asey, and he said as much.

"And you come right in," he concluded, "and stay to dinner."

"Dinner?" Asey said. "You got me for a week. I'm the official Wellfleet del'gation, or somethin'. Weston bullied me into comin' over an' bein' picturesque for the tourist trade. D'you mind?"

"Mind? I wish I'd thought of it myself. Has he got you a badge? Well, I'll get one, and I'll see you have a place in the reviewing stand, and banquet tickets, and all. Wait'll I put it on my list." He pulled a notebook out of his pocket. "More of Weston's ideas, these lists. Very handy. You write things down, and give the pages to someone, and forget all about it. Girl Scouts, or the Ladies' Aid, or someone, do the hard work. For a bachelor, Weston does know how to make women work—"

Sara took Jeff by the arm and started toward the house.

After dinner, young Zeb Chase suggested a trip to town.

Sara threw up her hands in horror at the thought.

"Jeff and I are going to bed early," she announced with a meaning look at Asey, "and get some rest. We've purposely not invited any company for the week, and we've begged out of a lot of events—old age is such a lovely excuse for not doing what you don't want to do anyway—but there is still a lot to tire us. You go with Zeb, Asey, and see if the midway's the gyp I think it's going to be."

"Midway?" Asey said. "But I didn't know that anything started till tomorrow."

"It's a preliminary," Zeb informed him. "To see if things work, and to give the local boys and girls a chance to see things first. We've got a ferris wheel, and a shooting gallery, and a place where you toss rings over electric clocks, and another where you throw darts—all good clean fun, and no fan dancers. Aunt Sara really wanted a fan dancer, but they voted her down. There'll be fireworks, too, and the band's giving a concert. Come one, come all. I'll drive you up."

Once in the car on the way to town, Zeb grew suddenly serious.

"Am I glad you've come! I know more than Aunt Sara thinks. Saturday was my night off, so I came home, and was in the living room reading when I heard the shot by the garage. Sara wouldn't let me go out, but I slid out later, and prowled around. It was a dark night. Down by the foot bridge over the creek, I bumped into someone."

"Who?"

Zeb shrugged. "I chased him, and lost him—and don't look like that! I chased him for twenty minutes. And Bill Porter'll tell you that my only contribution to society is a 4.17 mile. Finally I went back to the house, and after I got in bed, I heard this funny laugh. God, it was awful! I never heard anything like it. It was like a loon, only—well, I can't explain. Believe it or not, I got up and locked my door."

Asey nodded slowly. Weston had mentioned hearing a laugh, when he related the story of Saturday's shooting.

"Oh, well," Zeb was annoyed by Asey's silence. "Maybe it was all done with mirrors. I don't know."

"What time was this shootin' at Leaches'?"

"Around eight-thirty. Aunt Sara and Jeff had gone up for the mail, and they planned to be home for some radio program they listen to. I was just switching it on when I heard the shot."

"That tallies," Asey said. "Wes got his around eight-fifteen, an' the Brinleys don't know exactly, but it must have been in between the other two. Wes an' the Brinleys ain't so far apart, an' it ain't more'n two miles to Leaches'. Zeb, you keep your eye on the Leaches for me—my, my, if this is a sample—why, the World's Fair's a penny candle beside it!"

They drew up at the brightly lighted ball park, and as Asey got out of the car, Weston came up.

"I called up Sara, and she says you're staying there. Look, here's your visitor's badge, and your police badge, and here's a badge Lane of the state police sent along with his compliments when he heard you were going to be here. Put'em on."

Asey surveyed them with distaste. "All? All three?"

Weston pinned them on. "There. Now, I want you to meet General Philbrick. He says he always wanted to ask you about the Blight case, and Vincent Tripp wants you on three programs, so—"

"Gee, look there!" Asey said.

Weston wheeled around to look at the street. When he turned to ask Asey what he meant, Asey and Zeb were gone.

Ten minutes later Zeb called Asey, hidden in behind one of the carnival trucks.

"You can come out. He and Philbrick and Tripp have all driven away. I think you'd be peachy on the radio, Asey. Whyn't you do what the nice man wants? Maybe—" He ducked. "Oh, if that's the way you feel about it! Come on, let's see how good we are."

Within an hour, Asey knew the pitchmen by their first names, and the whole town knew that Asey Mayo had won eighteen blankets, ten boxes of candy, a hundred and seven cigars, four clocks, and an even dozen Shirley Temple dolls. A herd of small boys followed him and Zeb wistfully from booth to booth.

"Nothing left but the glass blower," Zeb said, "and would you really want a glass pen after you got it? And I wouldn't go back to that shooting gallery until I gave the lad twenty bucks for some new gadgets. The bell's busted, too. And look, I take back all my pooh-poohs. If you carry on in other fields as you have here, then you're all they say you are. Wha—"

"A nice doll," Asey said, "for a nice sentiment. Play with it when the bean business is dull. We ain't been on the ferris wheel yet, Zeb. Come—"

The siren on the nearby firehouse broke through the midway noises.

"Two purple lights," Zeb said, "that means out toward the beach. Come along in my car. That's right. Two long and two short. That's the beach. And bells—that means woods, not a house—"

Asey dumped his trophies on the ground and ran after Zeb, and the children panted after him.

"Hey, you left your things! You—"

"Keep 'em." Asey swung onto the running board.

Zeb laughed as they sped along.

"What a problem," he said, "plunder, or the fire? They'll go mad."

He drove too far on the beach road, and by the time they found the brush fire it was practically out. Zeb raced off with a broom, but Asey sauntered over to Slade, who was nursing a burned hand.

"Slade, I met you once in P-town—"

"Hullo, Mayo. Damn these tourists, whyn't they take some care of their filthy fires? Seen Aunt Sara?"

Asey pointed to his badges. "Yup, an' see what it done. I feel like the Women's Club Parlor. Slade, I want to chat with you."

"I want to see you, too. But right now I've got to get this hand fixed, and then move my junk from my studio. If someone hadn't spotted this, the studio'd have gone up in flames. It was headed for it. How's for tomorrow morning?"

"At Sara's." Asey turned away abruptly as he saw Weston, with Philbrick and Tripp, approaching.

He couldn't find Zeb, and the car keys were in the boy's coat pocket. And Weston was clearly hunting for him. Asey grinned, and started back to town on foot. When they inveigled him onto a radio program, it would be because he wanted it.

Deliberately he chose the network of back roads, preferring to get lost than to be picked up by Weston. It was damp there in the lowlands, and he pulled the collar of his shooting jacket up around his neck.

There was a name for this part of town, he thought as he strolled along. Something Hollow. It took him minutes to recall the name. Hell Hollow, that was it. Hell Hollow. There were a lot of stories about it, too, and about the curling mists that rose at night from the swamps and tiny pools.

He tried to remember the legends he'd heard about it years ago in his childhood. It was a place youngsters were threatened with. "Be good, or the bogey man from Hell Hollow'll get you." There was something about a witch, too. The early settlers had ducked her in one of the muddy ponds and packed her off to Boston. Oh, there were lots of things, but he couldn't sort them out. He'd ask Sara about it the next day.

He came suddenly onto a tarred road. He looked ahead, then jumped back and put a hand on his gun.

Ahead of him, under the dim street light, were three weird figures, two women and a man. Two women in bonnets and hoopskirts, and a man in a tall beaver hat and a tail coat. The mist blew around them—they hadn't faces, or feet!

Asey blinked, and then laughed.

Dummies, of course. Dummy figures. Yes, he could see the sign beside them. "Antiques." There was another sign on the street light. "Mrs. Larkin Randall. Antiques."

Asey laughed again. So Mrs. Larkin Randall, the antiquer, had changed the name of Hell Hollow to Pleasant Valley! No wonder he hadn't recognized the location when Jane Warren spoke of it. Pleasant Valley, in this god forsaken hollow full of swamps, and dampness, and that chilly curling mist!

He walked on toward town, past the dummy figures and the squatty house beyond. That house, he recalled, had been a favorite rendezvous of the gay blades of Wellfleet, back in his boyhood. Hell Hollow Minnie had lived in it then. Hell Hollow Minnie wore aigrettes in her hat, had a spanking turnout, and was built on the same general lines as Mae West.

Fireworks began to splutter in the town, and colored balloon lights floated out of the jets of sparks, and then dissolved one by one.

FIGURE AWAY

As he stood there wondering how General Philbrick expected to compete with this lavish display on nights to come, a car whizzed by him, then braked and backed up.

"Where'd you go?" Zeb demanded. "I've hunted high and low and in between for half an hour. How'd you get here?"

"Oh, I been roamin' around," Asey said, "delvin' into the past, like. Your girl friend's fancy figures was like to scare me half to death. I never saw anythin' so creepy, with the mist crawlin' around 'em. If I was a drinkin' man, I'd have signed the pledge an' gone on the wagon by now."

"A lot did," Zeb observed, "the first week those figures were put up. It's a scurvy place anyway. When I was a kid, and we spent summers out at the old beach house, I used to stick my head under the blankets and shiver till we got to the clearing. We never had a horse that could go fast enough past that place to suit me. Boy, look at the General, spreading himself! Aren't they loud? Look, Asey, I want an excuse to call on Jane. Drive back with me?"

"No," Asey said. "Zeb, if this's just the initial blow-out, what's Philbrick plannin' to work up to, a panoramic view of the world war, with special ref'rence to the bombin' of Paris?"

"It's the old come-hither, I guess," Zeb said. "Wow, see that! Yes, I gathered from the gossip at the store that he was going to put on the blazer of a show tonight. By tomorrow, the whole Cape'll have heard, and come to see more. Asey, come on and come calling with me, there's the old sport!"

"No," Asey said, "why should I? B'sides, I want to watch these things. Never had anything like 'em in my day. The most I—"

"Come on," Zeb persisted. "Haven't you any respect for young love? I know Jane's home all alone, because I saw Eloise

Randall up by the ferris wheel. Mary Randall goes to bed at sunset, practically, and either Jane or Eloise has to stay there with her. What's the matter, didn't you like Jane?"

"She's pleasant," Asey said. "Nice lookin'. Wee mite metallic, maybe—"

"Why shouldn't she be a little soured?" Zeb demanded defensively. "Her father was one of the brokers who jumped out of windows in '29, and her mother went off and married a fat Argentine, or some sort of Spig, so as to keep up her standard of living. But Jane and the Spig—oh, well, you've seen it in the movies. Anyway, she's a nice girl. I wish she'd pause and reflect on what a fine catch I am. There's where you could come in, Asey. The old build-up. I need a better build-up. If I bring the great detective along, she'll—boy—was that an explosion! Sounded like a gun. It's spelling something—listen to *that* crash! I bet it's spelling out the words of 'Billingsgate Beautiful.'"

"Get along," Asey said, climbing into the roadster. "Hustle. Turn around an' get going, will you?"

"What? Oh, back to Jane's? Changed your mind, have you? Softened by the glow of Phil—"

"Turn around, an' hustle!"

"What's your hurry?" Zeb backed the car around. "What's the matter with you? First you say no, no calling, not on your life, not by the well known jugful. Next minute you're harrying me to get there in a hurry. Perverse, huh? A new slant on the Mayo character—"

"Will you," Asey thundered, "hurry?"

"But—"

"Stop your chatter, and get there!"

"Oh, all right."

There were things in Asey's tone which compelled Zeb to obey without further flippancy.

He glanced curiously at Asey as he shifted. Odd sort, he decided. Chipper one moment, grim as hell the next. Why, the old boy seemed almost afraid of something!

He shrugged, and pressed his foot down on the accelerator.

It had not occurred to Zeb, as it had to Asey, that the blasting sound of the last piece of fireworks had preceded the flash of lights by a good ten seconds. It had sounded like a gun because it was a gun, behind them somewhere in Hell Hollow. And in that interval between the gun shot and the real sound of the fireworks explosion, Asey's keen ear had caught something that sounded like the cry of a loon.

CHAPTER
3.

JANE WARREN opened the door to Asey's lusty knock, but he noticed that she didn't slip off the guard chain until she saw who was outside on the step.

"Mr. Mayo!" she said. "Why, come in. Look, I'd no idea this afternoon that you were *the* Mayo, the Great Asey! Sara didn't tell me. But Mary said it must be. She was quite excited. She wanted to see you about something, and if she hadn't been so dead tired, she'd have driven over to Sara's. Go into the living room and sit down—oh, turn that radio off, will you, Zeb? The static is simply terrific. I've been trying to get a London concert on the short wave. I'll see if Mary won't get up. It's time for her hot milk, anyway, and she might as well have it in here—"

"Tender way to greet your suitor," Zeb grumbled as Jane went out of the room. "So tender and touching. 'Turn off the radio, punk, the static's lousy.' We might almost be married. Asey, what eats you? Why this Man in the Iron Mask attitude? You wanted to come here, didn't you? You virtually forced me—oh, sit down and stop being grim and tight-lipped! You make me— Jane! Jane—"

FIGURE AWAY

She wavered on the threshold, clinging to the door knob for support. Her face was ghastly under its tan.

"Look after her," Asey said. "She's goin' to faint. Grab her while I see what—"

"What do I do?" Zeb asked helplessly.

"Grab her 'fore she topples, chump! Put her on the couch."

He hurried into the lighted bedroom on the other side of the front hall, stopped short, and swallowed.

For ten minutes he stood there. Then, locking the door behind him, he returned to Zeb and Jane.

"She's dead," Zeb said. "She— Asey, she won't come to!"

From under the girl's shoulders Asey removed three sofa pillows, and thrust them under her knees. Then he swung her head over the side of the couch.

"What're you doing?" Zeb said. "Her head—"

"The idea," Asey informed him, "is for the blood to run that way. Find some whiskey, or spirits of ammonia—find *somethin'*, can't you? Haven't you ever seen anyone faint before? What you modern boys do miss. Prob'ly wouldn't know even how to cut a stay string—"

"Asey, what's happened? What's the matter with Mary Randall? I'm going to see—"

"No, you're not!" Asey grabbed him. "Someone," he said firmly, "that's been killed by deer ball ain't a nice sight to think of, let alone see. If you act this way over a faint, you'd probably faint, too."

"Someone's shot Mary? How? Who? No one in this house—"

"It wasn't anyone in this house," Asey said. "She was sittin' in a chaise longue by the window, an' apparently she leaned forward past the window. As she did, someone outdoors let go with both barrels of a shotgun. Deer ball. Marble size. Now, tend to that girl." He picked up the telephone. "Oh, she's comin' to? Well, get water. Is this a private line?"

"Billingsgate 327," Zeb said vaguely. "I guess so."

Asey cranked at the phone bell. "Hullo, Nellie? Hi. Say, get me Doc Cummings. He is? Get his wife—she out too? Oh. Know where they are? Oh, I see." Asey laughed. "Well, listen. Get him for me, will you? The Warren girl's—yes, up to the Hollow. She's fallen, and knocked herself out. That's right. Fine. Have him call me right back."

Zeb stared at him. "What *is* this?"

"Cummings' wife," Asey said, "is stuck on the ferris wheel up town. That is, the ferris wheel's stuck, an' she's up too high to get down. She's havin' hysterics, an' the doc's havin' a different variety on solid land. Nellie'll get him."

He strolled out into the kitchen and brought back an electric percolator.

"Plug this in, Zeb," he said. "When it seems done, feed Jane some. Okay, youngster? Lay there, an' don't think. You—ah, there's the doc."

He didn't bother with the formalities of saying hello, and asking who it was.

"Listen, Mary Randall's been killed. Shotgun. Deer ball. Through the window. Keep it quiet. Get that state cop Lane, and Weston, and come over. Your wife?" Asey chuckled. "She'll keep. Hustle."

He was still chuckling at the thought of the portly Mrs. Cummings aloft on the ferris wheel when he turned around to the white-faced couple by the couch.

"Asey," Zeb said, "you knew, back there on the road, that it was a gun? That explosion?"

"I wondered," Asey said. "Feel better, Jane? Look, you was here in the house. Didn't you hear the shots? You must have."

She shook her head. "I had the radio going. Not very loud, but it was on the table right by my ear. The static was awful on the short wave, and then the fireworks kept banging. I did hear one awfully loud noise, but I thought it was the fireworks finale. Is she really dead, Asey?"

" 'Fraid so. Jane, did your aunt—"

"Godmother."

"Did she have any enemies?"

"Never heard of one. Dealers and customers both liked her. She—"

"Relatives? What about them?"

"Her husband's dead, her people are mostly in England, and the few over here live on the west coast. She has a daughter, Eloise. She went up town for the goings on, with Mr. Prettyman."

Asey raised his eyebrows. "Mister Who?"

"Prettyman," Zeb said. "Tertius Prettyman. He's in the insurance business. Old Prettyman at the point's son. He's fifty-odd. Look, have you met Eloise, Asey?" He caught Jane's eye. "Oh, well. Well, she's all the near relations Mary had, anyway."

"All and only," Jane said. "I— Asey, I appreciate the way you're beating about the bush, but let's have the worst. What is it?"

"Without meanin' the least disrespect to Mrs. Randall," Asey told her, "the worst'll be to blow this Old Home Week sky high, an' to put the town in debt so much it'll never recover. This sort of thing acts two ways. Some few folks'll come to gape. But the majority'll leave as fast as their cars'll start, particularly when they learn how this happened. I'd say that ninety-five percent of the people who've planned to spend the week here, they'll look at the thickness of their walls, an' consider how many times they pass by a lighted window, an' promptly exit. Until we get to the bottom of this, the headlines'll be 'Madman Loose,' or 'Maniac At Large.' You, an' Miss Randall, you'll get headlines too."

"For me especially." Jane gulped down some coffee. "Because whereas you've not made a point of it—well, they'll arrest me, won't they? No one will ever believe in this world that I could sit here in this room, and not hear what happened. And there's a shotgun out in the shed, too."

"Whose, yours?"

"It belongs to Zeb. He left it here once, and forgot about it," Jane said.

"My God, Jane, did I?"

"You did, and I wasn't going to dash after you with it. You're so impulsive, you might have misunderstood. Anyway, the gun's there, and I'm here, and all the town heard me say up in the Club Parlor today that I hadn't a cent except what Mary gave me, and that I was afraid of being fired almost any time. I was joking, but it won't be a joke tomorrow."

"They won't," Zeb said. "They can't!"

"I'm used to headlines," Jane told Asey. "When father died, I was five hundred miles away at school, but you might have thought I pushed him out of the window. When mother married the Spig—oh, but why go on! I'm used to it. Shakespeare wrote a sonnet once about how if you got the worst at first, then you were more containder about the remainder. Or something. Maybe it was Nash. Zeb, aren't you glad I never decided to marry you—"

"If you'll marry me tonight—" Zeb said.

"Don't be quixotic!" Jane said. "Think of your father and the headlines. 'Baked Beans Heir Jilts Suspect Fiancée. Romance Ends in Old Home Killing'—d'you suppose they'll call it 'The Old Home Killing'? Asey, I don't mean to gabble on so, but I feel wound up. I—well—I feel desperate, if you want to know. Oh, Asey, I simply adored Mary, and she's been so marvelous to me!"

Zeb put his arm around her, and she cried on his shoulder.

"Look after her," Asey said. "I hear a car."

He went out as Dr. Cummings, and Lane of the state police, both calm and professionally expectant, got out of a sedan. In the back seat was Weston, sitting like a statue. Despair was written all over him.

"Oh, come, Wes," Asey said. "It's bad. It's awful. But nothin's as bad as you look. Cheer up, man! Lane'll settle this for—"

"It's the end," Weston said. "It's in the contract."

"In the what?"

"Contract. Philbrick's contract. We're going on the air as a quaint old-fashioned New England town. And if—"

"If you ain't, you get the air? I see. Well, come in, an' let's see what we can do."

Dr. Cummings looked around the bedroom and backed hastily out into the hall.

"Someone loathed her like poison," he observed, "or else we have a maniac loose. So someone waited outside, and shot at the shadow of her head on the window shade? What a— Asey, I feel responsible, in a way. She wasn't well when she first came to town, and I suggested among other things that she go to bed early, since she had her business to run during the day. She kept the early-to-bed habit up, I don't know why. Everyone in town knew about it, of course. There's a book—was she reading?"

"Guess so," Asey said. "N'en she leaned forward to get a cigarette from that box. Tell me, what was she like?"

"Mary was very pleasant, and she knew her business. Used to be a buyer for some New York firm, and it blew up, and she landed here. Seemed to enjoy burying herself out in this hell hole. Said she made a living. She's got some fine stuff out in her shop in the barn. Had a lot of customers, and did her rubbing and restoring and finishing all herself. Great worker, very competent woman."

"Enemies?"

"She got on well with everyone. Of course she got the women up on their heels once in a while, but they all like her except Brinley's wife. Damn fool, that Brinley woman. Thinks she knows it all. Took a course in interior decorating once, and no one's allowed to forget it. Awful row over the Club Parlor."

"Who won?"

"Mary, hands down. Then Bessie claimed that Mary was only after a chance to unload her antiques, and make a profit. Lot of fuss. Turned out to be a nice room, though. Well, let's get busy. Going to be nasty for the town. Any way out?"

"Of keeping it quiet? Maybe," Asey said. "Maybe, if—say, what's the daughter like?"

Dr. Cummings looked at him over the rims of his glasses.

"I'm not a psychiatrist, or a psychologist," he announced cryptically. "I'm just a plain country doctor, with the misfortune never to have delivered anything more bizarre than triplets and a two-headed calf. Will you tell Lane and Weston to come here, and bring Lane's camera, and all that stuff."

FIGURE AWAY

Half an hour later, Asey went into the living room.

Zeb and Jane still sat on the couch, staring at the pattern of the hooked rug before the fireplace. Weston, his face a yard long, sucked at a dead pipe in the corner. He wore the sort of expression usually reserved for funerals, or automobile accidents, or various other forms of sudden death.

"Where are the rest?" Jane had passed the stage of flippant desperation, and was now resigned and nearly normal except for the redness of her eyes.

"What rest?"

"Oh, police and all. Coroners, and reporters, and things like that."

"Doc's medical examiner for this part of the world," Asey said. "Wes is the town, an' the law, an' I'm actin' head of the police here. Lane's the state outfit. Don't need more, unless you want it to be fancy. Lane's a detective. He's done what you might call the needful. Say, when is Eloise due?"

"She should have been home long ago," Jane said. "It's awfully late for her. You don't suppose—but then nothing could happen to her. She's with Prettyman."

"She's stuck on the ferris wheel," Weston said dismally, speaking for the first time in twenty minutes. "Top seat, with Tertius. No ladders to reach, and she said she wouldn't crawl down one anyway. Neither would Mrs. Cummings. She's just below, with Bessie Brinley. The rest were all kids, and they managed to wriggle down somehow. Oh, I knew something would happen! I knew, it was bound to. I knew it would!"

"What would happen," Jane interrupted, "if we didn't let anyone else know?"

"Why, we've got to!" Weston said. "Haven't we, Asey? How could we keep it quiet? We can't."

"You're the town," Jane said, "and you know. Your police chief knows. The state cops and the coroner, or whatever you call him, they all know. And Zeb and I. Eloise'll have to, but why any more? Why can't we keep it a secret until after the week is over? It's all so horrible, and letting people know will be even more horrible—"

"We can't," Weston said. "There's the funeral, and the undertaker, and that smashed window, and the mess of that room. All sorts of things. How'd you explain about Mrs. Randall's not being around? How could—oh, it's just impossible. It can't be done."

"Wait now," Jane said. "I hear the beach wagon coming up the drive. Eloise—she probably took Prettyman home. I thought I heard it going past a few minutes ago—"

Asey watched the door expectantly. This Eloise had been mentioned any number of times, but people had shied away from personal description. Usually that meant someone was crippled or disfigured. Perhaps she had a wart on her nose, or was minus an eye. He didn't even know if she were in her twenties, like Jane, or if she were in her forties.

Forties. He almost said it out loud as she entered. Middle forties, stoutish, reddish brown hair beginning to show streaks of grey. Nothing the matter with her that he could see; she had the proper number of eyes and ears and arms and legs.

She looked from one to another in the group.

"Why, Jane! I didn't know that you planned— I mean, I didn't hear you say anything about a party! I'm *sure* Tertius and I would have preferred—so very distressing, up on that wheel. You know I'm always glad to help. Always. Sandwiches, or even a cake. I'm sure there's no necessity for your making

FIGURE AWAY

any secret of your parties, my dear—tch, tch!" she clucked her tongue. "And that coffee pot, right on the rug!"

She put her hat on the table, and somehow managed to knock off two books, an ash tray and a lamp in the process.

"I'll fix'em," Zeb said. He was watching Asey out of the corner of his eye.

"Very nice of you, I'm sure—won't the rest of you gentlemen sit—oh, Mr. Mayhew. I'm *so* glad you're here—I think it's only fair to tell you that the ferris wheel—really, the things those men who owned it said! So very unsafe—oh, why, Dr. Cummings! Your wife is so very distressed! She couldn't find you—"

"She'll survive," Cummings said brusquely. "Asey, you tell her—no, on second thought, I will. The rest of you go into the kitchen, or somewhere."

Asey drew Zeb out into the hall.

"What—"

"The doctors," Zeb said, "call it loose association, if you mean Eloise. Myself, I'm inclined to be a little more Freudian about Miss R. Tell me, *is* there any chance of keeping this reasonably quiet for a while?"

"D'pends on Eloise. Tell me, do they keep any servants here?"

"Only Lina for washing and ironing. I think she comes a couple of days a week. Eloise and Jane do most of the housework between them—what did you say?"

"I said," Asey informed him, "I'd hate to have to make a Lady Baltimore cake with Eloise at my elbow. I'd end up with mint sauce. On the other hand, I wonder what kind of a cook she'd be—oho. Doc's back. He got through it quicker than I thought he would. What's the verdict?"

Cummings wiped the perspiration from his forehead. "It

was easier than I hoped for. She took it very well. Feels badly, of course, but—she wants to see Jane."

"Really," Cummings added as Jane went back into the living room, "I hand it to Eloise. I was all set for some first-class hysterics, but she rose to the occasion like a lady. You have never seen hysterics until you've seen what Eloise can do along that line. That time she fell overboard from Baxter's boat! Well, maybe we can swing it, Asey."

In a few minutes Eloise called to them.

"Will you come in here? Jane, you tell them what we have decided—although I'm sure I can't help feeling that there's something very wrong about it, but of course if you and the rest feel that—I suppose the majority always knows—tell them, Jane."

"Mary loved this town," Jane said. "I think that matters tremendously. So does Eloise. Mary would have hated to think that because of this awful thing happening to her, and us, and all, that the town should suffer the way it will if this is all made public right away. It's an awful thing. A terrible thing. We're going to find out who did it. But we think if it can be kept quiet until next week, why shouldn't it? After all, everyone knows who's supposed to know, and there's no law about having to tell Winchell and the tabloids and the papers, is there?"

"But I don't see how we can!" Weston said. "How can we, Asey? We can't, can we, doc? Lane, what do you think?"

Asey picked up a pad and pencil from a desk.

"Let's go into a huddle," he said. "Let's see. First of all, I can fix up the window and the shade so they won't be noticed. We can fix the room itself and lock it up. Now, Wes, you can make a note of Mrs. Randall's death in the town records, but do you have to tell?"

FIGURE AWAY

"In the town report, it—"

"And the town report comes out once a year. In other words, note it, but don't tell till you have to. Don't even put the notation where anyone might see it."

"I *got* to—"

"All right, then enter it and put your book in the bank vault. That's that. Now, Cummings, you can manage the death certificate and an undertaker, can't you? Haven't you some relative who's an undertaker?"

"Well, he calls himself a mortician," Cummings said, "but he owes me for his last two children and his appendix."

"All right. Doc, you an' Lane'll have to go to him tonight, in the beach wagon, an' leave the car there. I'll—no. Zeb will follow, and bring you back. Can you fix things with your wife, doc, or shall I?"

"You, very definitely."

"Okay. I'll see to it, an' I'll drive to Weesit an' phone Porter in New York, an' have him phone back here to Jane."

"Why?" Jane asked.

"He'll pretend to be a cousin, an' say Mrs. Randall must go to New York b'cause of serious illness in the family. A telegram won't do. It would be phoned here from Hyannis tonight, an' I want the phone girls here to know about it d'rect. Help spread the news. Anyway, it's got to appear that Mrs. Randall's gone to New York, drivin' alone in the beach wagon."

"This is a charming house," Eloise said timidly, "of course as I always said to our friends, lovely panelling, fine lines and all, but—well, I mean, it's just a wee, wee bit—"

"Remote," Asey finished for her. "I thought of that. You an' Jane had best go to Sara's. Day times you can come back an' carry on, but nights you spend there. You can explain it by sayin' that you want to be near the cel'bration at night, an' haven't any car. Everyone knows that keepin' you would be like Aunt Sara—"

"There," Weston said, "see? Then Sara'll have to know. And Jeff, too. You see, you can't keep it quiet. It gets complicated right off the bat!"

"Sara already knows a lot, Wes. She an' Jeff are safe, anyway. Now, let's make a stab at this, an' see how long we can hold out for Billingsgate's budget. Lane an' doc an' Wes an' I will get to work."

"But I've got Old Home Week!" Weston protested. "I've got—"

"You got it like a rash," Asey retorted. "Well, you go an' Old Home Week, an' we'll get started. I'll use some of Lane's men, I know most of'em. Now, we'll get into the d'tails, an' get our stories fixed, an' get to work."

At half-past-four the following morning, Asey and Zeb wearily returned to Aunt Sara's. Jane and Eloise had been brought there earlier.

"Asey," Zeb said as they undressed, "d'you understand any of this? Things at first seemed to be directed against the town, but this—what's anyone got to kill someone like Mary for? It's a maniac—remember that laugh?"

"Yup, I heard it t'night."

"When?"

Asey told him. "It's all the same thing, Zeb. Shotgun—'course, it was deer ball an' not buckshot, but that don't matter much. The first shootin' was just a warnin'. This was meant to be— an' was—final. It's all part of the same muddle."

Zeb didn't believe it.

"Oh, come now," Asey said. "'Member what Jane said tonight, that Mary was anxious to see me about somethin'? My guess is that Mary Randall found out somethin' by accident, somethin' more'n you an' Sara an' Wes an' I ever knew. Someone discovered that she found out, an' someone seen to it she never had a chance to tell. She—say, hear that? Listen!"

Asey snapped off the light.

"What—"

"It's our friend, givin' us the razz—no, get away from that window. No, we ain't goin' out, neither. Not on your tintype!"

"Why not, Asey? It's that laugh—"

"Do you want a deer ball through your head? He's hopin' real hard we'll fall for it, but we ain't goin' to. When anyone taunts you like that, you can be sure you'll lose the tag game. Roll over an' get to sleep. I am."

He turned over on his side, and within ten minutes he was producing light but convincing snores. Then he half sat up in bed and made some experimental sounds, but Zeb was too fast asleep to hear them.

Grinning, Asey picked up his rubber-soled shoes, and Zeb's sweater, and slid out of the room.

The window at the end of the hall was open. He unhooked the screen, leaned out, and gripped the branch of the maple tree that rested on the slant roof. The window was small, but he squeezed through and swung onto the branch. Slowly he edged down the branch to the trunk, propped himself there some twelve feet above the ground, and waited.

The breeze rippled through the leaves and swayed the branches above him. Over by the swamp, frogs were croaking. Far away on the shore road an automobile horn barked. He could just hear the boom and smash of the breakers on the outside beach— Asey opened his eyes wide. Someone was coming, up from the swamp. Someone had just crossed the narrow wooden foot bridge over the creek.

He leaned forward and peered through the branches, but it was still too dark to distinguish anything.

The footsteps came nearer, scrunched across the gravelled space by the garage, tapped on the flagstone walk that led from the garage to the house. If the person, whoever it was, stayed on that walk, he would have to pass directly beneath Asey.

Quietly, he pulled aside a branch, and waited.

CHAPTER 4.

ASEY'S hand flashed under his sweater and his borrowed pyjama top to the old forty-five nestling in his shoulder holster. Then his hand dropped.

It dawned on him belatedly that the person was a woman, and that the tapping on the stones came from her high heels. And now he could hear the swish of silk, and see a skirt swirl in the breeze.

The woman strolled past the tree, and Asey very nearly fell on top of her.

There was no mistaking that white hair. The woman was Sara Leach.

Open-mouthed, he watched her walk to the front door, open it, and disappear inside the house.

Asey slid down the tree trunk, jumped and noiselessly followed.

"See here, Sara," he demanded, "what's the idea of this? What—wha—"

Aunt Sara finished locking the front door, put the key carefully under a jade vase on the hall table, walked past him without saying a word.

Keeping just behind, Asey followed her upstairs and along the hall to her room. The door closed softly as she went inside.

Asey leaned against the wall and wiped his forehead against the sleeve of Zeb's sweater.

Only once before had he ever encountered a sleepwalker. That was on the "George P. Cram"—no, it was the "Joshua N. Cram," and he had waked up just in time to wrench a machete from the hands of the West Indian cook as the latter swung at the second mate.

With a shrug, he tiptoed back into his own room and crawled into bed.

It was unthinkable that Sara had anything at all to do with this business, with the shotguns Saturday, or the killing of Mary Randall, or anything else. But her wandering around made him uneasy. Very likely it was a regular habit of Sara's to take a stroll every night down by the swamp. But how long had she been there, and what about that crazy laugh? It was all screwy.

Out of the whole mess only one real fact emerged; someone had something against Billingsgate. It might be a grudge against the town itself, or perhaps someone wanted to blank the celebration. Anyway, the person had issued plenty of warnings about how he felt, and now he was getting right down to business.

Why, Asey wondered, all this paving of the way? Apparently the fellow had nothing against Brinley or Weston or the Leaches. The selectmen didn't figure. If they did, why hadn't the fellow shot at them instead of just aiming to one side of them with buckshot?

Anyway, by some accident Mary Randall had become aware of whatever this person had in mind, probably stumbling

FIGURE AWAY

nearer to the truth than she comprehended. At least, she understood enough to want to see him and tell him things. But someone anticipated that, and took good care that nothing of the sort happened.

That led to Jane.

He didn't know about Jane Warren. She had been a bit sour on the antique business that afternoon. What was that crack of hers— "All work and no pay." Something to do with the Randalls or the antiques had annoyed her. But if she were as destitute as she claimed, and if she was supported solely by Mary Randall, it hardly seemed that Jane would deliberately kill her benefactor and employer. Perhaps in some way she would benefit by Mary's death. Maybe she inherited the antique business or some money. Perhaps it was something more indirect; clearly Eloise was too scatterbrained to carry on by herself, and Jane would profit thereby.

With the radio going, and the static and the fireworks, it was possible that she had not heard the shotgun. Offhand, it wasn't very credible. And most people, when they were confronted with a murder, promptly began to tell how innocent they were. Jane had taken the other attitude and offered herself up as a sacrifice.

After cleaning up Mrs. Randall's room and fixing the window, Asey had gone over the entire house from attic to cellar, and investigated Zeb's shotgun in the shed. It was covered with the chips and sawdust and dirt of the woodpile, and the barrels hadn't been touched for a month of Sundays. He could find no trace of any other weapon, nor could Lane. But that didn't mean that there wasn't any.

After Jane and Eloise had gone to Sara's, he had even read through Mary Randall's diary, but that cast no light on the affair. From it he picked up enough to know that Mrs. J. Arthur Brinley was more of a thorn in Mary's flesh than anyone guessed, and that Jane cared far more about selling antiques than rubbing or restoring them, or tracking them down. Mrs. Randall had been rather plaintive about Jane's lack of what she called "stick-to-it-iveness." There were numerous items about Eloise. A lot dealt rather resignedly with her clumsiness, like breaking some Stiegel glass, and smashing up the beach wagon's fenders again, and once or twice she mentioned Eloise's inability to take a stand or make a decision. Asey remembered one sentence, "She is so good to me, and works so hard, and means so well, but she does clutter, with the things she says as much as the things she does."

Asey thought he knew exactly what Mary Randall meant.

Well, Jane would have to be looked into. For fun he would check up on Aunt Sara, although he knew it was a futile gesture. Zeb didn't enter into it, or Eloise. That ferris wheel was a rock bottom alibi, if ever one existed or was needed.

He turned over, closed his eyes and slept soundly until Aunt Sara banged on his door at nine o'clock.

"Asey, Jeff and I have to go," she called to him. "Zeb's already driven the girls to the hollow, and gone to work, but he said he'd leave any time if you wanted him. Sally or Bertha'll be here all day long, and get you any meals you want. I'm leaving a program for you—"

"Hey," Asey scrambled out of bed, "wait till I—"

"I simply can't wait. Really. I'm the sheep and lamb sorter for the Old Returning Settlers! Bye—"

Asey looked out of the window at the open official car with its flying blue and yellow streamers in which Jeff and Sara drove off in state behind a uniformed chauffeur.

FIGURE AWAY

"All they need," he murmured, "is ticker tape."

At breakfast he propped the official program against his coffee cup and read doggedly through the events of the day.

Tuesday was Old Settlers' Day, and began with a town flag-raising at nine-thirty. School children, the chorus, and the soprano would render "America."

"Aha," Asey said. "Render is right, but rend'd be better—don't mind me, Bertha, I'm just carried away by it all."

After "America" and "Billingsgate Beautiful," the remainder of the morning was devoted to a reunion of Old Settlers at the various churches, an address of welcome at the Town Hall, and at twelve-thirty there was to be a luncheon for the lambs, given by the selectmen in the Women's Club Parlor. The sheep and goats had to buy themselves a box lunch, which a footnote described to the last stuffed olive.

The afternoon was more or less mutilated by baseball, Billingsgate All-Stars versus Philbrick's Fireworks Nine. That night, Upjohn's Merrymakers would hold a grand open air concert at the canopied dance floor next to the ball park. Free. The midway carnival offered fun for all, and the movies were right on deck with two brand new features for the price of one, free souvenirs, a sterling-silver-plated coffee urn for the prize ticket, and a Mickey Mouse to boot. Everything ended up with fireworks. Events marked with an asterisk would be broadcast.

Asey sighed. "Just readin' it," he told Bertha as she brought in more coffee, "makes me feel tired an' old before my time. If they keep up that pace all week till Sunday, they'll be limp slivers of skin an' bone."

"Tomorrow's Governors' Day," Bertha said. "Three governors. It'll be like today, except all the things to do with them, and speeches and a banquet. Thursday's Billingsgate Day. Tag day for the new hospital they want, and they're going to lay the cornerstone of a new library addition. Everything's to do with the town, sort of. Friday's Historical Day."

"What's that?"

"I don't know, much," Bertha said honestly. "Speeches, I guess, and drives to points of interest, like where the British nearly landed in 1812, and where the Pilgrims didn't land, and where they think those Icelanders passed by. You know."

Asey nodded. "History marches past, or Chance-to-get-a-good-rest Day. Go on."

"Saturday's Cape Cod Day. That's going to be swell. Water sports and field sports. All the towns got teams entered. Yacht races, golf matches at the club, and all. Dances, and a Great Mommoth Ball, all free. And that's the day they give the prizes for the expositions at the Town Hall. I've got some beachplum jelly entered."

"If it's anythin' like your marmalade," Asey said, "it gets my vote right now. Couldn't enter popovers, could you? No, I suppose they are kind of perishable. Say, I tell you what. I'm goin' to give my prize for'em right now."

He pulled out his wallet and impressively counted out ten crisp one-dollar bills.

"For me?" Bertha's eyes opened wide.

"For the popovers. 'Course, you got to figger it's only six dollars, what with money leapin' around. Bertha, tell me about Sunday, an' then I won't have to look at that yallery-blue program any more. What's Sunday?"

"Church Day. Did I tell you about the broadcasts, and the fireworks, and the clambakes? And parades, and horribles, and the band? And the summer camps, they're putting on a show, and Mike Slade has some sort of show, too—"

"Say," Asey interrupted, "that r'minds me. Did Slade come here this morning for me?"

"No." Bertha hesitated. "What do you make of him?"

"Seems all right. Friend of yours?"

"I went out with him a couple of times when he first came to town. It wasn't much fun, he talks all the time. He said it was wrong for me to work here. Can you beat it? Like I told him, anyone who works here is lucky. Good room, and food, and wages, and you always know what's going on. Where else'd I work, I asked him. Who's going to support my mother if I don't, I said. But he said I was being exploited. I looked up 'exploit' in the dictionary, and it said, 'brilliant achievement.' I couldn't see anything wrong about that. Aunt Sara laughed when I asked her, and said exploit meant my cooking—"

Bertha chatted on, and when she showed any signs of running down, Asey supplied new subjects. Gradually he led her to talk of Sara, but at the barest suggestion of her sleepwalking, Bertha shut up like a clam and retired to the kitchen.

"Huh," Asey said.

He took his roadster from the garage and drove over to the little one-roomed house Slade had built for himself on the outskirts of town.

The door was open, and the house was empty. On an unmade bed were laid out immaculate white flannel trousers and a blue coat with brass buttons. There were fish hooks and lines on the table.

"I bet," Asey said, "he's playin' hookey an' gone fishin'. But—"

A young man came to the door as Asey left.

"Mike there? Damn him, where is he! He's not at his studio, either. Never saw such a—have you seen him? Well, if you do, tell him he's got work to do, and to get to the Town Hall in a hurry. If this is the way he—"

Grumbling, the young man got into a blue-and-yellow-draped car and tore off.

Asey drove back up the beach road to Hell Hollow. Jane waved a hand to him from the shop, where she was taking care of a dozen customers. Lane, in dirty khaki pants and a flannel shirt, was mending a lawnmower.

"I wouldn't know you," Asey said, "how do you do it?"

"Rumpled my hair, dirtied my face, that's all. There's an advantage in being nondescript. People who've seen me in uniform don't know me in plain clothes, and the other way around. Asey, this business is not so hot."

"Can't find any trace of a shell?"

"I've raked high and low, and not a thing. He stood in a line—what's the matter?"

"I'm lookin' at them fool figures," Asey said. "Those dummies. There are four of'em. I only counted three last night."

"One fell down," Lane said. "It was on the ground this morning. Has dropsy. It's fallen down four times since. I'm going to mend it after I'm through with this mower. Listen, from where those balls were in the wall, he stood in about the line of you and the house and that big pine. That's the line. I wouldn't know what distance away. Probably over by the garden. Asey, this lad's got us. D'you realize that?"

Asey nodded. "No shell, no nothin'. We can't tell anythin' about any gun unless we have that shell. Whyn't he use a pistol, so's we'd have somethin' to work on with a bullet? Anyway, without the shell we can't tell the gun, an' without the gun we can't tell the man. An' even if we guess someone, an' he's got a shotgun, that don't prove a thing. We got to find that shell, an' we got to find it here."

"Probably," Lane said, "the gent thought of that, and deposited the shells and gun out in the Atlantic. I've been wondering about the ball end of it. We might find out who bought any deer ball at Harry's—"

"But the ball could have been bought in Timbuctoo," Asey said. "It's like tryin' to find out where someone bought a stick of chewin' gum from the wrapper. This is kind of a clever way of killin' someone, ain't it, Lane?"

"We've got a dozen shotgun murders on the files," Lane said. "One since 1914. We still putter around with it in our spare time. I sort of think, Asey, you're not going to have any Garrison finish in this case. You might just as well dig in for the winter. All you've got is the fact that she was killed last night by someone with a shotgun out here."

"And the laugh."

"That? It's probably a real live loon, or someone faking. And have you thought, Asey, that there are going to be a lot of fireworks to come?"

"It's preyin' on me," Asey said. "Too much free noise for our lad to fire under cover of. While we might be able to keep one murder quiet, we can't cope with any more. Gimme the wrench—"

He bent over the lawnmower as some of the customers approached the figures.

"Mornin'," he looked up and spoke to Jane. "Wonder if I could bring over that footstool for you to fix up? Do I hear that Mrs. Randall's gone to New York?"

The two local women in the group drank in the information.

"Illness in the family," Jane said. "I'd be glad to tackle the footstool—oh, and Mrs. Porter's things!"

"I'll have to take'em piecemeal," Asey said—all this conversation had been previously arranged, "they're sort of breakable, an' need a lot of packin'. I'll be round for'em. Thanks." He nodded towards Lane. "If he don't do a good job for you, let me know. So long."

It was on his way back to town that he met with the soprano who had been practising with the chorus the day before at the Town Hall. She was pushing a bicycle with a flat tire, and Asey gallantly stopped and offered aid.

"Like to put it in the rumble an' drive back?"

"Thanks." The woman was rather massive, and Asey suspected that she was more or less unaccustomed either to bicycling or walking. "I didn't expect this. And I tell you now, as far as bicycling goes, my figure can stay where it is!"

She was so emphatic about it that Asey grinned.

"You're the soprano, ain't you?" he asked as he lifted the wheel into the rumble. "Madame—"

"M-e-a-u-x," she spelled it out. "Not Moo. The next one who moos at me is going to get his teeth pushed in. You," she surveyed with admiration the sixteen-cylindered Porter, "are not a native, are you?"

"Not of this town, so go as far's you like," Asey said. "Tell me, what do you *really* think of 'Billingsgate Beautiful'?"

Madame Meaux looked at him. "Don't! Mrs. Brinley brought me here—she'd heard me at a Women's Club convention—and I'm grateful, and all that, but I didn't know about 'Billingsgate Beautiful' until I got the contract signed. She wrote the words, and the music. And the music, mind you. Let's just pass over Sister Brinley. I want to have kind thoughts about her till Sunday night. I get paid Sunday night. She pays me. Words, mind you, and music, both! Why, the words alone should carry twenty years to life with'em! Say, after you leave this bicycle some place, could you take me down the road a bit? I want to see a man named Slade."

"Mike Slade?"

"Yes. I didn't know he lived here, but I bumped into him last night at the carnival. I was with Sister Brinley—say, she got stuck on the ferris wheel, and I nearly died laughing! Anyway, Mike gave me the high sign—I guess he and Mrs. B. don't click—and later when he got a chance, he said to drop in on him. Great lad, Mike."

"Known him long?"

"Well, I was working on a theater project a couple of years ago, and he was on an art project, and we were in the same office. He got kicked out. Too wordy. Gee, he was sore last night about something. He looked just the way he did when Blickstein—he was our director—fired him."

"That must have been after the fire near his studio," Asey said. "He was only a little sore when I saw him—but say, he ain't home. I just been there. He's probably been found and put to work by now. He's a big shot here, you know."

"He's all right, really," Madame Meaux said, "except he likes to talk, and he gets sore easy—well, if he's not around, leave me here at the garage, and I'll get home on that thing somehow. I ought to rest, anyway. I got to sing with the rhythm cats tonight, and I need a rest—"

"With the what?"

"The yokel swingsters. Upjohn's Merrymen, or whatever they call themselves. Thanks. Be seein' you."

Asey waved and set off for the Town Hall. He had a higher

opinion of sopranos, somehow. And it would take considerable force, he felt, to compel this one to warble the ditty about tying apples to a lilac tree.

J. Arthur Brinley stopped him as he entered the Town Hall by the rear door. Asey knew it was J. Arthur, because his badge said so. There was even a hint of proclamation in the inch and a half high letters.

He was a short, fat pompous little man, and Asey wondered if the shoulder seams in his blue flannel coat could take it until Sunday.

"Er—Asey Mayo? I understand from Weston that you're helping the town, and I want you to know we appreciate—"

Asey barely listened to the little speech. He had a definite feeling that J. Arthur wanted something, and he waited rather impatiently for the preamble of thanks to finish.

"Now I know," Brinley said, "that you will be able to do the town one great service. I refer to Slade, who has—well, I hate to say it, but he has communistic tendencies. I know, Mr. Mayo, that you will be able by tactful methods—or other methods if necessary—to restrain him."

"What's he done?" Asey asked.

"My wife and I have always felt that Jeff and Sara Leach rather overstepped, if you know what I mean, when they campaigned for him, and actually allowed him a place on the town board. When you allow a communist, an avowed communist, to become a town officer like anyone else, well, as I said to my wife, that is stretching the democratic form of government a little too far!"

"Well, yes," Asey said, "seems that way, don't it?"

His bland expression never wavered as Brinley looked at him sharply.

"Well," Brinley said, "you will restrain him, won't you? Why it was disgraceful last night, the way he was ranting around about that brush fire! All over town. Some of our guests were most disturbed, and indeed they had every right to be! It's what comes, as I said to Bessie, of letting—"

"Uh-huh. But after all, his studio did nearly burn up, an' he charred his hand. Sort of had some provocation, don't you think? He wasn't just rantin' for the sheer love of it, was he?"

"Why, I—"

"Brinley!" Vincent Tripp beckoned to J. Arthur from the door. "Brinley, quick—er—quickly!"

J. Arthur bustled off, and Asey followed leisurely to the large assembly hall, which was overflowing with people. Old Settlers, he assumed, since most of them looked both old and settled.

Up on the stage Sara looked cool and poised and unperturbed. Jeff, sitting directly beneath the American flag, was picturesque and imposing, and more of a McGuffey's statesman than ever. He caught sight of Weston in the background, issuing orders like a major-general.

"The welcome," J. Arthur was saying, "the welcome of the town to you former residents who have returned to do honor to Billingsgate, the welcome is the welcome your mother would give, and so Mother Billingsgate extends it. In this changing world of ours, with its noise and confusion, its airplanes and fast cars and tall buildings and—er—streamlined trains, still two things remain sacred. Home," he paused, "home and mother. A mother's love is the most beautiful and sacred thing in life. The older we grow, the more we cherish the associations of childhood, and our old school friends and our old school days. And so, those of us who have stayed here in Billingsgate, so we sent the clarion call out to you, who responded by travelling from all parts of our country, and some of you from foreign lands, to come back home. Home to Billingsgate. Home for this week of celebration. All of us here have banded together in one great thought, to make this home-coming a real welcome to you, a welcome—"

Asey's eyes met Aunt Sara's.

Hurriedly, he edged his way back to the roadster.

But it was not Brinley's oratory that puckered up his forehead. It was the absent Slade. Brinley was substituting for Slade. Why should a wordy fellow like Slade pass up a chance to talk his head off without interruption in front of so many people? Something was wrong. After all, why fish in silence when an audience that size was waiting?

"Mr. Mayo!"

He hardly needed the badge to identify Mrs. J. Arthur Brinley. Like her husband, she was short and fat and pompous, and her face was red and perspiring. He knew it would be. She reminded him somehow of an old table someone had given his father, a table made of sixty million different little chips of wood. Perhaps it was her three strings of beads, or her rings, or the buttons on her big-figured chiffon dress—anyway, she had a built-up look.

"I do hope," she said, "that my husband has seen you? He has? And he told you about that Slade? You will restrain him, won't you? Rushing around with that shotgun! It was disgraceful! A town officer, brandishing a shotgun, with all our guests! People were shocked! I said to my husband, Arthur, I said—"

"Look," Asey interrupted, "let's get to the bottom of this. You an' Mr. Brinley tell me that after the brush fire last night,

FIGURE AWAY

Mike Slade was uptown, brandishin' a shotgun. Am I right up to that point?"

"Well, he wasn't exactly brandishing it, but he had a shotgun with him openly, and it upset a number of people, including many Old Settlers. It upset them very much. Naturally it is upsetting when—"

"Yes. But what did he have a gun along with him for? Decoration, or use, or what?"

"Didn't Arthur tell you? Arthur tried to restrain him, and Slade was very rude, and told him to go away and lay an—oh, he was just as rude as you'd expect someone like him to be. He said—why, the things he said!"

"Yes, I know. Outspoken sort. An old spade caller. But what expl'nation did he give your husband?"

"Why, it really wasn't an explanation, at all, really. The man was either drunk, or crazy. He said he had a shotgun with him, and he intended to carry it with him as long as he felt like it, and certainly until he got the chance to shoot back at whoever had been shooting at *him* with a shotgun. Oh, no. He said, whoever had been trying to shoot at him, or something. Now you know that's absurd—"

"Yes," Asey said.

"What? But it is absurd! I'm sure that many people might have *wished* they could do something about him, but no one ever did—after all, we're civilized people, and we—why, certainly no one tried to shoot him! And—why, where are you going, Mr. Mayo?" Mrs. Brinley sniffed. "And in such a terrific hurry. Well, *I* don't care," she continued to talk as the roadster shot down the street, "what Arthur Brinley thinks, I think that Mayo is crazy, too! Dashing off like that—"

CHAPTER
5.

"YOU don't mean it," Aunt Sara said. "You can't mean it, Asey."

"I do," Asey assured her firmly. "You think I'm jokin'? D'you think I'd try to be funny, under the circumstances?"

"But I simply can't believe it." Sara shook her head as she poured out another cup of tea. Jeff was having a nap after the excitement of the day, Zeb was still at the store, and Jane and Eloise had not yet returned from the hollow. She and Asey were out under the maples in the front yard. "Dear me, I do wish Jeff hadn't insisted on our staying to that ball game. I've never understood baseball, but it gives me such an appetite, and it'll spoil my dinner entirely to gorge myself now. No, Asey, to get back to Slade, I don't think you're joking, but I do feel that your conclusion's somehow wrong."

"I have hunted Mike Slade," Asey said, "for six hours. All I know is, his best pants an' coat is on his bed. His Old Home Week badge is sittin' on a copy of Karl Marx, an' his brand new buckskin shoes are on top of somethin' called 'Tender Buttons'—say, you ever read that? You try it some day. I'd like to see how you felt afterwards. An' the rest of his wardrobe, what there is of it, is sort of strewn around casual."

"Where's his pocketbook? Gone?"

Asey laughed. "Sort of a middle class touch. He'd hidden that in an empty sardine tin an' stuck it in his ice box. Anyway, Mike Slade hasn't been any place he's supposed to go, today. He hasn't been home, his milk's on the doorstep. He hasn't been to his studio. No one's seen him since last night. Those are—"

"The facts in the case, to coin a phrase," Sara said.

Asey didn't let her sarcasm bother him. "They are. An' his shotgun ain't around, an' he has two empty cartons in his book case, an' the labels on'em say deer ball an' buckshot. You can figure it out any way you please. You can figure that he killed Mary Randall an' exited in haste, or you can figure that the person who got Mary also got him. There you are."

"I never thought of that," Sara said, "the possibility that he might be harmed. That must be it. I'd never believe he had anything to do with Mary. Asey, what are we going to do? Don't you think we'd just better let Billingsgate go, and let the thing be made public? After all, suppose someone else is killed? We've no right not to let people know of danger, if there is any!"

"The human'tarian aspect," Asey said, "is sort of muddled. It'd be too bad if anythin' happened to anyone else, but after all, the fellow can't keep up any massacre on a large scale. An' if we let Billingsgate down, pop goes your whole town. Workin' on the greatest good for the greatest number theory, Billingsgate an' its finances are the most important."

"But if people knew, wouldn't you be able to ask more questions, and find out more things? I mean, here's the problem of Slade. He's gone. If you weren't handicapped by keeping this quiet, you could ask around and find out things."

"I have. Lane an' I have both asked around an' found out nothin'."

"But you keep assuming that he's alive! Suppose he's dead? Shouldn't you organize a posse, or something?"

"And drag ponds, to find him alive an' fishin'? Nope. I don't think."

"Why are you so sure he is alive?"

"Because," Asey said, "if I had some idea of killin' Slade, an' then I seen him cavortin' around with a shotgun, as he was last night, promisin' death an' d'struction to the person who had any such ideas, I think I'd hesitate. That man's a born fighter. I think he'd scare me off."

Sara got up from her chair and walked over to the garden.

"I always thought I was rather bright," she said plaintively. "But I don't understand any of this. Why, if someone actually did threaten him, why didn't he come to us last night? He knew about things, everything but Mary Randall."

Asey chose a bachelor button with care, and drew it through the lapel of his coat.

"That's what makes me think he's all right. P'raps he thought that by comin' straight to us, he might give somethin' away. P'raps he figured if he could make it personal, he might get farther into understandin' things. As I get it, someone did somethin' to him after I left the fire last night. Probably some sort of warning, like the shotguns Saturday. He warned right back, as loud an' obvious as he could, that he was ready to meet all comers. N'en, I think, he decided to lay low. He may have some idea of his own that he's working out. From the little I saw of Slade, I know he wouldn't take any risks, like movin' past lighted windows. No, I give him credit. An' at the same time, I don't entirely write him off the list as innocent, either—"

"Car's coming," Sara said. "Let's talk about the governors, all three of'em—no matter, it's your cousin Weston. Did you hear his speech today? It was good, in spite of the fact that he sounded a little like the late Mr. Coolidge—Hullo, Wes, are you exhausted?"

"I'm a little tired," Weston said, "but it's gone all right so far, hasn't it?"

"It's a triumph of organization," Sara said, "and I mean that sincerely, Weston. Everyone had a grand time today—what's that you've got?"

"It's the strangest thing ever. A note from Slade. I just found it in my mail box, in front of the house. I don't often look into that box, I get my mail at the post office, but the flag was up. It says," he opened the note and read from it, "'Dear Mayhew, I was called away suddenly. Back soon. Slade.' Now, what do you make of that?"

"Is it genuine?" Sara asked. "Let me—why, it looks like his writing. Wait. I've a note from him in my desk, and I'll bring it out."

As far as they could tell, the writing on the two sheets of paper was identical.

"Same kind of paper, too," Asey said. "Same kind of ink. I'll give'em to Lane, to make sure."

"What do you make of this?" Weston demanded. "What's he found out?"

"Nothin' I know of," Asey said. "This is all Slade's own brain wave. What do you think?"

"I don't think he possibly could have had anything to do with Mary Randall," Weston said slowly. "He's a fighter, but he wouldn't fight that way. He'd rather shoot you full of words. And he wouldn't have left any notes for me. What I think is, he's been scared off. He's led a funny life, and his past is shady, and what I think is, he recognized someone, some visitor, who'd known him before, and someone he didn't want to meet again. He play-acted around last night for an alibi. That's what we think—"

"We?" Asey said. "You an' who, Brinley?"

Weston turned pink.

"Well, yes. They were very upset about him last night. They felt—"

"Don't tell me," Asey said, "I know how they felt. Well, this is just somethin' else to delve into."

"Honestly," Weston said, "I've gone through the day like I was sitting on a bunch of thistles, with a sword hanging over my head and a bottomless pit at my feet. So far, so good—but what's going to come? How long can we keep this quiet? It's driving me crazy! And here I got so much to do—"

"Run along an' forget it," Asey said. "You do the Old Home Weekin', an' leave the worryin' to us—"

But Weston refused to be soothed. He was still audibly worrying when he left.

"Somehow," Sara said as they watched his car disappear over the hill, "the Billingsgate branch were never the calm, imperturbable brand you have in Wellfleet."

"Oh, I dunno," Asey said, "it's just that they ain't happy in the abstract. Just the samey, Brinley an' Wes may have somethin' there." He told her about Madame Meaux. "She was headin' for him. Maybe he's dodgin' her. I think I'll hunt her up later, an' look into it. Meanwhile, I'll see Lane an' find out if this note's genuine. If it is, at least it'll mean he's alive."

With Lane was a man whom Asey greeted with open arms.

"Hamilton, I'm glad to see you. I can use you—Lane, can I, or is he just here for the ride?"

"The boss thought you might want me," Hamilton said. "He said to tell you he'd seen the woman, and he'll do what he can to help keep it quiet this week. He thought he might get down with the governor tomorrow. He—what's that, a handwriting job? Your department, Lane."

"My kit's indoors. Come in, and—Asey," Lane said, "can't you do anything about that woman Eloise? She's driving me nuts. I'm telling you, there's something the matter with her. I finally showed her my wife's picture, and told her I had two kids in high school, but she kept right on."

"It's your fatal charm," Asey said. "Come on, we got to settle this, an' then I want to lay some plans with you fellers. An' by the way, Lane, can you get one of your men to lurk around here tonight, too? I think we'd better keep on havin' someone here. And at Sara's, an' Brinley's, an' Weston's, if you can manage. Got enough men? Any excuse'll do, like protectin' the town officers from bein' disturbed, or protectin' the antiques here. N'en if anything happens, we at least took precautions. Say, who took the women home from here, did Zeb?"

"Two local men, one was from the point," Lane said. "Curious bird. Wanted to know just what relative was sick, and where, and how bad, and all. Jane took him on, and played him like a piano. Say, what about that girl, Asey? She seems pretty clever."

"We're lookin' into her tonight," Asey assured him. "Lookin' into lots of things."

At dinner, back at Aunt Sara's, Zeb announced his intention of working most of the night.

"Orders!" he said. "My God, you never saw so many orders in your life. Matt's daft. Thought he had enough for this week, and we had to phone Boston fifty times. Matt's ordering carload lots now. And Baked Beans'll be up ten points by the end of the week. It's awfully funny. You say, what about a can of beans, and they say, why yes, they'll be nice to have in the house. It seems you don't ever buy baked beans to eat, you buy them to Have in the House, like coal or flowers. I've sent father a wire. Something's radically wrong with his advertising. Say, Jane, you'll have to go with Asey tonight—"

"I already asked her," Asey said. "Miss Randall's goin' proper with Jeff an' Sara, an' sit in a blue-an'-yellow draped box, but Jane an' I, we're goin' to mingle with the hoi p'loi an' eat peanuts."

"I'm going to flirt with the trumpet," Jane said. "He asked me for a date, Monday, and when I asked him who he thought he was, he said he was the best solid sender in the business. It must mean something, he was quite proud of it. While I'm busy with him, Asey, you—"

"I'll be chattin' with Madame Meaux. Hustle, Jane. I want to hear her render the openin' number. Maybe she's better with lights an' spangles than she was in the corridor the other day."

Madame Meaux was rendering "America The Beautiful" when they reached the ball park, and Asey admitted that she was doing it rather well.

"Maybe so, but I never liked that song," Jane said. "It's so blatantly smug. As if no other country ever had spacious skies, or amber waves of grain, or purple mountain majesties, or anything. It doesn't seem to sound right here, either. There are spacious skies, but—"

FIGURE AWAY

"Well," Asey said, "you can sing 'Oh beautiful for bay'bry bushes, for lots an' lots of sand,' if you like. No one'll ever notice."

Jane laughed. "Now this one—what's this? People have been singing it at the drop of a hat for weeks, and I never yet have understood a word. I asked Mary—" she stopped and bit her lip. "Mary didn't know. She said she just hummed a sort of obbligato."

"That," Asey said, "is Billingsgate's crownin' opus. That is 'Billingsgate Beautiful.' The town anthem, by the fine Italian hand of Bessie Brinley."

Jane shivered and gritted her teeth. "Wow! Why do they sing it? How can they? I mean, after all, you don't try to sing something like that from choice, or just to be nice to Mrs. Brinley."

"Well," Asey said, "in a cel'bration like this, you got to sing something for brotherhood an' the cause, like—oh, like—like the 'Horst Wessel.' "

"That name," Jane said, "always sounded to me as though it should be some sort of black sausage—well, that's over! Thank God! Asey, where are you—are you really going to talk with her? Well, can you tie that!"

Madame Meaux greeted Asey with a dazzling smile. In evening dress, and with makeup, she was a far different woman from the hot perspiring bicyclist of the afternoon.

"Very nifty," Asey said. "You had 'em hanging on the ropes."

"Sister Brinley," Madame Meaux told him, "wanted a soprano with volume, and she got one. I can make that trumpet sound sissier than a penny whistle. Say, have you seen Slade?"

"That's what I wanted to talk with you about—got a few minutes?"

"I've got an hour before I have to tear off Old Favorites, if that'll help."

"Fine," Asey said, "get your coat an' come along with Jane Warren an' me—"

"If you mean your girl friend, she's walked out on you. Joined the local swells in that box. And you'd better know you're being watched, if that sort of things matters to you."

"Half the fun of these things is the nice new gossip," Asey said. "Billingsgate'll r'member for years how I upped an' made off with their soprano. Hop along."

He gave no indication of seeing either Aunt Sara's wink or Jane's annoyed stare as he escorted Madame Meaux to the roadster.

Once in the car, he had a bad moment. All he wanted was to ask questions about Slade, but he had forgotten that the eyes of Billingsgate were upon him.

Madame Meaux solved the problem.

"What I'd like," she said, "is a couple of dogs with mustard, and a sundae with a lot of marshmallow. Sister B. has this feeling that sopranos don't eat."

"We'll remedy that," Asey said gratefully. "By the way, is— er—M-e-a-u-x your real name?"

"My real name happens to be Emily Slade. And I know who you are, because I asked that guy at the garage."

"Relation to Mike?"

"His brother was my first husband. Died five years ago, and don't say you're sorry, because no one was. Charley Slade was a punk. Now," her manner changed, "let's get some food, and you tell me why the great detective wants to know about Mike. You do, don't you?"

"First we'll eat," Asey said, "an' then we'll dally with him."

She ate her hot dogs and devoured two sundaes with a wholehearted abandon that charmed Asey.

"There," she pushed away the dish, "now what's the trouble?"

"Are you," Asey asked, "enough of a menace in Slade's life for him to decamp at the sight of you?"

"Well," Madame Meaux said thoughtfully, "he owes me around four hundred dollars, and he knows it, and I admit I had some hope of prying it out of him. I helped him with a hospital bill. That's all I can think of. He and I got along all right. Oh, it was true, what I told you about working on those projects. We did. But I didn't know who you were then, and it didn't seem necessary for me to tell you any more."

"Quite right. So he owed you money. That may be why he's vanished, leavin' what seems to be a genuine note sayin' he'll be back next week. But we kind of wondered."

"Must be. But don't let that give you any wrong ideas about Mike. He's a right enough sort. My money's safe with him. Say, he hasn't done anything, has he?"

"Not that I know of," Asey said. "But—say, it's time I got you back. Only—if you see him, or he gets any message to you, will you let me know?"

"Sure." They got up from the table. "I don't understand —hm."

"Hm what?" Asey inquired as they got into the roadster.

"Your specialty is murders, isn't it? And the town's making money—no, don't say anything. I shan't. Maybe I'll pick you up something. You hear a lot in a town like this, in a place like mine. Singers and manicurists, they hear everything."

"How," Asey had no fear of telling her anything, even if she guessed the whole business, "how'll you know what to listen to?"

"I shall probably hear enough about you," she said, "to last a lifetime. Drop me here, will you? Thanks. I got to see Upjohn. Sorry I can't ask you if there's any number you want. Upjohn and Brinley planned everything—and you'll hear me sparring over 'Chloe' with that trumpet, clear in the next town. So long!"

Asey left her at the rear of the band stand, and then went to join Aunt Sara and Jeff.

"Jane is pretty sore," Sara told him. "She's not accustomed to being left for blondes—Is she as much fun as she looks, by the way? I thought so. Women like that either have a sense of humor, or they don't. No two ways about it. Anyway, Jane's a little dazed, and I'm sure it's doing her a world of good. Jane is just a little too engrossed in Jane, I think."

"It's all her fault for not believing what she's told," Asey said. "Where'd she go?"

"She's dancing with the Mitchell boy. Eloise is helping with refreshments. We get'em free. Ah, the graft us politicians' wives do get!"

"It's somethin' fierce," Asey said. "Canned fruit punch an' two fig newtons. What about Jane, Sara?"

"Go easy with her. She's got a heart of gold, but—"

"But gold is metal," Asey said. "Soft, but still metal."

"She has that manner, but it's indigenous to her particular generation, I think. She'd be first to cry at the sight of a run-over dog. And right now she's scared stiff. Go easy with her, Asey. Don't rush, and don't bully. You'll find out in time what you want. She's awfully scared, and awfully mixed up, and she wants to lie down and cry. I think there's something more than Mary that's bothering her, too, even though she adored Mary. And you'll find—hullo, Jane. The prodigal's returned."

"Thinks he's going to be welcomed back into the bosom of our select group, does he, after gallivanting—"

"I guess I know," Asey said sadly, "when I'm not wanted. Yessiree, One-Hint Mayo, that's what they call me. I'm goin' over to the Town Hall an' look around, an' leave you dance-mad things to your fate. See you later."

He expected to find Weston over at the hall, and the usual number of bystanders remembered seeing him just a few minutes before, so he waited in the exposition rooms, where the local antique collections, and the flower and vegetable and preserve entries, held sway.

J. Arthur Brinley came up to him.

"Good evening, viewing our entries? Er—Mayo."

"Yup."

"Weston tells me that Slade has left town for the time being. He," Brinley nodded knowingly, "says Slade was scared out of town, but Bessie and I know that you managed it. I wanted you to know that we appreciate it, sir, we appreciate it deeply!"

"Don't thank me."

"Ah, modest, as everyone says. But you know *we* know." Asey wondered what sort of reward that was supposed to be. "And—Mayo."

"What?"

"Er—some of the ladies, they want to take down their quilts for the night. I don't want to be rude to our guests, but on the other hand, it's a chilly night, and the quilts—you know what I mean. Have you any suggestions?"

"There's General Philbrick over there," Asey said. "Tell him to take out his watch, and announce in that voice of his that the exposition will close in five minutes, but will open tomorrow at—well, whenever it does. Then close the door, an' the ladies can rip down quilts to their hearts' content, an' no feelin's hurt."

"Wonderful!" Brinley said. "Thank you! I never thought of—oh, thank you!"

Ten minutes later the antique quilts of Billingsgate—pine trees, log cabins, rising suns, birds and baskets, ship's wheel, rose of Sharon, duck's foot in the mud—and all the hundred and one other kinds, were on the way to their respective homes to warm the tourists and the old settlers.

Asey grinned and strolled upstairs towards the town offices.

A man coming down brushed by him hurriedly, taking the steps down four at a time.

Asey glanced after him curiously, for the man wore the first dark, city-like clothes he had seen in a long while.

Then, at the selectmen's offices, Asey stopped short.

The glass-topped door was open, but there was no light in the offices beyond.

He could see the marks where the lock and door had been forced.

CHAPTER 6.

ASEY stood there and surveyed the situation.

There was no sense to romping downstairs and trying to pursue the man, for the chances of catching him were something less than slim. If the fellow continued his original pace, he was now beyond pursuit, anyway. And in the confusion outside the hall, with dozens of cars starting and turning and departing, it would be next to impossible to find anyone. Not without creating a lot more confusion.

Weston appeared at the head of the stairs.

"Brinley said you wanted me—is anything the matter? What's this?"

"A gent," Asey informed him, "has been pryin' into that which don't concern him. Come on an' let's see the damage."

Weston nearly wept.

"Asey, has someone broken in there? Who? Did you see—let's go after him!"

"He's not important, rel'tively speakin'," Asey said, "but what he may have found or got or done or taken away matters a lot. Come see."

Nervously, Weston went to work in the office.

"He hasn't touched Jeff's desk, and he hasn't touched Brinley's desk, but he *has* been at *my* desk—what are you laughing about now, Asey Mayo? This isn't—"

"You sounded so much," Asey said, "like Goldilocks an' the three bears. Go on, Wes. I'm sorry."

"He didn't touch the files. They're all right. He didn't touch the safe, thank God, because I've got a hundred times as much cash there as usual. As far as I can see, Asey, he only went to my desk, and everything seems to be in the right order except my lower big drawer."

"What d'you keep there, ledgers?"

"Yes. Mostly I've got committee lists and plans for this week—I did keep'em in the safe, but lately I've just left them out. Everyone knows'em. They weren't important, because everything in them has been copied and printed and mimeographed. I—oh," Weston added lamely, "I did used to keep my ledger of vital statistics there. Just jotted things down, and copied them later. We don't have more'n a couple of dozen births, or deaths or—"

"Did you or did you not hike that ledger over to the bank and put it in the vault?" Asey demanded.

"I did. I was out front this morning when they opened the bank at eight. Well, I don't understand this much, do you?"

"Only that someone wanted to peek at that ledger. Certainly they didn't want Old Home Week plans, with the streets knee deep in'em, so to speak. Well, well. An' I didn't even get much of a look at that fellow, either. He had on dark clothes an' a felt hat, but he didn't limp, or smell of garlic, or have any outstandin' features. Huh. You was goin' to have a guard here at night, wasn't you, in the hall here?"

Weston shook his head. "You know there's never been a

FIGURE AWAY

burglary in this town, unless boys broke into summer houses, or something. Why?"

"It'd seem that you had a would-be burglar here among your guests," Asey said. "Wes, don't lose sight of the fact that you're not just copin' with natives here. You've got a good many outlanders, an' some of 'em are goin' to act outlandish. We'll have a couple of cops left here."

"People will want to know why."

"Tell 'em, to look after your antiques, an' exposition, an' all, an' for the benefit of anyone desirin' aid or assistance. Billingsgate's gesture of safety for its guests. Two cops constantly on call. Make a hit, I shouldn't wonder."

"Well," Weston was dubious, "I suppose so. But how can we explain this door?"

"Blame it on me. My car keys got locked up, an' I broke in. Now grab the phone an' get a locksmith an' have him fix things up. Got one in town, ain't you? Get him, then. Weston, I don't know as I ever saw a man jitter the way you can when once you get started! What's the matter with you?"

"Matter? It's like sitting on a powder keg! You can't tell what'll be the last straw that'll leave you holding the bag—"

"Weston," Asey said, "get the locksmith, an' stop this foolishness! I'm goin' over to the fireworks. It's most time for 'em."

"There!" Weston said. "There's the next thing! The fireworks! What'll happen tonight when they have the big display? Who'll be shot tonight?"

"No one."

"How do you know? For all you know, someone might shoot at you!"

"That is exactly why," Asey said, "I'm goin' right plumb up to the field an' stand in the middle of the crowd, teeterin' on my toes. Sara an' Jeff, an' Eloise an' Jane are goin' to stay there, an' I'm goin' to send a cop to stay with you. In fact, you're going to have a guard yourself, tonight. Does that help your blues?"

"What use is a guard, if someone's decided to kill me? Suppose I did keep out of the way of windows, and had a guard with me. If anyone wanted to shoot deer ball at me, all they've got to do is figure where I'm sitting, or sleeping, and fire—right through the walls. Suppose someone does take to shooting through walls? Up at Aunt Sara's, for example?"

"Won't get far there," Asey said. "That's an old house, an' built on the foundations of an older one still. There's a solid four-inch thickness of brick between the clapboards an' the wainscoting. Aunt Sara was tellin' me today, an' about how it cost 'em a young fortune to have the place wired for electricity. If anyone wants to pop at me under the circumstances, they have my permission. Now, call the locksmith, an' I'll send up a trooper. Don't worry, you'll be taken care of."

"But who was this man here?" Weston said. "What did he break in for?"

"This is a new one," Asey told him. "This isn't the first one."

"Someone else?" Weston said. "Oh, my God! What makes you think so?"

"The first fellow stole your keys, didn't he? Or the duplicates, or skeletons? Well, why should he stoop to lock breakin'? This is two other fellows. Weston, cheer up, will you? I—oh, goodbye. I'll see you later."

General Philbrick, who managed to look as though he had on a full dress uniform even when he wore a white flannel suit, was waiting with Jeff and Sara for the fireworks to begin.

"And I hope," he said to Asey after greeting him effusively, "that you'll find time to say a few words to our radio audience before the week is out. We want you. I know you'll be glad to hear the preliminary reports on our program have been most favorable, and the evening papers gave us fine publicity. Splendid. Now, you have a large following, and people are interested in you and your work, and Mr. Tripp wants to—"

"That's real nice of you an' Mr. Tripp," Asey said. "You—er—think this is going to help your business?"

"No question about it, no question about it at all. The American people have unfortunately outgrown the habit of —perhaps I should say, grown out of the habit—of using fireworks of the ornamental type at their—"

"Oh, but the fire," Eloise Randall interrupted. "I mean, I do think they're pretty, and so colorful—but so dangerous, don't you think? I remember torpedoes—of course you can hardly see the scar on my finger now, but that was a long time ago. Then Cousin Dorothy's boy—when he was younger, of course. He's an engineer now, and really doing quite well in spite of the depression—so hard for young people, don't you think? Like Jane, and—well, Gerald *would* have firecrackers—of course we tried to dissuade him, but he was a very firm-willed boy, always. I always said, Cousin Dorothy's family are *so* strong-willed about everything, I don't mind their sleeping outdoors in bags but I do feel it's an imposition for their guests —of course Gerald's eyesight finally did come back—"

"My dear woman," the General said, "modern scientific methods in the manufacture of—"

Asey slipped away to Sara's side.

"Let's beat it," he said, "to the edge of this mob. I'd like to hear that conv'sation, but I'm tired. When Eloise gets goin', she goes, don't she? Seems like she hung onto your words for the one purpose of b'ginnin' to talk just a split second before she thinks you're windin' up. Lane has had an awful time with her. He says she's coy."

Aunt Sara grinned. "Odd, but Jeff and Zeb have noticed that coyness, too. She set her cap for Weston, did he tell you? For a while last winter, the town was pretty much resigned to losing its bachelor selectman. Oh, dear, there goes the noise! It's beautiful to watch, but I do hate to listen!"

Near the parked cars on the side of the field, they waited and watched the General's display.

"What about fire hazard?" Asey asked.

"Oh, everything's been chemically treated within a radius of ten miles, or something," Sara told him during a lull. "By the way, you should have heard our evening broadcast. We were quite good. Upjohn's band outdid themselves, and your friend the soprano was fine. I think she cares more for 'Chloe' than she does for 'Billingsgate Beautiful.' And we had an impromptu amateur contest. At least they claimed it was impromptu, but I am sure it was pre-arranged. And there was a girl, a reporter, who did imitations. She was simply marvelous. Awfully interesting-looking girl. Red hair and freckly. She came over later and we met her. I liked her a lot. You will, too. Er—I—"

"Go on," Asey said. "Get to the point, Sara. And what happened next?"

"How did you know it happened next? What is this, thought transference?"

"It's the sensitive Mayo mind," Asey said. "Just a vast receivin' set— Sara, I know by the way you're going at this that you done somethin' you shouldn't. What's the story? What did you say that you shouldn't?"

FIGURE AWAY 85

"Well," Sara said, "she told me that the only accommodations she could find were in Provincetown, and so—"

"Sara Leach, did you offer to put her up? Did you? Did you get soft an' fall for— Sara, how could you?"

"She's a nice girl."

"Sara, she'll be into everything! And, honest, Sara, I could spank you! You should know better—lettin' a reporter—a reporter! Oh, God A'mighty! Here I worry what Weston'll tell in his jitters, an' that blurty Eloise, an' all the troopers an' everythin' else, an' you—the one person I never wasted a second of worry on, you go an' invite reporters in!"

"But she isn't the tabloid type, she's—" Sara began defensively.

"Listen, news is news! You give any reporter a scoop an' he forgets if he's workin' for the 'Daily Pulp,' or the 'Brotherhood of Coiled Bed Spring Makers Weekly Gazette and Herald'! He just scoops. An' furthermore," Asey was angry, "you'll leave the key of your room outside, because Jeff's goin' to lock you in an' hide the key. Do you understand that?"

Aunt Sara's face became as white as her hair, and she bit her lip until Asey was afraid that it would bleed.

"Oh, Asey, did I—have I been—"

"You did. Sara, I'm sorry to be so impatient an' abrupt, an' I don't mean to bully, but you have gone an' done the silliest thing you could do! What's her name? Can't I find her another place, an' head her off? Ain't there some way out?"

"She charmed Jeff, too," Sara said. "I don't see what we can do, she's already had someone take her luggage— Asey, what did I do? When was—of course it must have been last night. Oh, dear, dear, what shall I do if I'm beginning that again!"

She was more distraught than Asey had ever imagined she

could be, and she seemed suddenly to become rather a frail little old lady instead of the erect, brisk person he had always known.

"I'm sorry," Asey said again. "But you took to walkin' out by the swamp, an' our shotgun friend was in the vicinity, pretendin' to be a loon. When I found it was you, I near went crazy to think of what might have happened to you. Does it —do you—or don't you want to talk about it?"

"I don't, but I've got to. Let's leave this din—"

Asey helped her into his car.

"I've done it since I was a child," Sara said. "No one's been able to do anything about it. It drove mother frantic, and she made me so ashamed of it that it rather preyed on me when I was older. Father took me to doctors, and they figured out that it happened only when I was upset and worried about something, and usually when I was trying to keep a secret. The older I've grown, the fewer secrets I've had, and well—I thought it was all over. This affair must have started me going again. Asey, what shall we do?"

"Do locks stop you, or do you shinny out of windows?"

"Locks will do it, and I'll have to tell Jeff. I'll tell him the whole story, I think he suspects most of it. He knows about me, of course. He thinks it's funny. He claims he had to tie me, shortly after we were married, and father'd told me about some railroad bill in the Senate that was a tremendous secret. I've always kept it hidden—you can see why. Billingsgate would love a bit of news like that. The maids know, but mercifully they like me too much to talk. Oh, dear! What can we do about this girl? Her name is Kay Thayer. She's a good sort, really, but—oh, damn this Old Home Week! Damn it!"

"Why Sara Leach, how you talk!"

FIGURE AWAY

"I mean it, I've wanted to say it for months. Asey, if we try to shunt the girl, she'll get suspicious. And on the other hand, how can she help knowing, right there in the house? We'll have to cope with it somehow. Have you any ideas?"

"One," Asey said, "but—oh, Sara, oh, my!"

He waited at the Leach house until after the rest had returned from town, and then he set out for Hell Hollow, where Hamilton was waiting for him.

"This place," Hamilton said, "has my teeth chattering. Asey, I never saw anything like it. The way that mist comes out of the swamp, and those mud holes, and the noises—I never heard so many noises in all my life! Look, what sounds like this?"

He opened his mouth and produced something between a moan and a wail and a horse whinnying.

"It sounds like someone in a radio mystery," Asey said, "at the end of a chapter. I think it was a raccoon, though. When's your trooper due?"

"Twelve-thirty. He's a new man, and I hope he can take it. If I had to park here alone until tomorrow morning, I'd go crazy. Honestly, look at those figures! One of'em fell down ten minutes ago, and do you know what I did? I fell flat on my stomach and drew my gun. Honestly, I'd rather spend the night in the morgue alone than sit here with those figures! Look at'em. Watch'em sway! And don't," he added, "tell me I'm nervous!"

"I'll confess, Ham, I reached for my gun the first time I seen'em. Here's your man comin'. Tell him to put his car back of the house where it won't be seen, an' don't tell him how you feel!"

"I won't need to. He'll feel the same way in fifteen minutes. What's orders? Stick around and watch and listen?"

"Just about. Lane'll relieve him. Tell him we'll come back an' visit with him later on. May hearten him."

From the hollow they returned to Aunt Sara's, where another trooper stood in the shadow of the garage.

"I rigged up that gadget on the foot bridge," he said. "The fellow at the house and I did. Anyone who comes up from the swamp'll get a blank cartridge going off under his feet. I can see the rest of the place, and I've got some other noise makers around. Sure, I'll handle things."

The Brinleys and Weston both lived near the center of the town, and the troopers whom Lane had selected both assured Asey that they would look out for any emergency.

"I look after the fronts," one said, "Biff takes the rears. We'll see to everything."

"That's that," Hamilton said to Asey as they got into the car. "What's behind this, a crank? Sounds like one."

"I thought that way at first," Asey said, "but it's too bright for a crank in some ways, an' not bright enough in others. Besides, cranks like publicity. I been kind of waitin' today to see if some hint of this crept out. But it ain't. No one's questioned Mary Randall's goin' to New York to see a sick cousin. No talk, no gossip. If there had been, I'd have said crank. Let's drive around to Slade's place, an' see if he's been there."

The door was still open. Asey went in and made for the ice box.

"If he's dropped—aha!" he said. "Slade is alive an' kickin', an' he's had some milk an' eaten up some odds an' ends. Taken his money out, too. Now, let's look into the clothes situation."

The new white flannels and blue coat were still on the unmade bed.

"He's not bein' formal, anyway," Asey said. "An' here on

the floor is the flannel shirt an' dungarees he had on last night. These weren't here this mornin'. Ham, I should of left someone here. Let's look at the closet."

He peered so long at Slade's wardrobe that Hamilton became impatient.

"Taking inventory?"

"Nope. Ham, I'm awful dumb. He took a dark suit an' a felt hat. An' the lad who busted into Weston's office tonight had on a dark suit an' a felt hat. In this weather, with the whole populace in light clothes, an' wearin' straws an' panamas, an' yachtin' caps, that's just a little odd."

"Think it was Slade? Say, Asey, what about fingerprints? Think of them at the hall?"

"I did, an' so did he. He wasn't much of a burglar, but the door an' the top of Weston's desk an' everythin' else he touched was wiped off nice'n neat. Ham, I'm droppin' you off at the Town Hall, an' you roust up someone to stay here. Take one of the two at the hall—they got a car there? Well, drive one up here, an' you take his place."

Hamilton protested. "And leave you careening around the countryside? I don't like to, Asey. Everyone knows your car, and with this fellow loose—"

"Don't worry about me. Tell you what, though. Get Lane, an' have him park here in this shack tonight. N'en after you brought him here, come over to the hollow. I want to see if everythin's all right there. Somehow I'm uneasy about that place."

"So'm I," Hamilton said. "All right, I'll get Lane, and then follow you up. Asey, where are we getting in this mess?"

Asey sighed.

"To tell you the truth, I don't know. This seems to me the

jerkiest thing. We know we're on guard against somethin', but we don't know what. Everythin's scattered around. Disconnected. We got a murder, an' two blobs of deer ball. They're worth nothin' as clews. Nothin' we can tell about'em, except that someone fired'em out of a shotgun. Just a shotgun, no special one. Just someone, no special someone. We can assume it's a man. Deer ball is reasonably masculine. We can assume Mary Randall found out what he was up to. What she found an' what he's up to are both mysteries to me. Somethin' to do with this infernal town. That's all there is. What I'd give for somethin' to stick my teeth into, an' chaw on! This is just like pickin' at chicken bones or lobster claws when what you want is a good hunk of porterhouse!"

He wondered as he sped along after leaving Hamilton, if it really could have been Slade who broke into the office. If it had been, what did he want? And if it was someone else, who was it? He felt sure that this intruder was not the person who had killed Mary Randall. That man didn't do amateur, bungling jobs when it came to murder, so why should he be amateur and bungling when it came to burglary? And particularly in a building full of people, any one of whom might have happened in on him at any time.

This business of Slade dropping out of the picture was puzzling no matter how you looked at it. He might well be in hiding from Madame Meaux, but it didn't seem much like Slade. Certainly he couldn't be very conscience-stricken or very afraid of being caught, or he never would have returned to his house and so casually had a meal and changed his clothes.

"Huh!" Asey muttered. "Chicken bones! More like jack straws."

He slowed down as he neared the hollow, for the mist from

the swamp blanketed the road. First, he decided, he would drive out to Slade's studio, anyway, and then return and hang around with that trooper a while. Mentally he made a note to tell Lane to give the job to someone else the next night. One night's vigil at Hell Hollow was enough for anyone.

As he passed by, he turned and glanced toward the house, and then he eased the big roadster to a quiet stop and snapped off the headlights.

A thin pencil of light was flicking around in the barn where Mary Randall kept her antiques.

And that was all wrong. The trooper had no keys to the shop, and his flashlight was a big powerful thing with a wide beam.

Asey got out of the car and quietly began to circle his way toward the barn.

At the foot of one of the tall pines he stumbled over something limp.

He knew even before he bent down just what he was going to find.

CHAPTER 7.

WORKING feverishly in the darkness, Asey removed the twisted handkerchief gag from the trooper's mouth, and with his pocketknife sawed through the heavy cord binding his wrists and ankles.

The trooper groaned and put one hand up to his head, gropingly, as though he weren't quite sure what he expected to find there.

"Okay?" Asey said. "Not shot, or carved, or anythin' like that?"

"Groggy. He got me from behind. Garrotted me—"

"Shh! Not so loud. He's still there. Now listen to me. Stay here till you feel like movin', an' keep your eyes peeled. I'm goin' to look into things. Got your flashlight?"

"It's somewhere around—"

"It don't matter. Stay an' rear guard for me. Got your gun?"

"He took it." The trooper was bitter.

"Huh! Well, follow after me quick an' quiet when you are able."

He tiptoed around the barn and peeked in the window.

A man was sitting in front of the old Governor Winthrop

desk which Asey had admired earlier in the day. Jane told him that Mary Randall had called it her "Office."

"Somehow," Jane had said, "it has within it a cash box, and letters, and orders, and Mary's reminder lists, and auction lists, and customer files, and bills, and glue, and labels, and string, and stamps, and everything any business like hers needs in the line of stationery, and Lord knows what else besides. That only takes up the top part. We use the drawers for a number of varied purposes."

The man, whose face was hidden in the shadow, was methodically going through each pigeon hole, flicking through the papers as though they were a pack of playing cards. With a bit of celluloid he opened the small locked compartment and went through its contents, and then he turned his attention to the small drawers under the pigeon holes, and the carved wooden pieces that lifted out.

Asey could imagine his snort of annoyance as the fellow slammed them back in place and picked up the celluloid again, to open the first full-sized drawer underneath. His long slim fingers prodded under the old linen that filled the drawer, and then he impatiently pushed it shut. The remaining drawers were investigated, and then the man went back once more to the pigeon holes.

Clearly he knew just exactly what he was after. It wasn't money. He passed up the cash box with only the briefest examination. He didn't want letters, or auction lists, or orders, or stamps, or glue.

Asey could hear the trooper coming toward him, and apparently the man inside heard him too, for he turned off his tiny flash. Mercifully the trooper had sense enough to stand still, and in a few moments, reassured that he was alone and unobserved, the man snapped his light on again and went back to his investigation of the pigeon holes.

The trooper pressed his own large electric torch into Asey's hands.

"Go around back, quiet," Asey breathed the words, "an' then make a noise there. I'll fix him."

This time the man started to walk toward the sound before putting his light out. The instant he did that, Asey entered by the door and snapped on the trooper's torch.

"Reach," he said. "Reach, an' stand still."

To make it emphatic, Asey squeezed the trigger of the forty-five, unintentionally presenting a black eye to an unframed Currier and Ives lady tacked on a cross beam of the loft.

The trooper came dashing back.

"Take your gun," Asey said. "It's on top of the desk. That's right. Continue to reach, feller, an' turn around."

It was not Mike Slade, or anyone he had ever seen before.

"Know him?" Asey asked the trooper.

"No," the trooper's voice was choked and hoarse, "but you can bet I will before I get through with him, the—"

"Delve in the gent's pockets," Asey said, "an' see if he happens to have any callin' cards with him."

To Asey's surprise and to the trooper's utter amazement, the first object to come from the man's breast pocket was a tooled leather case of calling cards.

"Ah," Asey said interestedly. "A socialite. What's the name?"

The trooper held the card up to the light. "It says—oh, but it's a fake. That can't be right! It says, 'Tertius Prettyman.'"

Tertius Prettyman. Asey thought back. That was Eloise

Randall's boy friend. Old man Prettyman's son, at the point.

"Well, well, how do you do, Mr. Prettyman?" Asey said cordially. "My name is Mayo, an' this gentleman you was so abrupt with is—what's your name? Konrad? This is Konrad, Mr. Prettyman. Konrad, take some of Mrs. Randall's mailin' cord an' tie up Mr. Prettyman, will you? There's a nice yard stick over there, an' if you was to put it under Mr. Prettyman's knees, Konrad, an' then lash his wrists an'—ah. You know. That's fine."

While Konrad trussed up Mr. Prettyman, Asey turned on two lamps and drew the curtains.

"Cosier, I always think," he said pleasantly as he strolled around the barn. "Now you know, Mary Randall has some fine stuff here. That's a good piece of early Israel Trask, that pewter. Too good to be kicking around here. And she's got good chests, too." He paused for a moment in front of one and surveyed the sewing basket on it. "You much of a hand for old chests, Mr. Prettyman? I got a corker home. Not a family piece. I found it in the dump, an' brought it home, an' they tell me it's seventeenth century— Prettyman, just exactly what is your basic an' underlyin' motive, anyway?"

"Just exactly what do you mean?" If his cool calm voice was any indication, Asey thought, this fellow was going to prove difficult, more difficult than he had first imagined. It was not the voice of anyone easily moved or easily bluffed. In fact, the fellow was definitely amused.

"What did you come after, Tertius?"

"Really, that's none of your business, don't you agree?"

Asey pulled out the forty-five and twirled it by the trigger guard.

"Wa-el," he drawled, "it d'pends largely on your point of view," he looked down at Prettyman, "an'—when did you write that policy?"

"Put that thing away," Tertius said. "It might go off again. What did you say? When did I what?"

"You know," Asey said, "you look awfully like a trussed chicken down there on the floor. In fact, you look plain silly. I asked you when, more or less, you wrote that policy for Mrs. Randall?"

Tertius smiled, but plainly the answer was beneath his dignity.

Asey looked at him thoughtfully. Someone had said—probably it was Zeb Chase, that Tertius was around fifty. You had to look twice to believe it, for he was slight and wiry. His hands and eyes gave him away, and to a certain extent, his face.

Asey studied the face. In general it was weak, weak in a blurred way, as though the mould had been used too many times. But there was nothing pliable about it. Mr. Prettyman, he guessed, was the sort of person who would probably pursue the wrong course, but he would pursue it with vigor to the end.

Old man Prettyman—Asey tried to remember about the family. He knew something about them, if he could only drag the details from his mind. Old Prettyman had made a fortune from some patent medicine. Everyman's Elixir, that was it. And he'd lost the fortune in some scheme like getting gold from seaweed, or silk purses from sows' ears, or something. Asey wished he had paid more attention to gossip, and to Billingsgate gossip in particular. Anyway, this Tertius had inherited a lot from his mother, and still more from his father's people. But Zeb Chase had said that he sold insurance, which

FIGURE AWAY

meant that his inheritances had probably long since disappeared. He looked like the sort whose inheritances would disappear.

"Want him to talk?" Konrad inquired with a certain grimness.

"Don't bother, he'll get to it," Asey said.

"What's about a policy?" Konrad asked. "Whose policy? What policy? Where?"

"The policy our pal Tertius was hunting," Asey said. "Only he went hunting like a man, an' Mary Randall's a woman. She didn't bother to put it in her desk, or anywheres else special. She just stuck it in her sewin' basket, over on top of that oak chest there. You see, Konrad, Tertius sold her a nice life insurance policy, only it was a fake."

"It was a splendid policy," Tertius corrected him pleasantly. "A sterling policy. Mayo, you wrong me."

"Then why were you after it?"

"Say, I'll make him talk!" Konrad unstrapped his belt and prepared to remove his coat. "I'll show this—"

"Wait. Tertius, tonight you've busted into town property, you've assaulted a cop, stole his gun, an' you've c'mitted armed robbery. You—what's that? You didn't rob anything? Oh, don't be finicky with details. We'll fix that. You see, Tertius, d'spite your poise an' nonchalance, you're hardly in the driver's seat. Far from it. Now, will you talk? If you don't feel like it now, Konrad an' I can take you to the barracks, an' I'll almost guarantee you'll talk there. Much easier to break down right now. Konrad, bring that policy over to me, will you?"

Tertius smiled. "Don't bother reading it, Mayo. I'll tell you something that'll make you wonder if you are in the driver's seat as much as you seem to think. The beneficiary is your little friend Jane Warren."

"So," Asey said, "so it is."

"Your little friend Jane. Oh, aren't you and Zeb Chase going to be sorry you happened in here tonight! Twenty-five thousand, double it for death by violence. Who's in the driver's seat, Mayo? Fifty thousand dollars does make such a nice motive, doesn't it? Roll it over on your tongue. Jane gets fifty thousand if Mary Randall dies by violence."

Asey smiled back at him, but the smile was somewhat forced.

"Saturday," Tertius went on, almost dreamily. "She gets the policy Saturday, because I bring it over then."

It flashed through Asey's mind that the shotgun had first gone into action Saturday night.

"On Monday," Tertius said, "she's killed. Life is a strange uncertain thing at best, isn't it? One never knows, does one? Here, as the saying so cheerily goes, today. Gone tomorrow. By the way, Mayo, yours is a perilous occupation. How are you fixed in case of accidents and whatnot?"

"Tertius," Asey said, "I begin to see. Eloise didn't take you home last night, did she? She dropped you here, an' you was goin' to walk back, but you got curious about the cars parked outside, an' so you looked into the matter. Guessed what was up, an' d'cided to make sure, so you go to Weston's desk where you know he keeps that ledger. Not findin' any ledger, you smirked like anythin' an' come here for the policy. Shall I guess why?"

"Could I have a cigarette? It's a bit awkward here, trussed up—don't you think you'd better stop playing games and let me go? Oh, I do. Definitely, my dear Sherlock."

"Why?"

Asey knew exactly what was coming. He had guessed it ten

minutes ago, but he wanted more than anything to play for time.

"Well," Tertius said, "I'll tell you. You pretend to be a bumpkin, but old Captain Porter left you comfortably off. I've heard him and father talk about you. You're a Porter director, aren't you? And even if you weren't so richly endowed, your friend Bill Porter is, isn't he? Yes. And Master Chase has all those beans. And you and Master Chase are keeping a murder secret, aren't you? Because of Jane Warren. Zeb likes Jane Warren. Need I really go on? It seems such a waste of time."

"How much," Asey inquired, "do you want?"

"Call it—oh, fifty thousand will cover it nicely," Tertius said. "I think fifty thousand will do."

Asey nodded. "An' your plan—of course, I'm puttin' it awful crude, an' I know it'll hurt you, but you had a nice plan, didn't you? You come to get the policy an' change the name, an' send in a notice dated—yes, I suppose you could of managed it somehow. An' after makin' Eloise the beneficiary—honest, that was a brain wave, Tertius. Eloise wants to be Mrs. Somebody, an' I shouldn't wonder if she hadn't jumped at you like a starvin' dog at a bone. An' then you'd have had fifty thousand to blow. Tertius, that was smart."

"That is very crudely put," Tertius said. "But what, on the other hand, is fifty thousand to you and Zeb? Chicken feed. Now, Mayo, let's stop skirmishing. You can't arrest me. You know you can't."

Konrad rubbed his forehead. He was plainly bewildered. He wondered to himself who was the crazier, this hick detective that was supposed to be so hot, or the burglar who wasn't acting at all the way a burglar should act, particularly when caught in the act of burgling.

"How d'you figure that?" Asey asked.

"Can you prove I entered the town offices?"

"You was careful," Asey admitted, "about prints."

"And will you tell me how this cop can identify his assailant as me?"

"Say," Konrad said, "I know—"

"Maybe you do," Asey said, "but did you actually see who throttled you? No. There you are."

"Have I taken anything from this place? Did you find on me anything belonging to Mary Randall? See? If you arrest me on any trumped up charge, I'll blow this hush-hush business higher than a kite. If you just let me loose, and forget this fifty thousand, it'll be worse than that."

Konrad turned to Asey. "Can't you get him for the murder? How'd he know about it? If no one knows, and he does, didn't he do it?" The problem had been bothering him.

"Unfortunately, Tertius was on a ferris wheel at the time, an' 'steen thousand people know it, includin' Tertius."

"Think fast, Mayo," Tertius said. "Think fast."

"Will you let me tend to him?" Konrad pleaded.

"No, no, Konrad—for the love of God, don't touch him!"

"That's right, no crass violence," Tertius said. "Prettyman is not to be mussed. Mayo, you're hoist by your own petard, aren't you? Just think of the stink I'd make—horrid word, but so apt. What a stink! Did you know my revered father?"

"I never had that pleasure."

"Thought you might have, he went on Porter's yacht once or twice—what did you say? I thought you cast a pearl my way. Anyway, the old man was no damn Einstein, but he was an expert at two things, poker, and hue and cry raising. I don't

FIGURE AWAY

like to brag, you understand, but the Prettyman family has hue and crying down to a magnificent art. Honestly, can you think of any loophole?"

Asey strolled over to the oak chest, sat down and began to laugh.

"What's so funny?" Tertius was irritated by the sound.

"Tertius," Asey said, "did you ever hear tell of possession? There's a coarse, crass old adage that says possession is nine points of the law. I admit what you can do to us if we keep you or let you go. But that don't alter the fact, we *got* you."

"Embarrassing possession," Tertius said. "You can't keep me in your pocket. Or leave me here. Think of the long autumn evenings ahead—"

"With the frost on the punkin an' you a'mouldering' on the floor. I been considerin' that, an' I just found the solution," Asey said. "I never met your father on Porter's yacht, but I r'member hearin' about him, an' about you. You went on the Porter yacht once, didn't you? Aha. You do recall that? Gets you a little green to think about it, don't it? An' how they had to put back to port an' let you off, with you so weak from seasickness you couldn't even walk. Had to be carried off in a stretcher. Well, Tertius, over to my wharf I got a nice motor boat. All set to go, 'cause I was intendin' to take a week's fishin' trip. I call her the 'Rock an' Roll.' She's a nice boat, an' I'm sure you'll be real happy on her. My cousin Syl an' his brother Alf—what's that?"

Tertius' face was a horrible greenish white.

"You can't! You can't do that, it's kidnapping!"

"Well really," Asey said, "I can't see it's any more kidnappin' than what you was doin' here tonight was burglarin'! You said I couldn't call you a burglar. I'm sure you wouldn't want to call me a kidnapper! Why, perish the horrid thought! Course, you're a blackmailer, really, ain't you?"

Tertius' mouth was working.

"He's going to have a fit!" Konrad was alarmed. "Say, he's frothing!"

"He'll froth more, after two weeks on the 'Rock an' Roll.' You're an amiable blackmailer, Tertius, but adjectives don't make much dif'rence. How about it?"

Helplessly, Tertius tugged at his bonds and writhed around on the floor.

"Come, come," Asey said impatiently, "answer me! You're a blackmailer, ain't you?"

He repeated the question until Tertius admitted with a sob that he was a blackmailer.

"Fine, now we're gettin' some place. Sit up, an' stop this nonsense. You been tellin' me where to get off, an' now I'm goin' to tell you. Do you want to spend an indef'nite period on the 'Rock an' Roll'? All right. Bear that craft in mind, feller. If you don't want an extended cruise, you sit up an' answer my questions, an' answer'em truthful—what *is* it, Konrad?"

"What's got into him? He's sick—he's a pulp! What happened?"

"Just seasickness. He near dies of it. I'm glad I finally r'membered all the yarns about him. Now, Tertius, goin' cruisin' or not?"

"No!"

"Splendid. How did you know about this murder? Did you hang around last night like I thought?"

"Yes."

"Broke into Weston's office for the ledger? Yes. Slapped

down Konrad? Yes again. Now, what makes you think Jane Warren killed Mary Randall?"

"She was here, wasn't she?"

"That's not enough. Why were you so sure about Jane?"

"She and Mary had been fighting. They were at each other's throats. Have been for a month."

"How do you know?"

"Eloise told me," Tertius said. "It was about Zeb."

"What about him?"

"Mary wanted Jane to marry him. Said he was a good fellow and it meant security for the rest of her life, and all that."

"And Jane wouldn't?"

"Jane said he was all right, but she didn't happen to love him. Mary said at least she didn't hate him, and it was no time to bother with that stupid modern sentimentality." Tertius was beginning to get back to normal. "Mary's right, of course, in Jane's case. But she rubbed it in. And the more she rubbed, the stubborner Jane got."

Asey raised his eyebrows. This was a new angle.

"That's all the truth," Tertius said hastily. "You can ask Eloise. Eloise put in her two cents' worth for Zeb, too. She thinks Zeb is dear—such a nice boy. Of course the money helps," he mimicked Eloise's high voice, "I always say it helps. Not that money is all, but I always think—Cousin Eleanor's daughter—but then her husband wasn't nice, and Zeb is *so* nice! I'm sure it wouldn't turn out like that, with divorces."

"So Jane," Asey said, "got it from Mary an' from Eloise too?" That might well explain, he thought, her attitude on the previous afternoon, and her bitterness about the antique business and everything connected with it.

"And how! She couldn't leave. She hadn't any place to go.

All the usual Orphan Annie stuff. The Randalls were feeding and clothing and keeping her, and she couldn't talk back too much." Tertius smiled. "And then that policy comes Saturday. Well there you are. I suppose Jane's idea was to kill Mary, and collect on that, and marry Slade and live happily ever after, only not in his tar paper shack."

"Marry Mike Slade?" Asey stared at Tertius. "Look, is this your imagination?"

"Ask Eloise," Tertius said. "She'll tell you. They've been pretty sly about it. But Eloise caught on, and Mary did too. That was what galled them so, that Jane should play around with Mike, while the Baked Bean Billions stared her in the face. And mind you, Mary and Eloise didn't care so much for the money. But they knew Jane did, and does. Poverty doesn't agree with her. They weren't being snooty about it, or about Mike. They knew their Jane."

Asey got up and started to pace around the room.

This put a different complexion on the whole business.

From the start, he and Lane had done considerable figuring about Jane Warren. She was there on the spot, and she was the obvious suspect. On the other hand, they could think of no motive. And here, certainly, was the motive.

"That," Asey said, "is somethin'. But we still got the gun problem. Zeb Chase an' I got here seven or eight minutes after Mary was killed. We can't find any trace of a shell, or any shotgun except Zeb's, an' his won't do. Lane's plumbed chimneys, an' opened panels in the wainscotin', an' peered under floors, an' generally fine toothed the house an' the surroundin' scenery. Trees an' everythin'. No gun. Now if it'd been Jane, she hadn't time to hide a gun, an' if she hid it, we'd of found it. But—"

"Did you say shotgun?" Tertius interrupted eagerly. "Was that what did it?"

"A shotgun, an' deer ball. Why?"

"Asey," Tertius drew a deep breath, "I should like very much to winter in Florida or California, preferably California. I like the place. And I'll promise you on my word of honor never to breathe a word to anyone about this mess until you say so. And I can prove every bit of what I can tell you. Isn't it worth a winter in California to find out who killed Mary Randall?"

Asey looked at Tertius. The fellow seemed in earnest, but that meant little.

"What makes you think you know?"

"If it was a twelve gauge gun—was it?"

Asey sat down again on the chest. Lane had weighed one of the balls. It was an ounce ball, a standard load for a twelve gauge gun. But only he and Lane knew. Perhaps Tertius was making a stab, but—

"Well," Tertius said, "was it? And what about California?"

"You're half tanned already," Asey said. "Go on."

"Oh, it's Jane, all right," Tertius said. "You see, Jane bought a twelve gauge shotgun just about six weeks ago."

CHAPTER 8.

TERTIUS paused for a moment to let the information sink in, and then he surveyed Asey with a certain amount of irritation.

"Well, doesn't that please you?"

"It'd please me a lot more," Asey said, "if you could only prove it."

"I can prove it. She bought that gun from a mail order house. I have the cancelled check that paid for it. How's that?"

"Whose check? Yours?"

Tertius nodded.

"In that case," Asey said, "how about you bought it yourself? An' if she did buy it, how come it's your check? Nope, you'll never bask in any orange groves on the strength of that!"

"Listen. In June, she came to me and asked if I'd write a check for her. She wanted to order something, and had only cash. So—"

"Why didn't she use a money order? Why'd she come to you, of all people?"

"Jane Warren," Tertius said, "probably doesn't know what a money order is. She comes from a different social scale.

FIGURE AWAY

There's only one way of sending money that she understands. That's by check. She always sent checks, and not having any checking account at the moment, she gets checks from someone who has 'em. She's done it before. Once when she bought some present for Mary and didn't want to give the show away by asking Mary to write the check for her. See?"

Asey nodded.

"Anyway," Tertius continued, "I asked who was the present for this time, and she laughed and said it was none of my business. She had an order blank with her, but I didn't get a peek at it. But I found out when the check came back the next month—say, undo me, will you?"

"How'd you find out?"

"Oh, well. Well, there was a catalogue number written on the back, so I got out a catalogue and looked it up. What she ordered and what my check paid for, and what she got, was a twelve gauge anniversary special shotgun. And you can prove that, by the check, and by her order and by your store records. By the post office. Anything you want. There you are. Mary's killed by a twelve gauge gun. Jane bought one. Jane has a motive."

"That's all true."

"And if you haven't been able to find any gun," Tertius went on, "what about Mike Slade? Suppose Mike did the shooting. Or suppose that Jane did, and then gave the gun to him to cart away. Now, what about California—do I hear a car in the drive?"

"It's Hamilton." Asey drew a folding check book from his pocket. "Got a pen, Konrad?"

"Hamilton," Tertius said. "He's the one who got my license taken away. Speeding. That's why Eloise was driving me last night, and why I had to hitch hike over here from the hall tonight. I'm a marked man—hi, Hamilton."

"Hullo yourself. What are you tied up for?"

"Undo him, Konrad," Asey said. "Ham, come here."

After a lengthy whispered conversation, Hamilton grinned and Asey walked over to Tertius.

"Here you are," he said. "Ham's going to take you to your house to get that check for Jane's gun, an' then he's drivin' you to Boston. Are you goin' to play ball?"

Tertius' eyes bulged at the sum Asey had given him.

"My God! Really, this is very decent of you. Really. I mean, you could arrest me, and—"

"Ham'll see to things. You pop along. Konrad, you hang around an' keep your eyes open from now on. I'm leavin' in a few minutes, but first I want to paw around this desk—"

He sighed wearily after they left, and then he smiled to himself. Hamilton would put Tertius on a train, but at Tertius' side there would be a plainclothesman for some time to come. He was taking no chances on the Prettyman family.

He pulled out his pipe and sat down at the desk. It was odd that Mary Randall should have made no mention of Jane and Zeb and Mike Slade in her diary, but on the other hand it was an impersonal sort of diary that could be published on any front page without causing any consternation to anyone. She had mentioned several times that she hoped Zeb and Jane would get things settled, but that was all. That was—

A noise in the shed beyond brought him to his feet.

He reached for his gun. There were plenty of rats in the barn, but rats didn't say "Damn" in clearly audible tones.

Before his hand could lift the door latch, someone on the other side touched it.

FIGURE AWAY

A girl with red hair and freckles smiled at him and walked past into the barn.

"I caught on a nail," she said pleasantly.

Asey didn't need to ask who she was. He knew. This was Sara Leach's girl reporter. And it was only too clear that she had been making the most of an orchestra seat.

"That shed door lock," she went on, "is no earthly use. My nail file almost cut it in two." She stretched and wriggled her shoulders. "And whoever thought up that glued-to-a-keyhole idea was a master of the apt phrase. I've got sciatica or something in every limb. Look, I'm not going to bite, or break into little pieces or anything—"

"What brought you here?" Asey demanded.

"That shot. I heard it as I drove by. So I came in. Frankly, I'm a sucker for the sound of a shot. I can't seem to resist them —do I really discourage you as much as you look?"

"Miss Thayer," Asey said, "you do. You—"

"How'd you know my name?"

"Sheer detectin'," Asey told her.

He foresaw that it was going to be uphill work, disliking this girl. He wanted to, but he couldn't seem to get started. She wasn't hardboiled, like some of the lady reporters who had been sent to interview him at one time or another. She wasn't mushy or soppy, like that Viola Someone who'd knit him socks and mourned that he had to live all by himself in that great big house of his. She wasn't at all cocksure or arrogant, as she had every right to be when you considered what she had stumbled into. She was just matter of fact.

"Sheer detectin'," Asey repeated. "Miss Thayer, what do you want? Or puttin' it another way, what do you want more'n you want this story?"

Kay Thayer sat down, lighted a cigarette and looked thoughtfully around the room before answering.

"It's going to slay you," she said at last, "but I don't want anything. Not even a trip to California. I want the story, but I don't want it now."

"What?"

"You heard. At first I was all worked up to find you were hiding a murder. Then it occurred to me that you couldn't be hiding it. If the state cops knew, then various and sundry other authorities would know. And then, after a period of deep thought, I began to grasp it. If Billingsgate had a murder now, well—poof—"

"Poof, or boom. Honestly, you don't mean you'll keep quiet for a spell?"

"Why not? If I phone up what I've found out, the whole pack'll be here as fast as their cars'll carry'em. What chance would I have? None. But if I can go home with the whole story—well, I really do think that I can afford to be a little charitable about Billingsgate."

Asey walked over to her and extended his hand.

"It's always a pleasure to meet a logical female. It's an event."

She smiled. "And now, before I burst, will you fill in the cracks for me? Don't I deserve to know?"

Briefly, Asey told her all that had happened.

"And so," she said, "your obvious suspect bought a twelve gauge gun. That means that by tomorrow or the next day, you ought to have some sort of case, doesn't it, really?"

"It means nothin' at all," Asey replied coolly. "It don't mean one single blessed thing."

"What? But you told Tertius—I mean, you said—"

"Tertius was a fly in the ointment," Asey said. "He was the excess baggage. The monkey wrench. What comes of tryin' to keep things quiet. All I know is, he didn't kill Mary, an' I didn't want him. Fast or loose, Tertius could have been just as nasty a burden as he promised. Just a white man's burden. That's that. Therefore Tertius is goin' on a long, long journey, feelin' valuable an' virtuous, an' a plainclothesman'll tend him like a brother. At least, I hope he will."

"Then you did all that to get rid of him? Look, there seems to be a lot of things that elude me. What about the ballistics end of it? Is there one? I mean, there usually *is* a ballistics end to these things."

"Out of every ten shotguns sold," Asey said, "probably nine of 'em is twelve gauge guns. It's like findin' an arrow. Almost any bow might do, offhand. There's one, an' just one way of connectin' any shotgun with this murder. That's by findin' a shell. An' findin' a shell in this vicinity that you could more or less prove was left there by the murderer last night. You could say, the only connection was if we *had* found a shell. Because we ain't so far, an' I can't see how we will now."

Kay Thayer wrinkled up her nose. "But you have the ball —look, put it in words of one syllable, can't you?"

"S'pose," Asey said, "someone shot Mary Randall with my gun here. We take the bullet, an' we know it come from a forty-five. Now in our real case, we weigh the deer ball, an' we know it's a standard load for a twelve gauge gun. But—an' this is an important but. But in our case of the forty-five, we corral every forty-five we can find, near or far. Sooner or later, we find a forty-five that shoots a bullet that's got all the ridges an' markin's an' whatnot of the bullet that killed our person. Got that?"

"I'm plowing along."

"Then," Asey continued, "get to our real case right here. The deer ball's got no markin's. It might have been fired from any shotgun in Christendom, providin' it's a twelve gauge. Everyone with the slightest connection with this case might own a twelve gauge gun. They might have collections of twelve gauge guns. We couldn't do a thing. Not unless we find, or found, the shells in a place—well, like outside Mary's window somewhere. Those shells would have the mark of the hammer. Then we could begin to hunt shotguns, an' try to find the one that left the same mark on the shells as these did. See?"

"Sort of."

"An' mind you this. We'd have to prove the shells had some connection with this. That's a nice joker."

"In brief, a shell you probably will never find is the only connecting link between shotgun, deer ball and murder?"

"Just so. For fun, say we find the shell. Then we got to find the shotgun, which any sane person would have hove into the Atlantic last night after Mary was killed. Into somethin', anyway. Then we got to prove the ownership of the gun. Then, maybe, with the grace of God an' the hand of fate an' such, maybe we might prove that the owner was the person who was here last night an' killed Mary Randall. But you can see," Asey added drily, "there's some chance involved."

"In other words, even if Jane Warren bought a shotgun, and a twelve gauge, and even if she were here and had a motive, you still haven't a clew, don't expect to find any, and even if you did, they probably wouldn't help?"

Asey beamed at her. "That's a fine summin' up of this whole case. It's the works in a thimble. Now ask me, what good can I do? An' I'll tell you the honest truth, I don't see how in the world we can do a single thing."

"Then why do you keep on?"

"Guess."

Kay stubbed out a cigarette. "Not for what you can get out of it, that's a cinch. I—well, there are probably two reasons. One is that you've just stated the case from the official copper's point of view, and it's hopeless, but that you've got some ideas on the subject just the same, and you intend to work it out yourself. And the other reason—well, that you feel Mary Randall's murder is incidental to something else."

Asey nodded. "An' there's a third thing. I got a sort of hankerin' notion to find out who this clever feller is. I'd sort of like to meet him."

"Are you very sure," Kay asked, "that it's not a madman on the loose? There've been cases sort of like this. I've read about them."

"When everything else fails," Asey said, "you lay it to a maniac. But just the same, I tie this up with the things Sara an' Weston worried about. There's a plan somewhere. I can't tell where or what it is, or lay my hands on much of it, but it's there. We got odds an' ends an' corners, but nothin' to tell the shape of the thing. I wish to heaven this man'd make a move. He'd be a fathead to, because all he's got to do is sit tight an' say nothin', an' he's all set. But Mary Randall was killed for a purpose, prob'ly to keep her from tellin' somethin'. There is a plan here, I'm sure. I been hopin' if we sat back, some more of it would filter out."

"There's the Warren girl and Mike Slade. Perhaps they're the planners. He's connected with the town, and she's connected with Mary. Personally I should dally with those two."

"They'll be dallied with, never fear," Asey promised. "An' now, let's get back to Sara's. I'm tired. I—"

"Oh, I see how you knew me. You're staying there! Aunt Sara told you!"

"Swami Mayo," Asey observed. "Knows all, hears all, sees all. Let's get back there b'fore anyone else pops in. You know, I took Slade for the hot-tempered kind that flies off the handle easy, an' I thought he was tryin' to help, in his way—put out the lamp, will you? But now I'm lookin' forward to findin' Comrade Slade at an early date. Tomorrow, probably, while you're takin' down governors' speeches."

But his chance to dally with Mike Slade came much sooner than that.

As Asey turned his roadster up the lane leading to the Leach house, he noticed that the house blazed with lights at every window.

His headlights, as he shot the car forward, picked up the figures of three men on the front lawn. Four men. The place was swarming.

Swinging his car so that the headlights illuminated the front of the house, he shut off the ignition and ran towards the group.

It was Slade—Slade was fighting someone. Slade was fighting J. Arthur Brinley, and the trooper who'd been stationed by the garage was trying to separate them. Zeb stood there helplessly, watching, but not doing anything about it all. Just, Asey thought, the way he'd stood around when Jane fainted. No great shakes in an emergency, the baked beans heir.

Suddenly Slade stopped pounding Brinley's face and turned his attention to the trooper. J. Arthur hastily moved out of range and watched.

FIGURE AWAY

"What is goin' on—" Asey began.

"Thank goodness," Sara appeared beside him. "And *what* a time I had getting out of that room! I hadn't any idea where Jeff put the key, and he couldn't remember, but luckily he had one on his key ring that—"

"Sara, what's goin' on? Hey, trooper, stop! Slade, cut it out —hold it, you two!"

Slade and the trooper, rolling over and over in the grass, ignored his commands.

"What happened?" Asey asked. "Sara, stop watchin' them so avid an' tell me what happened, will you?"

"Oh, I don't really know," Sara said. "We just heard the screams, and then the fight. I don't know who's fighting who, or for what—really, I do think that the trooper is getting far the best of it, don't you?"

Asey strode over to Zeb.

"What *is* this?"

"I don't know," Zeb said. "Everyone's all right, I guess. Jane and Eloise and Jeff are indoors. Eloise," he added as an afterthought, "is having hysterics. Should I call the doctor, or—"

Asey snorted and turned to Brinley.

"See here, J. Arthur, what's the meanin' of this rumpus— oh, what's the use?"

Brinley was puffing and blowing after his tussle with Slade, making so much noise that he didn't even hear Asey's question. He was nervously dabbing a handkerchief at his lip, which was bleeding freely, and each time he saw the little spots of red, he puffed and blew more fervently.

Kay Thayer, who had parked her little coupe next to Asey's roadster, came over and stood beside him.

"What's the general idea?" she asked. "I mean, who's the trooper spanking?"

"Slade," Asey said. "Don't ask why. I don't know. No one knows, I guess."

"Aren't you going to take any steps?"

Asey shrugged. "Everyone's havin' lots of fun. Maybe if we wait, someone'll get bored with fightin', or watchin', an' let us in on things. Nope, I guess I'd better not wait at that. Slade's stagin' a comeback—"

He marched in between the two men and did something— Kay couldn't tell what because it all happened too quickly. Somehow, the trooper was on his feet, apparently none the worse for the scuffle, and Slade was flat on his back after a somersault through the air. Asey stood over him.

"Shut up, Slade. Keep quiet or I'll do it again. Trooper, what's this about?"

"Him." The trooper pointed to Slade. "I heard someone, see, and I thought I heard that laugh you spoke about. So I sneaked around, but I couldn't find anybody. Then after a while I heard someone moving, but I couldn't find anybody. And then I heard footsteps—"

"But you couldn't find anybody," Asey said impatiently. "I know. Get to the point, will you?"

"Well, finally I heard someone in the house scream, and then everybody woke up, and people started moving around, and coming out, and then I seen this guy here, getting down the big maple. He'd been up the tree, trying to get into a window, and I guess some woman in the house seen him and screamed. And then this fellow," he pointed to J. Arthur, "he come up out of nowhere, and he tackled the other fellow, and

FIGURE AWAY

they were hitting it up and then I tried to stop 'em, and then he went for me. That's all."

"It's not," Asey said, "the clearest explanation I ever heard, but— Sara, what's your version?"

"Someone screamed," Sara said. "Eloise, it must have been, for she's gone to pieces entirely indoors somewhere. I told Jane where the spirits of ammonia are, and she and Jeff are working on her. Jeff's awfully handy with hysterics. His mother had them regularly. Monotonous, I thought, but people always tore around and did things for her—"

"Slade," Asey said, "it looks like you had to provide the explanation yourself. What was the underlyin' idea behind your human fly act?"

"Oh, go to hell!" Slade said disgustedly. "You've busted my collar bone with your tricks! If I could move, I'd make hash of you—"

"It shouldn't be broken," Asey said. "Just sort of wrenched. But you r'sisted, an' I'm sort of stale at that stuff, an' that all makes— Kay, what are you snickerin' about?"

"Don't mind me, I'm the audience," Kay said. "And I do think this is pretty funny—hey, look out! Slade's trying to trip you!"

Asey moved back. "Trooper, you an' Zeb cart this fellow into the house. Sara, how about you take a hand with Eloise? I never heard anythin' so bloodcurdlin' as them screams! Kay, trail along, will you? By the lord Harry, I don't know what's come over folks. Brinley, are you back to normal yet? Where do you come in?"

"That man, that man is a menace!" Brinley spoke with difficulty. His lip was swelling and it gave him a slight lisp. "A menace. A maniac! He came to our house while we were all in bed—"

If J. Arthur hadn't looked so desperately miserable, Asey would have finished it up, "And you took a marrow bone and hit him on the head." But he only nodded, and told Brinley to go on.

"I was on the back porch," Brinley said, "I'd just come back from the clothes yard—that's where we keep our oil tank because it's handy, but out of sight. Anyway, I'd forgotten the oil before I went to bed—really, it's been a very tiring day! And I remembered it when I woke up, so I went out and filled the stove tank, because Mrs. Brinley likes plenty of hot water, and we have company anyway, so we had to have it, and Mrs. Brinley is particular about enough hot water when we have company. Madame—uh—the soprano, you know, is staying with us, and she—"

"You was on the back porch," Asey reminded him.

"And it seemed to me I heard a noise. I looked around, but I couldn't see anything, and—"

"Didn't happen to see any state cops, did you? No? Nice fellers, but not such hot guards. Go on."

"Well, I happened to look up, and there was this man, climbing down the Paul's Scarlet! Down the trellis, I mean. Well, Mrs. Brinley would rather *die* than have anyone break her Paul's Scarlet, you know. It's—why, everyone knows about it! You must have heard about Mrs. Brinley's Paul's Scarlet!"

"My fav'rite rose," Asey said. "What did you do?"

"Well, I thought rather quickly," Brinley was quite pleased at the rapidity of his thoughts, "and I said to myself, if I stop him now, he'll break the Paul's Scarlet. And I didn't want to wake Bessie, or Madame—uh—the soprano. They've had a hard day, too, and I knew Bessie would get worked up, and it's so bad for her heart, to get worked up, so I waited until he got down on the ground, and then—well—"

"Well, what? What happened?"

"Well," Brinley dabbed at his lip, "he seemed like quite a big man. And he didn't seem to be carrying anything, and I looked up, and the screens were in place, so I knew he hadn't got in, and besides, he hadn't waked anyone, and he would have if he'd got in. Mrs. Brinley is a very light sleeper—"

"So, you let him go?"

"For all I knew," Brinley said, "he might have been armed, and I only had the oil tank. And in my bedroom slippers, and just my pants on over my pyjamas, and my sweater, like I am now—"

"Uh-huh. But you turned up here. Now let's get into that side of it. Sort of wade on, Brinley."

"Well, I waited, and he slid around to the side of the house, and then I knew who it was. It was Slade, because he had a bicycle. Slade doesn't have a car, you know. He's against the car manufacturers. He says they exploit—"

"Slade got on his bike," Asey said, "and you did what, exactly?"

"Why, Madame—the singer's bike was there, so I followed. He came way up here, and left his bike, and I came after him and followed along. He cut through the woods, and then he came up to the house, and climbed the maple, and then that cop came, and—"

"Thanks," Asey said. "You done a nice job, an' I should expect it took considerable courage. Now, the cop'll attend to Slade, an' I'll take you home myself—"

"Not," Brinley said with a show of spirit, "until I know

what's going on here! Not until I am sure that menace, that maniac, is properly restrained! Taken into custody! Mr. Mayo, what *is* going on?"

Asey sighed. If he told J. Arthur, Mrs. J. Arthur would know, and that was equivalent to telling the whole town of Billingsgate.

"And this trooper here," Brinley said. "A lot of funny things are going on! Troopers at the hall. I saw them with my own eyes. And—"

"If you want to know," Asey made a desperate stab, "it's all on account of Slade. You know how he is. He wants publicity. That's why Weston had me come over, so none of Slade's stunts would get into the papers. Bad for the town. See that girl reporter? She knows, but she ain't written a word—"

He rambled on, and the more involved he got, the more inclined J. Arthur seemed to believe him. Just as Asey was beginning to feel that he had won, a car slewed up to the front walk, and Mrs. J. Arthur Brinley tumbled out and rushed up to her husband.

"Arthur—Arthur—oh, thank God! Madame Meaux said that Mr. Mayo would know—where is she? Madame Meaux, come quick! Come, show him that letter! Let him see it, quick! It's about a murder, and that awful Slade, he did it! He says so—"

CHAPTER
9.

THE ensuing quarter hour at the Leaches' house was never entirely clear or coherent to any of the people who somehow lived through it. As Sara said the next day, it was the sort of thing you used to date things by, like the night the old ice house burned down, or when the big tide washed away all those cottages.

Even when a comparative state of calm arrived, the confusion and uproar were considerable.

Slade emerged from it tied hand and foot on the living room floor, with the state trooper and Zeb trying to silence his roars of rage and threats of what would happen when he was set free. Before he achieved his recumbent position, he succeeded in breaking three chairs completely, and in rendering three others quite unfit for occupancy. The excited Eloise had run the entire gamut of hysterics. She had screamed and sobbed and laughed and cried, separately and all at once, and now she showed every sign of beginning at the beginning and repeating the exhibition. Jane, white-faced and tight-lipped, tried to soothe her. The process reminded Asey of old Barney Snowden, who decided one day that he disliked the Atlantic Ocean, and thereafter spent his time removing it, a teacupful at a time. Jeff, in a cambric nightshirt, with his whiskers askew, had appointed himself curator of the ice bags and cold cloths for Eloise. As fast as he got one in place, Eloise promptly threw it as far as she could send it. When she began to aim for the mantel, and Sara's pet collection of Toby jugs, Sara had removed them to a place of safety. Then, rather grimly, she stood on guard between Eloise and the rest of her bric-a-brac.

Mrs. Brinley pattered futilely around from Slade to Eloise, fuming at the former and giving advice as to the latter, and at intervals she stopped to embrace J. Arthur and sob on his shoulder. He was still nervously dabbing at his lower lip with the spotted handkerchief; it happened to be his upper lip which had really suffered, but he was beyond the stage of caring much about details.

After the first flurry, Kay had disappeared with Bertha in the vicinity of the kitchen. Madame Meaux had followed them, and then drifted back to the most comfortable arm chair she could find. She sat there, surveying things with interest, and occasionally grinning.

"Where've you been?" she asked Asey after he made a third trip to the hall. "What's going on out there?"

"You ain't missin' a thing," Asey said. "I'm tryin' to get Cummings on the phone. He's out on a call, an' they're tryin' to locate him for me. Eloise is in too much of a state to be handled by amateurs. What are you havin' such a lot of fun over?"

"'Billingsgate Beautiful,'" Madame Meaux said. "Look at Sister Brinley. She makes me think of a turtle, I don't know why."

"She looks," Asey said critically, "like a full ash can the

day after Christmas. Wouldn't it be charitable to r'mind her of that cold cream?"

The soprano lighted a cigarette. "What an outfit," she said sadly. "My God, what an outfit. No wonder J. Arthur is a discouraged man—after all!"

She herself was no more fully clothed than any of the other women, but somehow she seemed dressed for the occasion. She wore no curlers like Eloise, or cap like Sara, nor was her hair mussed like Jane's. A hairdresser might just have finished with her. Her satin negligee was a rather too vivid shade of orange, but it was unwrinkled and shining.

"One thing about my business," she said, "it teaches you to be smart about emergencies. Now if this had been a fire, Sister Brinley would clutch the pillows in her arms and take them carefully downstairs, and then toss the glassware out closed windows. I know. I've often wished that thirty-six weeks on the Chautauqua circuit was compulsory for all women—look, don't you want that note?"

She passed over a crumpled piece of paper.

"'Mail me all the money you've got to the Weesit P.O. General Deliv. There's been a murder and I'm in a spot. Mike. P.S. Don't say anything. You'll get your money back.'" Asey frowned. "The fool—no wonder—look, how'd Bessie Brinley get hold of this? What happened?"

"As far as I can make out," Madame Meaux said, "the Brinleys moved out of their bedroom and turned it over to me, and then they moved to their guest room. Mike climbed up outside and flipped this in the top of the window. It hit toots there in the face. He didn't know about the room switching. She blew into my room and blew up. I got her into the car and over here to you. I thought it was a job for you to handle. Besides, at the rate she was going, all the town would have been up in a few more minutes, and I got the impression that whatever was going on, you wanted to keep it quiet."

"Thank God you did," Asey said. "What a mess, what a mess!"

"You may think so," the soprano said, "but you haven't been driven by Bessie in a sweat, and I have, and it has aged me horribly. She wouldn't let me touch the car, because Arthur never lets strangers drive it. The angels nearly had the wheel, the last mile. Look, let's stop this din, what do you say? I'll cope with Eloise. That isn't hysterics now. It's temperament. I know all about temperament."

"Go to it," Asey said. "I'll fix Slade. In fact, I just got the wherewithal out in the kitchen—"

He pulled a piece of laundry soap from his pocket and strolled over to the still shouting Mike.

"Gimme your handkerchief, Zeb. Got one? Fine."

As Slade opened his mouth for a good bit of oratory, Asey inserted the soap, and then tied the handkerchief so that the soap would stay in place.

"There. That's the old-fashioned treatment for small boys, Slade, an' you d'serve it. How—wheee!"

Madame Meaux had crossed over to the couch; she watched Eloise dispassionately for a moment, and then leaned over and slapped her face. It was a resounding slap, and it made Eloise blink.

"Another peep out of you, and you get another," Madame Meaux announced. "And then some. No wonder you lead a single life if you act like this very often."

She returned to her arm chair and lighted another cigarette. The silence was electric, bristling with undercurrents.

FIGURE AWAY

"Well really," Mrs. Brinley said, "I never saw anything quite so brutal—"

"But how effective," Asey said, "how effective! Kay, is that coffee? Sara, feed your guests, an'—ah, there's the doc."

They got Eloise upstairs.

"I'll look after her," Cummings said. "I don't know what's going on down there, but it looks as though you were needed, Asey. Why must some women be like this? Her digestion'll be shot to hell for a week, and it's none too good anyway. I've told her a thousand times to lay off that medicated hay and straw. What she stuffs into her stomach in the guise of food would leave anyone itching for hysterics, just for sheer relief."

Asey went back to the living room. He had a task before him, and he didn't look forward to it.

He went straight to the point.

"Mrs. Brinley," he tried to make his voice solemn, "you an' your husband have been the victims of a plot."

Mrs. Brinley squealed and looked around her anxiously, as though something on the order of an octopus was about to pounce on her from a corner.

"Slade." Asey pointed to the figure on the floor. "I was telling your husband about it when you came. Slade wanted to get you two all worked up, for the publicity. That's why Weston asked me to come over here. To forestall anything like this. Now," he turned to the trooper, "do you know anything about any murder? You don't, do you?"

"No, sir!"

"Zeb? No. Jeff, if there had been a murder, you'd know about it, wouldn't you?"

"Good gracious," Jeff said in his best McGuffey's statesman manner, "who brought the matter up? It's preposterous! Murders, indeed! Was that what Slade has been saying? Why, the idea!"

Aunt Sara swallowed hard.

"Now, Miss Thayer, you're a reporter. Have you heard of any reports about a murder?"

"If I had a whole fat murder story staring me in the face," Kay said with utter truthfulness, "I should not be here. I promise you that."

"There," Asey said, "see? It's a horrible thing, Mrs. Brinley, but you see, you an' your husband is influential, an' Slade knew if he could start a story through you, people would believe it. It's—uh—exploitin'. The—uh—rich, I mean, the influential folks always gets this sort of thing, in any community. You was bein' exploited by a ruthless publicity seeker, that's what."

"Ruthless?" Jeff Leach said. "It's dastardly!"

"Just so. Now, for the best interests of everything, Mrs. Brinley, Zeb'll take you home. You an' your guest. I want you to leave the rest to me. I," he added meaningly, "will fix this. I will—"

"Nip it in the bud," Sara helped him out.

"I want justice!" Mrs. Brinley began to lapse into her Women's Club manner. "I want justice, and justice will be done! Justice, or—"

"There's only one thing," Asey said, "an' Jeff'll agree with me. If there's any scandal now, with the Old Home Week goin' on—well, I certainly would hate to think of the effect."

He talked on until he was tired, and then Sara came to his rescue. She had never in the past been very cordial to Mrs. Brinley, but she made up for it.

At last the Brinleys gave in. To save Billingsgate, to leave un-

FIGURE AWAY

marred the escutcheon of Billingsgate and Old Home Week, they would forget their personal feelings. They would leave everything to Asey. They would never mention the affair. Never whisper about it.

Zeb drove them home in Asey's roadster. Madame Meaux, who had also allowed herself to be persuaded to save the town, winked at Asey as she left.

"What an M.C.," she said, "show business lost in you! I'll lay it on some more for you when they get back."

Finally Cummings got Eloise to sleep, and Asey got the rest of the household off to bed.

"What are you going to do with him?" the doctor pointed to Slade.

"Him an' me is goin' to have a little seance out in the barn. Help us take him out, doc. There's been enough to do in this house for one night."

After Slade had been deposited on the barn floor, Asey turned to the trooper.

"Go on back an' see none of them folks decide to come help us after all," he said. "If they don't get to sleep right away, they'll probably decide to lumber out an' assist."

He removed the handkerchief and the piece of soap from Slade's mouth and stood back to await the torrent of abuse he fully expected would issue forth.

But Slade just lay there sullenly and never uttered a word.

Asey looked at him thoughtfully. He could see how someone like Jane would fall for a fellow like that. Slade was no moving picture idol; his nose was too long and his mouth too wide, but his dark hair had the sort of crinkly wave in it that women seemed to like, and his black eyes had probably made any number of conquests. About thirty-five, Asey decided. Younger than he had at first thought. And even bound hand and foot, there was a tremendous vigor about him.

"Huh," he said. "I can see where you would make Zeb Chase look like skim milk. An' I see why Sara give you a chance. Slade, what's the big idea?"

"Go to hell."

"Now you know," Dr. Cummings sat down on an overturned lobster pot, "the trouble with Slade, Asey, he never made enough to live as an artist, and on the rare occasions when he did make anything, he never bought proper food. Now he has this town job, his disposition's improved some. He doesn't rant quite so much. You know, Asey, I've always thought communism is a sort of religion, and the people who get any religion really violently, they always have some quirk somewhere, and usually it's the digestive system. A well fed person doesn't care two cents for causes. They accept things. But you take a digestion—"

"Ain't you," Asey said, "sort of harpin' on the digestive system tonight?"

"Well," Cummings said defensively, "I read a book about it last night. Tonight—anyway, before I got into bed a while ago. The fellow goes too far, of course, they all do, but—oh, go on!"

Asey didn't remind him that he hadn't been given any chance to begin, let alone to continue.

"Slade," he said, "I'm tired. Let's get this over with. How'd you know about the murder? Man alive, I don't like this nonsense any more than you do! But if you smash up furniture and act in general like a fool kid, what can we do? Now, come on. Who told you about the murder? How'd you know?"

"Jane wrote me a note. I got it this evening. She's frightened to death, and why shouldn't she be, with all of you bullying her—"

"No one's bullied her, Slade. Don't be foolish. Why did you want all the money Emily Slade could give you?"

"Oh, to get away, you fool! To get Jane away—that's why I came here tonight. To take her away from all of you, and all of this before it's too late!"

"But—"

"And I would have taken her, too, if that damned Eloise hadn't gummed it up!"

"What's he talking about?" Cummings asked curiously. "He doesn't smell drunk—"

"Drunk? I'm not drunk! But I know what I'm talking about!" Slade yelled. "It's a conspiracy! It's all a conspiracy! The dirty Chase money they've piled up out of their filthy baked beans—"

He went on at some length about the dirty Chase money.

"I'm wrong about the digestive system," Cummings said while Slade paused for breath. "I don't think it's the digestive system at all, Asey. It's glandular. On the other hand—say, Mike, do you have many headaches? Does it ever seem to you that your hands, or arms, or head—or any part of you—just floated in space? Because—"

Slade got his breath and began again.

Asey listened to the tirade, trying to piece together some sort of story from it.

Slade had made up his mind that Asey and the rest, with the consent of the police and the town officers, had decided to shield the real murderer of Mary Randall. He was very set on that point, and he illustrated his ideas with any number of cases from Czarist Russia, Fascist Italy and Nazi Germany. But because eventually the murder would have to come to light and be made public, Slade felt that Jane Warren had been picked as the official scapegoat.

"And while you're bullying her, and getting your fake case made as water tight as you can, you withhold all the story from the public. From the people. From everyone who has any right to know. All to save your lousy town, and its moneymaking schemes! It's a conspiracy."

"It's indigestion, that's what it is," Cummings said. "What did you have for supper?"

"Baked beans." Slade was caught off guard by the doctor's professional tones.

"No wonder," Asey said, "why, in your situation, I think Chase's Baked Beans would upset me. Let's get this idea of yours about Jane and Zeb again. You wandered off and mixed me up when you footnoted on Spain."

It was simple, Slade said. Jane would be arrested for the murder. If she promised to marry Zeb, then the dirty Chase money would get her off. Obviously, to get off, it would take the dirty Chase money, and she couldn't get the dirty Chase money without taking dirty Chase's Zeb along with it.

Asey laughed when he finished. "I can't help it," he said. "You've gone all around Robin Hood's barn—honest, you couldn't be more wrong. Did Jane write you in this note that anything like that had been suggested?"

"No, but she said Eloise had suggested and hinted at it. But I know. You can't pull the wool over my eyes. I—"

"Slade, listen. Jane bought a shotgun. Where is it?"

"She bought the gun for me, for a present! She knew I wanted a new one—"

"Fine. Is that the gun you was brandishin' the other night up to the midway?"

"No, that was my old one. But shotguns don't make any difference—"

"They do," Asey said. "Where's your new gun now?"

"Oh, it's been stolen! It was stolen from my studio the night of the fire. Don't you see," Slade demanded hotly, "it's a conspiracy? Someone steals the gun that Jane gave me, that night, and kills Mary Randall with it. Then you find it, and then—"

"Now," Asey said, "we're gettin' some place. Jane bought a gun, give it to you, someone steals it from you on Monday night. Was that what made you run off an' hide, after shootin' your mouth off all over town, an' gettin' Brinley's goat, an' workin' up the Old Settlers?"

"No, you fool!" Slade said. "Of course it wasn't! My God, and you're supposed to be a detective! Can't you get anything straight at all?"

"With a mite of cooperation," Asey said, "I might pick out the gist of this, but right now you put me in mind of Mrs. J. Arthur Brinley. Well, we'll go to it again. Maybe we'll get it by degrees. I saw you Monday night at a brush fire near your studio. You was burned, an' worried about your paintings. Next thing, I hear you're rampin' around town with a shotgun. Why, exactly?"

"Because the fire was set, don't you see? Someone intended to burn down my studio! I found places later where kerosene had been poured around! And someone had stolen my gun, too. And I was mad. So I took my old gun and went up to town to show people that they couldn't intimidate me! I'm no—"

"You're no kulak," Asey said. "We know. Doc, your wife was caught on the ferris wheel when it stuck, wasn't she?"

"And," Cummings said feelingly, "and how! She and Bessie Brinley both. What they told the man who runs it isn't fit to print. She'll never get over that. It was better than the time she got stuck in an elevator in Boston, for eight hours, and they threw ham sandwiches in at her from the fourth floor. She seems to have a bad effect on elevating machinery, somehow. Hexes it, I shouldn't wonder."

"Doc, you was there at the midway, wasn't you, at the time?"

"My, yes, I gave moral support until Nellie sent someone to tell me that you wanted me. My wife—"

"How long, now," Asey said, "were you there before Nellie sent someone?"

"Half an hour or more. They were up there an hour and a half, all told. And, by George, all told, too!"

The doctor laughed heartily at his own joke.

"Uh-huh. Now, did you see Slade?"

"Man alive, everyone saw Slade. Couldn't miss him. He and the stuck ferris wheel were major attractions. Lots of people thought he was some sort of clown connected with the midway. He made quite a sensational appearance—"

"Doc," Asey said patiently, "I'm gettin' at something. Was Slade there when you came?"

"Oh, yes. He was practically the first person I saw, and I was going to offer some helpful suggestions about bed and the necessity for relaxing—that's another trouble with you, Mike. You don't relax enough. You're getting along in your thirties now, and you've got to realize that you can't keep up your youthful pace forever—"

"Doc!" Asey said. "Listen to me, will you? Slade was there when you came, an' that was half an hour before you was called to the phone. Now, is that right?"

"Yes," Cummings said, "why?"

"He was there during the last part of Philbrick's fireworks display?"

"I'm sure of it. He stood near me—why yes, he was there. He made some crack about the last piece—"

"That's all I want to know," Asey said. "Mary Randall was killed just before the final piece of fireworks went off. If Slade was up at the midway, that accounts for him. Seems to me it took a lot of pryin' to get that out of you two. Now, Slade, let's get back to your yarn again. Your idea in flippin' that note was to get enough money from Madame Thingummy to take Jane an' beat it. That's what you was climbin' the maple for, huh, to get Jane? Did it ever occur to you that the fellow who runs away is most usually considered the guilty one?"

Slade opened his mouth and closed it again. "Why—uh—why, no. But we wouldn't be running away from—"

"No. But it wouldn't help you any to run, would it? In fact, if you was in my place, how'd you feel if the two of you beat it?"

"I suppose I'd—oh, what the hell!"

"Just so. Will you give me your word, Slade, not to try to beat it with Jane?"

"She and I are free, and we have every right to come and go as we please—"

"You got the right," Asey said, "an' I'm the first to agree, but why be a damn fool? Will you promise to tuck that leavin' idea away in lavender for the time bein'?"

"Oh, well. Well, we haven't the money, anyway. We've just got to stay here and be intimidated and exploited and—"

"You poor things, you." Asey said. "Let's get back to another point. I'll grant you that we're keepin' this murder quiet, but it's legal quiet. You like the town, don't you? Well, why not let the town make its money, instead of blowin' things sky high over a murder? You blow, an' your job goes, b'cause the town goes bankrupt. Thought of that angle?"

Slade clearly had not.

"Well, consider it. Now, why did you rush off an' hide after Monday night, if you didn't know about the murder until Jane let you know?"

"I've told you, I won't be intimidated! And I was going to hang around, and lay for whoever started that fire and stole my gun, and wrote that note! He thought I'd leave, and I was going to let him think I'd left, but I was going to stay around and see—"

"*Who* thought you'd leave? Slade, can't you stop fiddlin' an' tell me what you're talkin' about? Who suggested your leavin'? Who's intimidatin' an' conspirin' against you, an' for what?"

"This Old Home Week! I've got—that is, I had—a lot to do. He was jealous. He tried to scare me into going, and leaving my part for him, that's what, and I won't be scared! Not by him, I won't. And you can tell him as much for me, too, and I'm—"

"Who?" Asey asked wearily. "Who? Who? My lord, I sound like a hoot owl, an' I feel like hootin'. Who on earth are you talkin' about?"

"Brinley," Slade said. "What a detective you are! You don't seem to know anything! Brinley, of course. Little J. Arthur, he's behind all this!"

"You mean that poor fat henpecked man? That piece of

Milquetoast? Oh, come now, Mike. Brinley's a lot of things, but he ain't hardly any master mind! That's goin' too far!"

"What about the message he left after he started the fire up at my studio?"

"What about it? Now, don't say again that I'm a punk detective. But you ain't mentioned this before, you know. This is news to me."

"Fish in my pants pocket," Slade said. "You'll find it there, a half sheet of notepaper, unless your filthy Cossack of a trooper spilled it out."

Asey found it, a much folded sheet of official Billingsgate town office paper, with the town seal and the names of the selectmen engraved upon it.

Written on it in large three-inch letters were four short words.

"Get Out. Stay Out."

"Brinley's writing," Slade said. "Now do you see?"

CHAPTER 10.

IT was nearly noon the next day before Asey began his solitary breakfast in the dining room at Aunt Sara's. On the table before him was the message that Slade had found in his studio, and a packet of letters written by Brinley to Jeff, which Sara had found for him.

There had been little doubt in his mind that the "Get Out. Stay Out" message was in Brinley's handwriting, and Lane, who had just left, confirmed his opinion.

"I can send it up to Max in Boston," he said, "if you want me to, but I don't see the need. I don't often say I'm positive of things, but I am about that. Now, I'm going back to Hell Hollow and grub around for shells."

"Ain't lost hope yet?"

"See the sky?" Lane said. "We're going to have a thunder shower today. Paper says rain, but I think thunder showers. It's a chance."

Asey nodded. "You think there's a chance of something washin' to the surface?"

"There's always a chance of something coming to light, and I'm hoping for shells. Sounds crazy, but in that Bernstein case we had last year, a knife washed out of a mole hole after a storm, after we'd practically dug the place up. You can't ever tell."

"No," Asey agreed. "Only I looked around for mole tracks an' couldn't find any. But more power to you."

"Thanks. What about Brinley?"

"I wouldn't know," Asey said, "I wouldn't know. I got to brood."

He brooded as he ate his breakfast, to the intense annoyance of Bertha, who finally couldn't stand it any longer.

"What's the matter with those waffles?" she asked tartly.

"What waf—oh." Asey looked down. "That waffle? Bertha, it's one of the finest I ever put into my mouth. I want another."

"Was Slade drunk last night? Aunt Sara said so. He made an awful racket, didn't he?"

"Certainly did. You won't talk about it to—"

"Oh no. Aunt Sara told me not to."

Asey ate another waffle, and still another, and still the problem of J. Arthur Brinley and the fire at Slade's studio and the message left there all puzzled him.

To begin with, the fire hadn't been a very convincing fire; it hadn't been a very efficient fire, if Slade found evidence of preparation for it. And it hadn't been a very sensible method of scaring Slade out of town. Anyone who knew the man ought to know that opposition aroused him and he throve on it. Intimidation was the last weapon to force anyone like Mike Slade. The note was silly, just plain silly. It wasn't possible that even a chump like Brinley could think for a moment that Slade would be moved by that. He amended his thought: it would move Slade and arouse him to action, but it wouldn't move him out of town.

The whole business was the work of a fool.

"Whoa!" he said suddenly. "Oh, I didn't mean you, Bertha. I—well, another cup of coffee, then."

It wasn't the work of a fool. He had been the fool, working at it the wrong way.

The fire hadn't been set with the purpose of exciting Slade, or frightening him. The note might be genuine, but it didn't mean a thing.

Slade wasn't the point at all. The point was the murder of Mary Randall.

Fires drew crowds. People went to fires. It was as simple as all that. The whole crowd at the midway—everyone in town— everyone had gone to the fire. He recalled Zeb's comment about the children who had been following him and his trophies, something about their difficult decision, whether to get plunder, or see a fire. And the children, along with everyone else, had gone to the fire.

Now the road to Slade's studio ran parallel to the road leading to Hell Hollow for a mile or so, and then it branched off, like two fingers spread apart. But there were no hard-surfaced roads connecting the two after they left town.

There was the rutted lane which he himself had taken, but no car could possibly get through that swamp. There were other old wagon lanes, but none of them were passable as far as cars were concerned. Now the fire would draw crowds from the midway, and particularly, he thought, it would draw the men Weston counted on, the special constables and special firemen. It would draw people from the outer beach and the cottages there, people who might otherwise be passing by the hollow.

It was not a serious fire because it was not supposed to be

a serious fire. It had been planned so that by the time it was over, everyone would say, "Oh, the fireworks, it's time for the first fireworks to go on," and everyone would swarm back to town, leaving the murderer to take a short cut across to the hollow, even as Asey had, and to shoot under the cover of the fireworks noise. All in all, it was an excellent bit of thinking. It had rounded up a swarm of people not only from the midway but from all over town, and landed them all eventually at the ball park—except for the men who were still watching the fire, and those were the men who would have noticed anything out of order. And they were collected in one place, away from the hollow.

Magician's trick, that was it. While everyone was watching the right hand, two eggs and a rabbit came out of the left.

And everyone except Slade called the fire the work of tourists, and Slade was given the note for something to think about, to draw his attention away from the main issue. Just, as in all probability, the shots fired at Weston and the Brinleys and Jeff and Sara had—why, of course! He'd been stupid. All the some sort of thing. All a smoke screen. Get people worked up about one thing, and they'd miss something else.

He looked down at the "Get Out. Stay Out" message. It was written on an apparently genuine half sheet of official Billingsgate notepaper, with the town seal and names of the town officials engraved on the side.

"Bertha," he called. "Say, Bertha, you got a spare program? Can I have it?"

He flipped through the pages until he came to a facsimile letter, a greeting from the town officials to Billingsgate's guests. The heading was similar to the one on Slade's message, but there were several differences. Underneath the town seal were the words "Old Home Week," and at the foot were the dates of the founding of the first settlement and its later incorporation as a town.

Bertha glanced over his shoulder.

"That's a nice letter, isn't it? Aunt Sara wrote it. And that swell new paper. Uncle Jeff says that the new paper's worth the trouble of Old Home Week, all by itself. He likes nice paper, and he never could get them to buy that expensive kind. Aunt Sara said to hear him talk, you'd think the only thing he done for this Old Home Week was to get that paper."

"You can't tell much about it from this picture," Asey said, "is it colored?"

"There's a box full of it in Uncle Jeff's desk," Bertha said. "Why don't you look at it? He wouldn't mind. He shows it to everyone."

Asey strolled into the living room with Bertha, who produced the paper from a bottom drawer.

"See? White with blue engraving. Brinley wanted yellow and blue, like the town colors, but Jeff put his foot down."

"An' with due an' just reason," Asey said. "Yessiree, that's swell. That's a swell breakfast, too. Say, how do you feel about your jelly prospects up to the show? When's the judgin'?"

"Saturday they give the cups," Bertha said. "Silver cups. I thought mine was pretty good, but there's some mighty fine jelly up there. I went up yesterday."

"Don't give it a thought, how it looks," Asey said. "Looks don't mean a thing. I seen some that was done up all fancy, an' folks was sayin' how nice it looked, but it was what my mother used to call spindlin'. Yours is probably dark an' gummy, like it ought to be. Thanks, Bertha."

FIGURE AWAY

After she left, Asey took down the name of the printer from the cardboard box of town paper, and after several minor skirmishes with various phone operators, he got his man in New Bedford.

He hung up the receiver with a feeling of elation. The last lot of old paper had been delivered to Billingsgate long before Christmas. The new paper had been ordered and sent in January.

Asey sat down and pulled out his pipe. J. Arthur had written that message, but he had written it long ago, and it had been planted in Slade's studio by someone else. He looked again at the paper. It had been ironed over, he decided, but near the top was certainly a place where a pin had pricked through. He rumpled the paper and held it to the light. Yes, the paper had been pinned somewhere, but not at the studio. Slade said he found it on his table, held down by an ash tray.

"I wonder," Asey said, "if—sure!"

J. Arthur Brinley was an irascible sort. Suppose he were busy, making tax lists or figuring, and people interrupted him. Suppose it was around town meeting time, or the time of some celebration, and a crowd was outside as there had been the other day, laying for Weston. He could see J. Arthur, plagued beyond endurance, scrawling just that sort of thing on a paper, and pinning it up on the door outside, and feeling that he had taken a great step forward toward securing peace. It was a gesture that Weston or Jeff would never have found it necessary to make, but somehow it seemed like Brinley. At any rate it was a good guess.

Then someone had happened past the door and taken the paper off. Perhaps for the fun of it and without any plan in mind, and perhaps to save it for something like this—

Kay Thayer strode in and perched on the arm of a chair.

"Sitting here looking pleased with yourself," she said, "and breakfasting at noon! On waffles, too. I smelled 'em. It's disgraceful. It's decadent. I'm up at the crack of dawn, and I get corn meal mush. I hate corn meal mush. We used to have it at school. I tell you, there is no—"

"Don't say justice," Asey told her, "please. After listenin' to Mrs. Brinley an' Comrade Slade on justice, I don't want the word brought up anywheres near me for sometime to come. There's too many conflictin' ideas about it."

Kay laughed. "How did you squelch Slade, anyway? He was up at the station, dressed like a filthy capitalist in white flannels and a blue coat. He was being polite to tourists and guiding old ladies to front seats and generally being the well-dressed man from Cook's. Tremendously active man, and he seemed very efficient. How'd you work it?"

"The doc," Asey said, "is r'sponsible for Slade's comeback. He out-talked Slade, an' finally Mike give in an' said he'd behave himself. I think he was itchin' to get to his committees, really. An' he was gettin' sleepy, too, an' it was the easiest way out. By the way, ain't you playin' hookey from all the governors? Think of 'em, speechin' away."

"I did." Kay shuddered. "Of the three here today, two always station men around to make sure you don't get away with less than six copies of any speech they make, and the other one never says anything anyway. Jeff promised to tell me the general trends. In fact, he said if I were really anxious about it, he'd tell me before they spoke. I like Jeff. Asey, he seems to know all about the murder, but he doesn't say anything about it."

"Jeff knows," Asey said, "he knew last night. While I'm sure

FIGURE AWAY

Aunt Sara told him most everything, I give Jeff credit for havin' guessed it mostly beforehand. He's safe as a bank. That's how he spent all them years in Congress, you know. Preservin' a righteous exterior no matter how much he knew. I wish Slade took after him. Slade's theory seemed to be you ought to tell all you know—which is righteous enough, but not very wise. What are your plans for the day?"

"I'm free for a while. I sent up stuff about Philbrick and the golden-voiced Tripp—what an empty pot he is! Anyway, I banged out the celebrity stuff yesterday, and Shorty'll take it up. The governors aren't really my job. I'm supposed to be local coloring—oh, you haven't heard about Win Billings. You know him, the last Billings of Billingsgate?"

"I know the old duffer. They washed him an' dressed him up an' stuck him on display—did he get loose?"

"Well, he got a flock of drinks somewhere, and he stole the show at the station when the governors came. He kept yelling 'Hurray for Grant,' and fussing about the lack of decoration. He said when Grant came the time before, they had the station covered with all the best turkey red carpets in town, and urns with trailing plants, and the General, he thought it was *fine!* He said so. They finally got Win under control, but he escaped in the flurry of the special train coming in, and when Brinley got to presenting 'This distinguished scion of our founder's family,' Win was gone. Brinley nearly had to be taken away in a stretcher, he was so upset, and your cousin Weston took command."

"Did they find Win?"

"Oh, it was just a temporary loss. He was in the cab of the engine, pumping the engineer's hand. The engineer had a black beard, and he did look a little Grantish. Anyway, Win refused to get off the train, so they let him go along with it. He was an awfully pleasant engineer and he seemed to appreciate the situation. I had Shorty get a picture of Win earlier, and he's going to label it, Last Billings of Billingsgate Who Remembers Grant's Trip, Welcoming Governors. I thought it might please the old gent, if he ever sobers up. I sort of like Win. He's a rugged individualist, and oh, what he called Mrs. Brinley! It was such pure Anglo-Saxon that she almost didn't know what he meant."

Asey grinned. "That was a thoughtful an' charitable gesture of yours, the picture takin', but from what I hear tell of Win, he won't see the picture for some time. Kay, is Brinley a fool or a fiend?"

"Fool, of course. I knew you'd been finding things out. It's written all over you. What? Tell me."

"Oh, I been ramblin'." He told her his ideas about the fire, and the notepaper.

"That's something, of course, but—oh, it couldn't be Brinley," Kay said. "What a silly idea! Think of J. Arthur as Macbeth, with Mrs. B. spurring him on! It's absurd."

She lighted a cigarette, took a few puffs, then stubbed it out and walked over to the window.

"Looks like rain. Too bad for Old Home Week. How do you feel about the weather problems?"

"Thunder storm, maybe a little tempest. It won't last. At least I don't think so."

"There's a clambake up at the shore. Did you know?"

"Is there?" Asey was not overly interested in clambakes.

"Thought I might go. How about you?"

"Oh, I've got to see Brinley, when he has a spare moment. I don't want to tear him away from his duty."

FIGURE AWAY

"Where's Eloise?" Kay didn't sound as though she really cared a whoop.

"Upstairs, I guess. The other maid, Sally, is supposed to be lookin' after her." Asey hesitated. "Kay, what's on your mind? What's botherin' you?"

"Nothing."

"Nothing except what?"

"Oh, look—it isn't anything, really. It's—tell me, do shotguns kick?"

"They've been known to. Why?"

"Well, would they kick enough to make some mark, like a black and blue mark?"

"They might."

"Not going to help me out one bit, are you? Well, last night, after all the flurry, Jane and I had a cigarette together, in my room before we went to bed. She was in an awful state. I feel sorry about her. I remember all about her, now. Her father was one of the—"

"One of the brokers who jumped," Asey said. "I know. I heard about it any number of times."

"That still doesn't make it funny," Kay returned. "I say, it's odd how the depression worked, isn't it? Some people crashed through, and some slumped, and some like Jane—well, it just didn't touch them. Oh, she went through it, and it touched her in a way, but I don't suppose it's done a thing to the way she thinks. She won't accept things and make the best of them, she just gripes around—where was I, anyway, before I got all involved with the depression?"

"I think," Asey said, "you were about to break it to me that Jane had a funny bruise in the general section of her right shoulder. Was that it?"

"How," Kay said, "how you must exasperate some people! It took my eye, somehow. I couldn't seem to look away from that black and blue spot. When she saw I was staring at it, she got awfully embarrassed. She launched into a lot of unnecessary explanations, all about cellar steps and falling down them—"

"If you'd ever seen those cellar steps in the kitchen up there at the hollow, you wouldn't treat'em so lightly," Asey told her. "I nearly broke my neck on'em twice the other night. But she explained, did she?"

"Endlessly. I feel like a squealer, but it seemed a point to consider. Oh, you don't think so? Let it pass, then. Have I time for a swim before it rains?"

Before Asey could answer, Dr. Cummings arrived.

"Save me some questionin'," Asey said. "Mrs. Brinley was up on the ferris wheel with your wife, wasn't she? Do you know where J. Arthur was durin' that time?"

"That ferris wheel obsesses you," Cummings said. "I never knew anything like it. Open your mouth, and out pop the words ferris wheel—"

"He wants to know what makes the wheel go around," Kay said. "That's his trouble."

"Have your laugh." Asey lighted his pipe. "And then when you get through, tell me about J. Arthur."

"Lord, I don't know. I don't seem to recall even seeing him. He must have been around somewhere. I never notice him much, one way or another. And he wasn't carrying a gun, like Mike Slade, or being very spectacular. I wouldn't know about him. I'll think it over while I chat with Eloise."

He was grinning widely when he returned.

"Just don't know what," he said, "we're going to do. Just

completely unnerved, that awful face of that awful man, always did mistrust a communist, horrid people, no God, the poor Czar and those sweet little girls, deserved something much better I'm sure, although as I always say, there was Rasputin."

"You've caught it," Asey said, "but don't give it to us. It is catchin', the way she nibbles with things. An' say, now that I think of it, what was she up for, an' how come she had the opportunity to see the horrid man leerin' at her? That window he was at opens into the hall."

"En route, or returning from the bathroom, I shouldn't wonder," Cummings said. "I didn't ask, but I'm reasonably sure. That's another complication that annoys her, but I keep telling her, if she eats that muck she does, she has to expect certain attendant inconveniences. Going to get some rain, I guess."

"Looks like it."

"Maybe you'll get a nice batch of colds," Kay said. "Isn't that cheering?"

"Oh, I pin my faith on the banquets. Only ptomaine now, but I'll be reducing fat women all winter, and there'll be plenty of aftermath. You can eat just so much chicken à la King, and just so many charlotte russes—oh. They tell me uptown that Win Billings ate the paper cup to his. Wanted me to do something about it, but I didn't see the sense. After what that old duffer did to the lining of his stomach during prohibition, he could eat sheets of corrugated iron without the slightest difficulty at all. There was a legend that he used to eat the bottles. No one could ever find any—well, so long!"

"Now there," Kay said, "goes a character."

"Good doctor, too, in spite of all he talks. Look, do you really want to swim?"

"I do, and it's rank heresy, but I like fresh water. Is there any around?"

"There's a pond up near the hollow where people do go," Asey said, "though I wouldn't give two cents for it myself. Tourists wash there, and cottages without any bathtubs take a cake of soap an' dabble with the outer layers, an' any number of dogs get washed there, too. Thoph's Pond. It's notorious. It's got a slimy sort of bottom, with a few hornpout."

"How delightful," Kay said. "How attractive! Billingsgate Beautiful."

"Get along an' change, an' I'll take you. Bring somethin' to keep my car leather dry. I sort of favor that leather."

"So you don't," Kay said as they sped along later in the roadster, "put any stock in this bruise on Jane's shoulder?"

"It's nice to know about, but how could Jane have set that fire, or left that note for Slade?"

"Slade could have done that part, easily. He had and has access to the town offices. He could have picked up that 'Get out' message without any trouble. He could have faked the fire, easily."

"Then come back to Jane," Asey said, "an' tell me what become of her shotgun? Or any gun? Lane said he had three fellows on the line of that shot this mornin'—we know the line, even if we don't know the place on the line. Lane's still got high hopes of findin' the shells, but I'm sure he's doomed to disappointment. We worked it all out on a time basis, so many minutes to get her indoors after the shot was fired, so much time for her to get to a point where she could of shot—it's easier to work it backwards, see. What's left of the seven or eight minutes there was between the time Zeb an' I heard the shot an' got back here—that's the time anyone had to hide or throw away a gun. You see, that narrows you down. The time element was hair splittin'."

"And everything's been searched, all around?" Kay asked as Asey swerved off the tarred road onto a narrow rutted lane that slid at a sharp angle down to the pond.

"Searched, combed, dug an' prodded," Asey said. "Here's your fish bowl. Go swim."

"Is it safe to dive?" Kay asked. "Oh, what a simply glorious spot, Asey, and what grand blue water! It's a wonderful place, and how you did malign it! Can I dive?"

"There's a couple over there, divin' off that end of the ice house pilin'—see?" Asey pointed. "Makes off deep around there. Don't you wear a cap?"

"Hate them. I'll be quick—"

Asey watched her run along the narrow shore to the ice house, and make her way out to the end of the old wharf. She poised for a moment, and then shot cleanly into the water.

Nodding his approval, Asey bent over and lighted his pipe. When he raised his head, there was no sign of the girl, and the couple by the ice house were peering over into the water.

Asey dropped his pipe and set out on a dead run.

He reached the last pile in time to see a white hand reach up through the water.

In it was a shotgun.

"Well," Kay said breathlessly a minute later, "here's exhibit A!"

CHAPTER
11.

THE couple who had been diving from the wharf took an intense interest in the shotgun Kay had salvaged.

"Gee, Sammy," the woman touched the trigger with her finger, "isn't it funny, huh? Isn't it funny? You know, I *said* I seen something down there, don't you remember? But I didn't think it was anything but a stick, maybe. Sammy, didn't *you* see something down there too? Didn't you think you seen something? I thought you said you did."

"Yeah," Sammy said. *"I* seen something. I didn't think it was a stick. I knew it was a gun. I was just going down for it when she come."

"See?" the woman said to Asey. "We knew it was there, all the time! Now, I don't want to get sore or anything, but we knew it was there, and we was going to get it, so you—"

"It pierces my heart," Kay said. "It shatters me to small bits, but neither of you possibly could have seen it. I didn't see it myself. I felt it. Therefore, if any claims arise—"

"Well, now just you look here!" the woman raised her voice. "I guess we did see it too! I guess we knew it was there! I guess, if anyone's going to march off with that gun, we are. Do you hear that?"

"I think," Asey said, "they heard you over in Weesit Centre. And I rather think that you—"

"Fresh, huh?" Sammy demanded. "Want to start trouble, huh? Well, listen! We seen that gun, and it's ours, and who do you think you are, to—"

"Who do you think you are, you?" the woman chimed in. "My God, I never seen such a town as this! You hicks, you seem to think you—"

"And what's more," Sammy continued, paying no attention to the woman, "I lost a gun here in this lake last fall. My boat tipped over, and I lost—"

"Fiddlesticks," Kay said, wondering why Asey didn't make any more of a stand. He was fishing around in his pockets, handicapped somewhat by the shotgun firmly clutched under one arm. "Fiddlesticks, and pooh. I don't believe a word of it. You just think you can bully us into handing the gun over to you, that's all, and it's the most nonsensical notion I ever heard tell of."

"Listen!" Sammy shouted her into silence. "That gun is ours, see? It belongs to me. And we're going to have it, and take it—take—oh."

He and the woman stared at the two badges Asey was nonchalantly fixing on the lapel of his jacket. One said, "Chief of Police," and the other was a state police badge.

"Oh, well," the woman said hurriedly, "maybe it ain't your gun, Sammy. Yours was a bigger gun. It was a much better gun, too. After all, if they're going to get sore, why what's the use of raising a rumpus, I always say—"

"It's been nice," Asey said, "havin' this little chat with you. Any time you feel like continuin' it, you'll find me at my offices in the Town Hall. Ask for Mr. Mayo. So long."

Looking terribly injured and outraged, the couple departed. They were muttering, but they were wise enough not to mutter very audibly.

"Well I never!" Kay said. "How simply—what nerve! What gall! Asey, did you ever in your life see anything like that?"

"Tourists," Asey said. "Just tourists. They'd call a cop if you stepped foot on the lawn of their own house—always providin' they got either a lawn or a house, but travellin' puts the gypsy into 'em. I found some one day makin' off with my great grandmother's best hooked rug that I'd been airin' on the line."

"They were pinching it?"

"Oh, my no, what a horrid thought!" Asey said. "Of course not! They'd left me fifty cents. Offered me two-fifty before they left. Didn't seem wise at that point to tell 'em how much Bill Porter made me insure it for— Kay, how in time did you find this gun?"

Kay smiled. "I was trying to make a nice spectacular dive to impress you, and it was shallower than I thought, and I bumped. You were right about the nasty bottom. It's all muggy with weeds and things. I hit something in the weeds and grabbed at it for fun, and that's the story. Asey, is it the one?"

"It is."

"But you haven't even looked at it!"

"See that tag? Says 'Anniversary Special' on it. And the gun ain't been in the water very long, either. Under the circumstances, I think you've done a noble task. Will you finish your swim so's we can get back an' look into it in a large way? While you're gettin' the mud off, I'm goin' to put the car top up. Our shower's just about hoverin' over Ames's woods at this point."

"I'll hurry."

Asey strolled back to the car and put up the top, just as a few tentative drops of rain began to fall.

Kay hurried back and wrapped herself in a white terry-cloth robe.

"That's not bad, really," she said, "that water, I mean. It's warm, but the air's getting cold. I have a feeling that the clambake is going to be rather soggy. Asey, how do you get the car out of here? Can you turn around?"

"I can ease her out." Asey backed into a thicket. "That's the one trouble with this beast, she can take a pile of turnin' on these lanes. The blow comes if someone d'cides to drive down that little path as we're comin' up it. Someone, say, like Sammy an' his girl friend." He leaned out to gauge his distance from a clump of scrub oaks. "An' in that case we get a biff on the bumper or some scratched paint. Oho. My goodness gracious! Shan't you die!"

"What's wrong now?" Kay asked as he stopped the car and pulled on the brake.

"Look yonder, will you? There's food for thought."

Back over by the ice house another couple had appeared, but these two were no tourists. Not even a light drizzle could disguise the chubby figure of J. Arthur Brinley.

With him, a wrap over her bathing suit, was Madame Meaux.

"Tch, tch," Kay said. "Dear Miss Fairlawn, I always thought my husband was true to me, but recently we had a guest staying to our house, a Blonde Woman from Another World, and I find from my many warm friends that she was often seen in my husband's company, often in dishabille. Dear Miss Fairlawn, should I turn a deaf ear towards this entanglement, or should I bundle the little weasel into the meat chopper. Answer soon."

Asey chuckled.

"I wrote answers to a column like that," Kay said, "for six months, and for six months the world seemed populated entirely with Blonde Women and Tall Dark Men and Sprightly Widows and simply fiendish children, all violently demented. Asey, what is your Blonde Woman doing with that Faithful Husband?"

"Considerin' we're some of the Virtuous Wife's many warm friends," Asey said, "we'll park right in this thicket an' eavesdrop. It's a wife's priv'lege to Know All."

"They see us, don't they? They simply must!"

"They ought to, but they ain't looked over this way, an' the car's b'hind bushes—wonder if we ain't misjudged J. Arthur, Kay? See him pursue her behind the ice house? All the same, I bet on Madame. This is what you might call a new slant on Brother Brinley."

"I bet," Kay said as they waited for the two to return, "I bet he's an old pincher, when Mrs. B.'s safely out of the way. The firm young flesh school. Asey, something very definite has happened."

"Not happened," Asey corrected her. "Transpired."

Madame Meaux strolled to a little patch of sandy shore, took off her robe and folded it with immense deliberation, while J. Arthur hovered restlessly in the background. With the same pointed deliberation, she walked to the edge of the water, dabbled a foot in it, and then walked doggedly into the pond.

J. Arthur called out something indistinguishable to her, but she never turned her head.

FIGURE AWAY

He called again, and then shrugged and walked over to the ice house and the old loading piles.

"I rather think," Kay said, "that J. Arthur has been forward. Maybe he's even made advances. Asey, by heaven—look!"

Brinley, after picking up a piece of broken oar, had walked out to the end of the piling and was prodding around almost exactly over the spot where Kay had found the shotgun.

"I think," Asey got out of the roadster, "that we'll go chat with Arthur. If he seen us leavin', he might feel we was miffed with him. An' I don't know anyone I have kinder thoughts towards than Arthur. I shouldn't want him to think otherwise."

"Who," Kay agreed, "are we, to slink off like a couple of ships in the night?"

Brinley's head jerked up at the sound of their approach, and he began nervously to edge back to shore.

"Hi." Asey's voice was silky.

"Oh, hullo. How do you do? Er—how do you do?"

"Fine," Asey said. "Fine." After all, he thought, J. Arthur had asked him twice.

"It looks rather like rain, doesn't it?" Brinley dropped the broken oar down on the sand.

"It *is* raining," Asey said truthfully.

"Our dog," as Brinley walked up to them, Asey and Kay noted with delight the thick welt on his right cheek, "our dog, we—that is, we usually wash our dog here. It's so much easier, we find, than the set tub or the hose. He hates the set tub, it's so cramped for him, and he's afraid of the hose."

"That so?" Asey sat down beside Kay on a log. "I never had a dog myself, but—what's that, Kay?"

"Man's best friend," Kay said. "A true pal. Isn't that so, Mr. Brinley? By the way, where is the dog? I don't see any dog around."

J. Arthur looked a little bewildered. "Amos—oh, Amos is home. You see, the last time I brought Amos—he's a *black* dog, you see—the last time I brought him here, the license tag off his collar got lost on—I mean, the license tag on his collar got lost off. I don't know how it happened, but I told my wife that the next time I was around here, I'd poke around and see if I could find it."

"How's your wife?" Asey asked.

"Oh, she's quite well, if you mean after all that last night. She went to the banquet, and then she was going to the clambake. The women are running that, you know."

"No men allowed?"

"Oh, no—men can go. Oh, you mean, why aren't I there? I can't touch clams. They do something to me. Oh, no. I never touch a clam. And Madame—er—Moo, she wanted to swim, and the fresh water appealed to her, so I thought I might bring her here and look around for Amos's tag while she went swimming. Killing two birds with one stone," he added brightly.

"Combinin' business, as you might say, with pleasure," Asey said.

He and Kay smoked in silence, and Brinley stood first on one foot and then on the other. Once or twice he absent-mindedly touched the welt on his cheek.

"I—uh—oh, there's some goldenrod," he said, pointing vaguely towards the woods that framed the pond. "I told my wife I'd get her some—I think I'll get it now. I always say it's almost fall, when the goldenrod comes, don't you? Er— I'll go get it—"

FIGURE AWAY

He almost fled to the woods.

Madame Meaux came out of the water, put on her wrap and walked over to them.

"How do the canaries taste?" she inquired. "You two cats, licking your chops! Did Arthur dissolve or did he melt away?"

"He's going after goldenrod, believe it or not," Kay told her. "What a right to the face you seem to pack, or was it an overhanging bough that hit J. Arthur?"

Madame Meaux grinned. "I had a husband," she said, "who was in the fight racket. So Arthur's picking flowers, is he, the old president of Associated Button and Clasp Makers!"

"The old what?"

"Oh, once when I was broke, I was official soprano for that outfit's convention. Ask me anything about buttons and clasps. Well, as I said, any woman who can go to bed looking like that has no one but herself to blame. What are you up to?"

"Did he suggest coming here?" Asey asked. "Or was it your idea?"

"Do you honestly think," Madame Meaux inquired icily, "that I crave seclusion with J. Arthur—"

"You wrong me. Did he ever tell you that he had anything to hunt up here?"

"He murmured something about a dog," Madame Meaux took one of Kay's cigarettes, "but he may have been speaking in general terms."

Asey laughed. "The point is, where he was just hunting, we just found a shotgun. At least, Kay did. We wondered about the dog and the license tag story he told."

"That dog makes me jealous," the soprano said. "Gets much nicer meat than we have—did Arthur say he was after a license tag? He lies. I was playing with the brute this morning, and his collar was lousy with tags. Inoculation, and license, and a batch of others. One with the official Billingsgate seal, with that man dressed like a Pilgrim about to throw a fish at someone. Perhaps Amos is the Old Home Week hound. Look, can't we get somewhere where it's dry? Sitting in this rain will never make me render 'Billingsgate Beautiful' any better."

The door of the old ice house was slumping on its hinges, and Asey kicked it open.

"What a nasty smell!" Kay said.

"Salt hay an' stuff. I wonder they don't tear this down, they ain't used it for years. Tell me, Madame—look, can I call you Mrs. Slade?" Asey asked. "It's easier."

"Call me Emily."

Asey felt Kay's elbow dig into his ribs.

"Okay. Look, on Monday night you was up to the midway with the Brinleys. Were you there while Mrs. Brinley was caught up on the ferris wheel, maybe?"

"Oh, boy, was I?"

"Where was J Arthur?"

"I don't know. I rather felt he was a prospective Button and Clasp Conventioner, in a small way, so I hung around with the boys from the band. Arthur was around, I guess. He—oh, what lovely goldenrod, Mr. Brinley!"

"Isn't it?"

J. Arthur turned down his coat collar and mopped at his dripping face with a handkerchief.

"Really, it's quite a rain," he said. "I do hope my wife is all right at the clambake. And the governors, at the ball game— but Weston had planned an alternative program in the field house in case of rain. That man," Asey knew instinctively that he referred to Mike Slade, "was to put on some sort of show.

FIGURE AWAY

Tableaux or something. Weston has been very efficient about things like rain."

"Where was you," Asey asked, "durin' the time your wife was stuck up on the ferris wheel the other night?"

J. Arthur turned such a deep red that the shade was apparent even in the dim interior of the ice house.

"Er—when? I mean, what?"

Asey repeated his question.

"Oh. Then? Why, I was around, talking to the man and trying to see if someone couldn't do something to repair the car engine—it worked by a car engine, somehow. My wife was tremendously upset. Really, this week has been very hard on her, with that wheel and then that man last night."

"Don't care much for him, do you?"

"Slade? I hate him!" J. Arthur spoke with a bitter ferocity that startled Kay and rather amazed Asey. "I hate him! And I don't care who hears it! And my wife says, she doesn't think that Warren girl is a bit better than he is. Turning up her nose at the town, and making fun of everyone, and talking about how much better they do everything in New York! What's New York?"

He paused for a moment as though he expected someone to tell him.

"That's what my wife says, what's New York?"

"Concrete, carbon monoxide, a lot of noise," Kay couldn't resist the opportunity. "Sirens, dirt—"

Asey shook his head and she subsided.

"Brinley, I s'pose, if you had to, you could prove just where you was Monday night, from—say the time your wife got stuck on that wheel to the time the fireworks ended?"

"I don't see that it matters where I was!" Brinley said hotly.

"If you want to find someone you think killed Mary Randall, find Mike Slade!"

"And how," Asey asked blandly, "did you know that Mary Randall had been killed?"

Brinley's breath sounded like the air escaping from a child's balloon. It was weak, but gasping.

"How?" Asey asked again. "This is news, J. Arthur. Where did you pick up that tidbit?"

He reached over and caught Brinley as the latter started to dash for the door.

"You don't really want to go out into the rain," Asey said, "an' listen to that thunder! Come, J. Arthur, stay. Stay an' talk!"

Brinley's explanation was dragged out, item by item. In brief, Mary Randall was not at the hollow, Eloise and Jane were with Aunt Sara, he knew Mary Randall had no relations in New York, let alone sick ones, and Mary was too shrewd a business woman to leave town during a period when she could make so much money. Slade had spoken of a murder. Asey was hanging around. Police were around.

"Therefore, therefore," Asey said. "I see. Think this out last night?"

"No, today when Governor Skellings asked for Mary. He said, where was she, because he collects sandwich glass and pewter, and he had bought things from her before, and she said she had something for him, and he was planning to look at them while he was here. He asked Weston, and by the funny way Weston acted, it came over me."

"Maybe that explains the Israel Trask pewter," Asey said, "but it don't explain you. Where were you, durin' the time I asked you about? An' why do you prod for dog license tags when Amos has more than the usual collection, right this minute?"

"If you want your murderer, go for Mike Slade! Don't you—"

"Did you write this note, tellin' him to get out an' stay out?"

"I—that's my writing, but I—see here, just what are you trying to do?"

J. Arthur blustered for ten minutes, without seeming to stop for breath.

Asey made no effort to curtail the flood of words. Instead he walked over to the door and looked out at the rain which continued to drive down in torrents.

Kay had commented on the bright blueness of the water when they first came, but now the pond and the sky above were nearly black. Lightning jagged down in brilliant flashes, and the thunder was almost continuous.

"Quite a tempest," he said to Kay, who had come over beside him.

"Asey, he may not be a fiend, but I'm beginning to wonder if he's quite the fool I thought. What about this dog tag business?"

"Easy enough to check on."

"If only he hadn't been hunting Fido's tag—how flimsy that is! Don't you suppose he was after the shotgun? He was prodding pretty hard. I bet he wanted to make sure it was still safely there. By the way, where is the gun now?"

"Locked up in the car, an' the person ain't livin' who can get at it inside of three hours," Asey assured her. "One nice thing about havin' pull with the comp'ny, you get locks that don't pick so easy."

J. Arthur stomped to the door.

"Now, Mayo, I want you to pay some attention to what I'm saying!"

"When," Asey said, "you cond'scend to answer the questions I asked you, I'll pay so much attention you'll be flattered by it."

Brinley stomped off.

"D'you really think he guessed?" Kay asked. "About the murder, I mean?"

"I wouldn't know. I thought we had him pretty well convinced last night that it was all Slade's nonsense."

"Slade!" Brinley overheard the name. "Slade! There's your man. Slade and that Warren girl. Two people on earth who have the most to gain from Mary Randall's death. And what do you do? You—you park in bushes with young girls, malingering around while justice waits! You—"

"Poor justice," Asey said, "certainly is takin' an awful lickin' from the folks in this town."

"You," Brinley was thundering, "you call yourself a detective, you do! First you carry on with that woman," he pointed to Madame Meaux, "and then you take young girls—"

"Toots," Madame Meaux said calmly, "shut your face and pin it up tight."

"Don't you talk to me. I—"

"Toots," Madame Meaux said, "I told you to shut up. You shut up. Or maybe you'd like me to stage a little act for the benefit of your wife?"

"Wha—you wouldn't dare!"

"Oh, toots, wouldn't I? Keep in mind, Arthur, that you play ball with Asey, or very shortly your wife will find you in what is known as a compromising position with her star boarder, see?"

"You—what do you mean?"

"It would be so simple," Madame Meaux said, "to make a pass at you just as she comes in the room. And mind, toots, you're the one that does the explaining. Not me. I've got a contract. I get paid no matter what happens. No moral turpitude clauses in my contract. And I'm going to stay right through to the bitter end. But if you force me—well, I'm sure that dear old Mr. Leach would believe me if I said I was leaving because of your undesirable attentions. And Mr. Mayo's cousin told me when I came that I was to march straight to him with any complaints. He meant Pinky Upjohn and the boys, but you'll do. Asey, if the rain's letting up, how's for taking me home along with you two? I don't trust myself with Casanova here."

"Oh, you can't!" Brinley was on the verge of tears. "You've got to drive home with me! My wife would ask questions— she knows you started out with me!"

"And I'll tell her plenty, toots."

Brinley collapsed and never uttered a word until half an hour later, when the rain abruptly stopped.

"Okay, toots." Madame Meaux relented. "You can take me home, but just keep in front of your mind just what'll happen if you don't behave. Okay, Asey?"

"Fine," Asey said. "Keep him in hand for me. I'll see you later, Brinley, an' you better be thinkin' up a lot of nice expl'nations, because considerable checkin' is goin' to be done on you. So long—where's your car, on the east road? 'Bye."

Kay's teeth were chattering as she and Asey walked back to the roadster.

Asey gave her a coat from the rumble seat.

"I was goin' to stop at the hollow," he said, "but that can all wait. You're due for a hot bath an' dry things. I forgot you was wet to begin with."

But as they passed by the hollow and the figures out in front of the Randall house, Lane and two of his troopers hailed them triumphantly.

"Shells!" Lane shouted. "Hey, Asey, we got a shell!"

CHAPTER
12.

IN spite of Kay's appeals to Asey to stop and find out everything at once, Asey merely slowed up long enough to call out and assure Lane that he'd be right back. Then he continued on to Aunt Sara's.

"Don't wait," Kay hopped out of the car. "Hurry right back there, and when I'm ready I'm going to steam back after you in my percolator. Asey, do hurry—Lane was so excited!"

"I'm goin' to wait for you," Asey said. "Hustle up, an' put on somethin' that'll withstand the next shower we're goin' to get, because—"

"Asey, Lane'll be frothing at the mouth! He wants you, and—"

"Uh-huh, an' I want you. You got a job to do for me, young lady, so hustle up."

Kay rushed off.

While she took a brief hot bath and a briefer cold shower, Asey sat there in the car and puffed at his pipe. He was very pleased with the two discoveries made that afternoon, but not at all for the same reason Kay supposed.

He started the car as Kay appeared, dressed in a light tweed suit and wearing black and white sport shoes.

"I'm simply thrown together—what's the big idea, anyway?"

"You'll see."

Back at the hollow, Lane was annoyed at the way Asey had flipped past, and he went into the subject at some length.

"Nice way to treat the only clew we got so far," he said. "Zipping past in—"

"You may have the ham," Asey told him, "but we got the rest of the sandwich." He unlocked a compartment in the roadster and displayed the shotgun Kay had found.

"Where'd you find that?"

"Kay found it, over in the pond yonder. Now, let me gape at that shell, will you? An' then you play around an' see if it c'nects with the gun. That r'minds me, where'd Jane go to, anyway?"

"Jane shut up shop," Lane said, "and went tripping off with that Chase boy. She just ignored some customers. She—"

"With Zeb Chase?"

"Yes. She said something about a clambake. I said what should I do with the customers, and she said, the hell with 'em. No one's been around lately, though. They got rained out."

An hour later Lane lined up half a dozen shells for Asey's inspection.

"There." There was a note of joy in his voice. "There you are. See? The same. This is the gun that fired the shell that killed Mary Randall. There you are."

"This is the gun that fired the shell," Asey corrected him.

"I suppose you think—look, you come out here and let me show you where I found it."

Asey and Kay followed him out to a small and badly kept garden at the side of the house.

"Now, here's where the shell was. See how the rain washed it out of that hole? It's smack on our line, or near enough, anyway. Someone tossed it there, and covered it over. See— Asey, what's the matter with you?"

Lane was annoyed and impatient. Usually Asey caught on to things before you expected him to. This afternoon he was being unnecessarily slow.

"In spite of the rain," Asey said, "you can tell that these flowers ain't been watered, or dug around, can't you? The ground's hard as a rock, even a little under the surface. That was a heavy downpour, but it didn't soak in much. It's been pretty dry lately. And here, on this slant, the water run down an' off into the drive. See where it went?"

"What if the rain didn't soak in? It could have washed out the shell, couldn't it? Asey, don't you see where it was? It washed out, right there." Lane pointed to the hole again.

"It did," Asey said, "because it was stuck there this mornin', or last night, so that a good rain would wash it out. Lane, I'm not tryin' to muss this up, but can't you see? The ground around is hard. Where you found the shell, it's soft. It was dug up, an' the shell stuck in, just so it'd wash."

Lane said a number of bitter things.

"Yesterday mornin'," Asey said, "you raked this whole area, didn't you? Monday night you an' me took flashlights, didn't we, over this whole area? We raked it. We walked up an' down around this garden plot. We both said it was hard an' dry. Lane, how could we of missed seein' it? If the ground around were softer, I'd say it could have washed out. But it's hard. And this rain wasn't heavy enough to wash anything out of a hole like that. And if the shell had been buried here before, we'd have found it, see?"

"Listen," Lane said, "can't you figure that this means the case?"

"I can figure enough to figure that someone wanted me to think so."

"The Warren girl," Lane said firmly, "stood near here, probably in the lee of the apple tree, and shot Mary Randall, and then tossed the shell—"

"That's another point," Asey said. "Shell. Why not shells, Lane?"

"Tossed the shells aside— I bet you I can find the other if I dig up this garden—"

"Why," Asey inquired, "bury 'em sep'rate? Oh, Lane!"

"If I dig up this garden, I'll find another. Anyway, then Warren took the gun and beat it to the pond, and tossed the gun in the water. Then she came back and let you in the house, and let you find the woman."

"If it were me," Kay said, "I wouldn't have tossed a shell, or the shells, aside. Not if I intended to dunk the gun in the pond right afterwards. I'd have flipped the lot into the water, all at once. Why complicate things by leaving the shells here?"

"All women," Lane said, "don't think alike. Where are you going, Asey?"

"Kay an' I," Asey said, "are goin' to make a little geographical survey. While we're gone, you dig up the zinnias an' prod around the petunias, an' find the other shell for us, an' I'll bet any sum you want, you'll find it in a nice little hole dug just for it. So long."

"Now what," Kay asked as Asey took her elbow and propelled her toward the woods, "what is your idea, and what is your theory?"

"Someone," Asey told her, "after givin' the problem due thought, come to the c'nclusion it'd be easier for him if instead of makin' this a hundred percent mystery, we was allowed to find a suspect. First point is shells. So Lane finds a shell, in a place I personally grubbed every inch of. Shortly he will find another shell."

Kay walked along a few steps in silence.

"Then you think that the gun I found is planted, too?"

"Wa-el," Asey drawled, "now s'pose you wanted to get rid of a gun, yourself. You got two things handy. Thoph's Pond, an' the Atlantic. There's an undertow alongshore, an' you got a fifty-fifty chance of havin' your gun go forever, or havin' some bather find it at low tide. To do a good job with the ocean you ought to dump your gun in the channel, an' that needs a boat. Too hard. The pond's nearer. The pond's also more obvious like, ain't it?"

Kay nodded.

"But now," Asey paused for a moment, "s'pose you d'cided that Thoph's Pond was the ideal spot to get rid of your shotgun in. So what?"

"Why, you'd dump it there!"

"Sure," Asey said with irony. "You'd march right out on that old wharf pilin', an' you'd dump it right off the end, wouldn't you? Right where all the tourists dive, an' the summer cottagers get clean, an' where all the dogs, includin' Amos the wonder dog, get their weekly wash. A nice, safe place. Sure."

"I never thought of that," Kay said honestly. "I suppose you would at least hurl it off a bit."

"At least, you'd go round to the other side where no one

bathes, an' it makes off into the real mud, an' you'd pitch the gun as far as you could send it onto the mud bottom. Now, climb up on this stump. Can you see the pond?"

"Of course I can!"

"An' you can see the house?"

"In the hollow? Yes. For that matter, I can see the ocean, and the lighthouse, and two coalers off shore, and the Town Hall tower, and the belfry of the First and only Congregational church. What is this, a course in landmarks?"

"Exactly," Asey said, "and you are Jane Warren. I'll give you an hour to work out the shortest an' most direct route, an' the most passable, from Randall's in the hollow to the ice house. There are two paths. You take 'em an' get familiar with 'em, an' then we'll try a little experiment. Oh, it's rainin' some more. You mind? If you don't want to do this—"

"I only get about half the idea," Kay said, "but I'm willing to do anything that might help."

"This will. Now, this is your affair. Personally, I think the lower path is saner. If you want to make detours, or anything, you can."

"I won't need an hour for that."

"Oh, yes, you will. You pick your path," Asey said, "an' learn it. Think how this'll help you. Local color. Bay'bries, scrub pines, checkerberries," he picked a leaf and chewed it, "nice Cape air, an' a first-hand acquaintance with Cape rain."

At the end of an hour Kay returned to where Asey sat on the stump.

Her legs were scratched with brambles and one shoe string had broken, her face was smudged and her red hair was soaking under her beret.

"Add local color," she observed, "mosquitoes, red ants, two

FIGURE AWAY

snakes, three skunks—happily not very observant—and a splendid assortment of insect life and prickers. How did the early settlers take it?"

"I've always wondered," Asey told her. "When you've rested, we'll go back an' try this out."

Lane greeted them with little enthusiasm.

"It's the shotgun the Warren girl bought with that check of Prettyman's," he said. "I called Boston and checked on it."

"That bears out your ideas," Asey said.

"I suppose so. But the other shell—yes, I found it. It was dug in, like you said. What've you been doing?"

"I just been sittin'," Asey said. "Kay, she's been investigatin' our local flora an' fauna."

"What are you up to?"

"Well," Asey said, "this is a continuation of our timin' project—how you pick up these words! My cousin Syl has takin' to callin' his garbage hole a refuse disposal project. Well, Lane, Kay's goin' to stand by the apple tree, an' say 'Boom,' an' then she's goin' to pretend to dig two shells in—just for fun—an' then she's goin' to run to the ice house at the pond, dump a gun in, an' rush back to the house. In eight minutes I'm goin' to bang the knocker. Let's see if she can be back there to answer. Now look, we'll time this shell diggin', too. Let's see what happens."

Lane hesitated. "But Jane knew the ground," he said at last.

"Kay prob'ly knows it just as well, an' she's got the advantage of not havin' any shotgun to carry, an' daylight, an' the disadvantage of a light rain. That ought to even it all up. Set, Kay? Got your watch ready, Lane? You start her off."

Lane gave the signal, and Kay darted to the garden, where she dug two imaginary holes, inserted two imaginary shells, and covered them over with a brushing motion of her hand. Then she turned and set off toward the pond.

Asey and Lane walked over to the house.

"Guess you're right," the latter said. "You seldom aren't right, but damn it, no one ever solves a case of this kind, and I got carried away. Why the plant?"

"Find out someone who doesn't like Jane," Asey said. "An'—I must tell you about Brinley."

Lane interrupted him in the middle of his story.

"Eight minutes are up. Go on."

Asey had time to finish his story before Kay panted back.

"Eleven minutes over time," Asey moved aside to let her sit on the front step. "Are you done up?"

"Give me a cigarette!" Kay said. "I haven't done anything so strenuous since I played hockey in my youth—isn't it amazing, the way you get to lose the use of your legs as you grow older? Anyway, Asey, I went the shortest way, and I was like to break my neck I went so fast, and here I am. Even if you take time off for the digging process, I'm still way behind, aren't I?"

"That dishes that," Lane said. "Asey, Mike Slade couldn't have—oh, I forgot. You've got him placed uptown, haven't you? Her other boy friend was with you. She couldn't have done it and been back here by the time you and Zeb—look, did you know it all the time?"

"He's smug, almost," Kay said. "How did you know, Asey?"

"She had on socks," Asey said, "Jane did. It's been stickin' in my mind since Monday night that they was silk socks, an' no pulls an' runs in 'em, an' her legs wasn't scratched. Look at yours, Kay, just from rompin' around. We—ah. We have visitors, Sara an' Jeff, no less!"

FIGURE AWAY 173

He walked over to meet them.

"This is Jeff's contribution," Sara passed over a piece of paper, "but I thought of asking him about it. Anyway, this is a copy of the notation. Jeff gave her the permit himself."

Asey read through the sentences which announced that Jane Warren had, two weeks before, been given permission to carry a gun, "For defense of self and property."

"Gun license, huh? Who issued it?"

"I did," Jeff said. "She told me she was scared to death up here in the hollow sometimes, there were such awful sounds. I could see the sense of it, so I gave it to her. Edwards was sick that week, and with everybody so busy about this Old Home Week, I did all the red tape myself. She said she wanted to get herself a little gun. I asked if she could shoot—it always seems rather futile to me to give permits to people who can't. They do far more damage than good. Anyway, she said she was being taught by an expert, and she was picking up."

"Who was the expert?"

"Zeb, I thought. Under the circumstances, she probably meant Slade. He's done a lot of shooting ever since he came to town." Jeff looked curiously at Kay. "What have you been doing to the girl, Asey? She looks exhausted."

"She is," Asey said. "Take her along with you. I got to do some putterin' around, an' she's chatterin' wet again. Look after her."

Kay made no protest. "It's not that I'm tired of detecting," she explained to Asey, "but I'm going to leave the concrete detail to you for a while."

Asey grinned and went back to Lane.

"Well," he said, "here's where she got a permit to carry a gun, which she can't deny. Legal sort of step for anyone contemplatin' murder, ain't it? She's got a shoulder bruise that might of come from a gun kickin', but she says cellar steps. She bought a gun, an' Slade says she gave it to him an' someone stole it. Turns up in the pond, but Jane couldn't have stuck it there on Monday night, an' with you here or one of your men, I don't see how she could of since. Besides, where'd she hide it in the interval? She's got the nicest motive, an' she was here. What does that make?"

Lane shrugged. "You tell me. Let's look into Brinley. I'll call up some of the boys an' have 'em stay here. Let's grab at straws."

"An' while we do it, let's find out why someone plants the gun an' shells here for us. Lane, put two men up here tonight, will you? I don't know why, but every time I look at the place, I get a feelin' of what you might call impendin' disaster."

Up in the village he found Mrs. Brinley issuing orders to a group of tired-looking women. They brightened visibly when Asey managed to drag her away.

He cut short her stories of the day—of the soaking everyone got at the clambake, how the governors had been so nice, and General Philbrick and ex-Senator Mulcahey were looking after them until the ball that night, and whatever they were going to do about Win Billings, she didn't know, the man was an ungrateful wretch.

With a masterly display of patience, Asey brought up the problem of Amos, the black dog, and his lost license tag.

It appeared, finally, that Amos had lost his tag, though Mrs. Brinley was sure she didn't know why Mr. Mayo cared. She, Mrs. Brinley, had put on his last year's tag, that was all, because everyone knew they were honest people, and the records would show they had paid the fee anyway, and what with Arthur being a selectman, it seemed the best way out, and it was little things like dog fees, wasn't it, and three cent postage, and the gas tax, and gracious only knew what others, that all made life so hard. Mr. Brinley, she added, was beginning to think there might be something in the single tax, after all.

The question of where Mr. Brinley was during the stuck ferris wheel episode was harder to get anywhere with. Mrs. Brinley frankly confessed that she had never spent such a time in her life, and was too terrified to look over, anyway, and what would have happened if the thing had collapsed, Mrs. Brinley for one hated to think.

Asey finally managed to tear himself away. Outside the post office he met Lane.

"No one seems to know where Brinley was," he told Asey. "I've asked all the people with badges, claiming I thought I'd given one of them my glasses to hold while I went on the merry-go-round, and maybe it was Mr. Brinley, but I hadn't been able to find him. Of course they all said they was there Monday night, but I hadn't given them any glasses to hold, and on delving into the matter, not one of them remembered seeing Brinley there. Now what?"

"For my part," Asey said, "I'm goin' home an' get me an early supper. Lane, I ain't no seventh son, but this feller's b'ginnin' to act. Have your lads around everyone's place again tonight, an' give blazes to them outside Brinleys'. The whole blinkin' household skylarked out last night, as well as Slade's climbin' the Paul's Scarlet, but your men was two other places, doin' a lot of other things."

"Don't think they haven't heard about it," Lane said grimly.

"They told me something about some wandering woman from the midway, and I told them plenty, believe me. Look, Asey, this bothers me. When were the shells and the gun planted?"

"Slade claims the gun was stolen Monday night. It could have been stuck into the pond any time after then, but somehow I think it was today or yesterday. The shells—well, the house's had you or one of your men around since Monday night. Except when Prettyman had Konrad hogtied last night. Durin' the time I was chattin' with Tertius would have been a good time. Konrad was inside with me. Takin' a chance then, to plant'em, but it worked."

"I'm wondering about those customers, too, Asey. A lot of'em wandered around, looking at the figures, and I know that some went near the garden. I was so busy thinking of things that had been left, I never considered people leaving anything."

Back at Aunt Sara's, Asey ate his supper by himself out in the kitchen, to the accompaniment of Bertha's version of the day's doings. All these endless stories of the celebration were, he thought, rather like a comic strip or a cartoon. If you didn't see it yourself, someone was sure to tell you about it and explain, and usually twice, to make certain you got the point.

After he had eaten, he went up to the room he shared with Zeb, and stretched out on his bed. To judge from the last two nights, things started to happen late rather than early, and tonight he was going to be prepared.

Somehow he couldn't seem to get away from a feeling of impending trouble, and it worried him.

He had wanted this person, whoever he was that they were up against, to act. Now the fellow had begun to show his hand, there was no telling what to expect. The planting of the shells

FIGURE AWAY

had been beautifully timed, and so had the shotgun. This fellow knew what he was going to do, and he did it.

Asey got up and hunted out Sara, and tried to impress on her the necessity of being careful.

"We're all of us going to the governors' party," she said. "I'll see to everyone, I promise you. Yes, Eloise is going too. She's recovered, she thinks, but I feel for Mike when she sees him. Yes, we'll be careful. Zeb and Jeff and I will look after them, and Kay, too. I wonder, Asey, is Zeb's stock picking up again with Jane? She seems to have spent the entire afternoon with him, and Slade hasn't called or been near the house today. Dear me, I suppose I was just as odd when I was young, but it doesn't seem to me that I could have been, possibly. I know I wasn't."

"If what folks say is true," Asey told her, "you had Jeff Leach on his ear, an' forty-seven others practically in the asylum. An' you worry about Jane with two! Well, look out for 'em all."

Before the fireworks were due to begin, Asey climbed in his roadster and drove up to the hollow.

It had stopped raining, but the fog was coming in and the wheel was wet and slippery under his hands.

As he turned into the driveway, he was pleased to see two flashlights shoot at him from different angles.

"On the job, huh?" he asked Konrad, who came running over to him.

"Say," Konrad said, "this place is worse tonight than last. Honest, this fog is creepy, and it has more noises in it—"

"Thought you was to get tonight off?"

"Yeah. But Lane said two men," Konrad told him sadly. "I'm the other."

Asey picked his car flashlight off the clamp on the steering wheel. "I'll stay with you a spell," he said. "I want to watch this place, but I couldn't tell you why." He looked at the illuminated dial of his wrist watch. "It's most time for the fireworks to begin. Twelve minutes more. I think I'll—"

"You're slow—see, there they go," Konrad said. "Hear—hear that?"

"Shut up!" Asey said. "Listen!"

The other trooper loomed out of the fog. "Say," he said, "was that fireworks, or a shot?"

"They're beginning the fireworks," Konrad said. "Hear that? Now? That's another—"

But Asey and the other trooper were already pounding towards the woods.

That strange laugh Asey had heard before rang out somewhere in the fog ahead.

"Jesus!" the trooper said. "Hear that? That's a woman screaming, that is!"

"No," Asey said, "that wasn't, but what you hear now is!"

CHAPTER 13.

THE woman screamed again. The sound cut through the fog like a knife.

"This way!" the trooper grabbed at Asey's arm. "She's over here, somewhere—"

"No, she's—"

"This way! Come on, quick—"

"Stop a sec." Asey knew how many tricks fog could play with sounds. "Listen."

But with Konrad blundering and crashing along behind them it was useless to try and gauge the direction with any hope of accuracy.

"Go where you think," Asey said. "I'll cut over here. Wait—maybe," he pulled out the old forty-five Colt and fired a shot into the air, "maybe I might scare someone off—"

He fired again, and then started to run.

Once more he heard the woman's voice.

"Asey!"

Whoever she was, calling to him, at least she could yell. At least she was alive and apparently kicking.

He bellowed out an answer.

As he raced along he tried to remember how things had looked that afternoon. He had sat there long enough on that stump to memorize the whole surrounding countryside.

He could hear no footsteps except those of the two troopers pounding along; still everything pointed to some struggle going on.

But no sound of it. That meant—he swerved to the left, that meant they were in that patch of tall old pines, where the needles underfoot were deep enough to deaden the noise.

"Asey!"

He was getting nearer. And they were there in the pines. He could hear, now. The pine needles were slippery under his feet, and the low hanging boughs twice nearly dropped him in his tracks. He crouched low and sprinted.

At last, ahead, the blurred beam of his flashlight made out a figure against a tree. As he approached, it slumped and fell into a heap. Somewhere beyond he heard the rustle of someone hurrying away through the pines.

It was Jane, slumped down there at his feet. He recognized the camel's hair coat she wore.

He knelt down and gasped.

It wasn't Jane, but Kay Thayer who lay on the pine needles, her face streaming with blood.

"Kay! Are you hurt—"

"Go after him," she said. "I'm not—not really—" she made a tremendous effort, "really hurt. Just battered, that's all. Get the louse—"

Asey howled for the troopers.

"Hey, you! Here! This way, in the pines! Over here! Ahoy, there!"

He continued to yell until the two found him.

"Look after her," he ordered. "Take her back to the hollow, an' for God's sakes, look for—"

"Where are you going, Mayo?"

"After the fellow. No, don't you come. You watch out for her. Phone Lane, an' Doc Cummings if she needs him—"

Asey slid between two pines in the direction he thought the other person had taken.

Again he heard that strange laugh. The fog played with it and distorted it into something horrible and inhuman.

"Huh," Asey muttered to himself, "with a pig an' a canary bird, he'd coin money with Major Bowes—"

He couldn't tell from what point of the compass the sound came. But in all probability, the fellow would stick quietly in the pines for a little while, where the going was soft and wouldn't give him away. He'd have to make some noise when he cut out of the pine patch; the bayberries and scrub oaks and low underbrush would offer too good a sound track for anyone who might follow.

Asey paused.

Probably the fellow would wait to see if he were pursued. It was the sensible thing to do. Then, when he was certain that he was safe, he'd probably stroll off. There was everything to win by waiting, and everything to lose by making a hurried exit at this point.

"An' so," Asey thought, "I'll out-wait you."

Catlike, he swung himself up into one of the pines and prepared to wait.

By the greatest luck in the world, when he called the troopers he had given no hint of how many there were. Perhaps, if the fellow heard the two of them taking Kay back, he might figure it was Asey and a trooper, and that no one had started after him.

Closing his eyes, Asey listened with all his might and main.

The branches above him rustled. In the distance he could hear Kay and the others making their way back to the house.

He wondered what in thunder the girl had been doing out here, anyway. Sara had promised to look out for them all, and here was Kay, out in these godforsaken woods, being slammed around by their man. For all the good Sara was doing, she might be first cousin to the fellow. Sara would hear from him, Asey told himself. Marching around with her sleepwalking, and inviting this girl to the house—not that the girl hadn't been more of a help than a hindrance, but it was the principle of the thing. The shotgun was a help, and just being able to put herself into a position where this fellow had to declare himself, that was a help, too.

Kay would have told him if she had recognized the man. Obviously she hadn't. But she would be able to tell him something about him, whether he was tall or short or fat or thin, and if he had spoken, what his voice sounded like. Or if he smelled of fish or tobacco or possibly perfume. Asey gave Kay full credit. She would have picked out some detail or other. Most women would have gone to pieces entirely, but Kay was too matter of fact. She had probably been frightened to pieces, but she still had sufficient sense to yell her head off. She would have found something out for him.

Asey could no longer hear the sound of the trio returning to the house, but now the fireworks were beginning to boom and splutter. A perverse wind faithfully swept every decibel and every echo over to the patch of pines in the hollow, giving

Asey's quarry every chance in the world to leave, if he so desired; he could, Asey thought, beat a drum and still leave no clew to his whereabouts.

Mentally Asey cursed General Philbrick and his fireworks with all the vocabulary he had picked up in all his years at sea. Long before he finished, General Philbrick had been reduced to something you could hide in an envelope and drop into a letter box.

Once or twice he thought of giving up and returning home. The man was probably miles away by now. On the other hand, he had nothing to lose by staying.

For more than twenty minutes the fireworks boomed and crackled. Asey waited a quarter of an hour more and then decided to start back.

One foot was already reaching for the branch below when he heard another branch snap somewhere near him. A second later a light flashed on and then as quickly flashed off.

The fellow had returned to the place where Kay had been —of course! Dropped something, most likely. Something that he had no time to grab when Asey came running up, but something he had no intention of having found by anyone. That was how he had spent his time during the fireworks, edging back to that spot.

Asey dropped lightly out of the tree and started toward the place where the light had been.

He wanted more than anything else to race after the fellow as fast as his legs could carry him. But he restrained himself. Once he made a sound, the fellow would freeze into silence again, and while Asey tried to hunt, he would make an excellent target of himself. Using the flashlight was out of the question. In the fog, like a headlight, it would glow for a distance, but it wouldn't actually illuminate more than ten or fifteen feet.

Asey stalked along. At first he was sure that the man did not know of his presence, but as he continued he became less positive.

He stopped for a moment, to listen and make certain that he was still on the right track. A blackberry vine pulled at his ankle; it was caught between the upper part of his shoe and the rubber sole, and in pulling it off, he made just the slightest noise. To him it sounded like more of General Philbrick's fireworks, and he automatically drew back beside a tree.

Something whizzed past him, and he heard a popping sound.

Asey held his breath and tried to fit as much of himself as he could behind the tree.

The fellow was using a silencer.

Asey grinned. In his hip pocket was a full tin of pipe tobacco. He drew it out and threw it as far as he could to the right.

It hit a tree trunk and made a splendid clatter, and Asey waited, with his forty-five in hand, for the fellow to do something about it.

Two bullets thudded into nearby trees, and then two more.

"My, my," Asey muttered. "He don't like me."

He could guess now where the fellow was, so he answered with three shots.

Somewhere away off in the distance, three shots replied to his. Asey nodded. That was Lane, or some one of his men, and they would be heartily welcome.

As the noise of the shots died out, the fellow began to run, apparently realizing that Asey was having reinforcements. Asey went after him.

FIGURE AWAY 185

In the chase that followed, he began to understand how Zeb Chase had felt the previous Saturday night.

No matter how grimly he continued, or how many times he tried to raise his speed, the man was always ahead, and just far enough ahead that Asey actually never once saw him. Once he took a pot shot, but a pot shot had no effect on that speeding, twisting, dodging human.

"If," Asey thought, "the man *is* human!"

By degrees they circled around to where the ground sloped to the pond and the surrounding marshes.

When they reached the beginning of the marsh land, Asey slowed up.

He had no knowledge of this particular spot, but he knew enough about those treacherous muddy marshes in general to be very wary. In his childhood the marshes near his home had been to wandering cattle what the automobile later became to wandering dogs. A series of pictures flashed through his mind —the time his father's best mare had gone down in a mud hole over by Holbrook's, and the hastily improvised blocks and tackles, and the lanterns flickering, and finally his uncle borrowing a shotgun from Nate Holbrook.

The strange laugh floated out ahead of him, but Asey stood still. Not even on the chance of catching a murderer would he let himself be manœuvred toward that ground.

Instead he sat down and loaded his forty-five.

According to his calculations, he was on the edge of the swampy land east of the pond, and not over three hundred yards from the ice house where he had been with Kay and Brinley and the soprano earlier in the day.

Somewhere, this fellow must have a car. There were two approaches to the pond, the short narrow lane which he and

Kay had used, and the road where Brinley had left his machine. The latter road was by far the better, but it was also farther from the pond and harder to reach in a hurry. But it seemed to Asey that if he were in this fellow's shoes, he would prefer having a greater distance to cover in an emergency to the chance of being bottled up in that narrow path. It was about three to one that the car was parked on the east road.

Asey decided to abandon the chase and investigate the line of retreat. Trying to catch this fellow was on a par with trying to catch the greased pig at the old Barnstable fairs, the principal difference being that the pig at least was visible.

After three unsuccessful attempts, he finally reached the east road.

A parked car loomed out of the fog directly ahead of him, and the sight nearly made him whoop.

He waited in the bushes, flashlight in one hand, forty-five in the other. This business was going to come to a finish, right then and there.

At last the man came, sliding out of the underbrush so quietly that Asey almost missed him.

The fellow was panting, Asey noted with pleasure. His breath came in short quick gasps and he walked as though he were utterly exhausted. Asey knew how those feet felt. His felt exactly the same way.

The man was abreast of him.

Asey's light flashed into his face and the forty-five ground above the fellow's belt buckle.

"Reah—my God! So it's you, is it, J. Arthur? Brother Brinley, the old—say, it *is* you, isn't it?"

J. Arthur was shaking from head to foot.

"It's me—who—are—is it Asey?"

"Old Mayo," Asey said. "Nurmi Mayo. You turn around. That's it. Keep on reaching. That's right, J. Arthur. You don't mind if I admit to bein' flabbergasted, do you? I'd never suspected it in a hundred years. Feel this gun borin' into your back? You do? Well, J. Arthur, you behave, or it'll go off, with r'sults that'll be a rev'lation to you."

With the flashlight propped between his jacket buttonholes, Asey's free left hand patted Brinley's pockets.

"Not in a shoulder holster—my, my, what'd you do with your pop gun an' silencer?" Asey asked. "Dropped 'em into the pond, did you? Or what?"

"What do you mean? I—"

"Brinley," Asey said, "there's no two-year-old in the world who wouldn't tell you this is not the time to bluster. Pick up both feet, laddie, an' march along the road. We ain't takin' to the bush no more tonight. That's it. Just you hep right along. I'm behind you. March."

Brinley marched.

"Can't we," he said breathlessly after a minute or two, "go in my car? That's my car, there—"

"I just couldn't trust myself to take rides with you, J. Arthur. Not after tonight. I somehow feel I mightn't get a chance to walk home. I might just be tossed out. No, I think we'll walk it."

Before they reached the main road, Brinley stopped short.

"Carry on, feller," Asey said.

"It's my corns," Brinley said. "Really, I would like to take my shoes off. They hurt. And do I have to go along the main road with my arms up like this? I'd hate to have anyone see me—and besides, I don't understand what this is all about, anyway! What is this all about?"

"The trouble with people like you," Asey said, "is that other people don't take 'em serious until it's too late. When you get a comb'nation of a henpecked husband, an' a Mister Milquetoast, who tries to be pompous an' blustery, it's sort of misleadin'. You don't expect—whoa—you don't turn around, J. Arthur, you—"

"I will so turn around!" Brinley said. "What I do is my business, and you have no right to interfere!"

"You might just as well save your breath," Asey said, "an' march along—hey, who's that?"

Someone was calling his name.

"Asey, Asey Mayo! Where are you?"

Asey bellowed back, and shortly Hamilton appeared from the woods.

"You got him! Who—Brinley? Well, I'm damned!"

"He's tryin'," Asey said, "to be innocenter than a new born lamb. I hand it to him."

"What went on?"

"I don't know about the first part of it," Asey said. "But he's been givin' me a workout I won't forget in years. Had a little silencer arrangement, an' used it lavish. Tried to bog me, too, but I r'fused to be bogged. How's Kay? You seen her?"

"I guess she's all right. She was up at the house, and Cummings was looking after her. Had a scalp wound. Just a scratch, but it bled a lot. I didn't wait to hear her story. I started out for you. Lane's out, too, and a bunch of his boys."

"Did you get Prettyman off all right?" Asey asked.

Hamilton laughed. "That guy is a pip, Asey. He got on the train and walked smack up to Burley and said, 'Let's be friends, it's so much easier that way.' They got a wire from

Burley before I left Boston. He said they were getting along swell. He said—hey, what's the matter, Brinley? Get going!"

J. Arthur turned around.

"I will not," he announced firmly, "move one more step until I have taken my shoes off, and I will not move very many steps after that! I tell you, my feet hurt!"

"With Hamilton here to help cope with you," Asey said, "I can afford to be gen'rous. Go ahead."

"Watch out," Hamilton warned. "Wait, Brinley. I had a guy nearly kill me once, taking a stone out of his shoe. Little gadget in his shoe fired a slug. I'll take the shoes off for you. Stick up a foot."

Despite Brinley's protests that he was perfectly able to remove his own shoes, Hamilton pulled them off.

"Okay," he said. "And what fancy shoes you wear—"

"Say," Asey interrupted, "I got a—let me see them shoes, Hamilton. I didn't think to—"

They were white buckskin oxfords with leather soles.

"Put on your light an' watch him, Ham," Asey said. "I want to look into these things."

They were not just white buckskin shoes, they were the whitest buckskin shoes Asey had ever seen. There wasn't a scratch or a mark or a smudge on them. They were brand new.

Asey looked down at his own rubber-soled brown leather shoes. Briars and blackberry vines had scarred the leather in two dozen places. There were broken pine needles stuck in the lacings. The toes were wet. Lumps of dirt and mud from the lowlands showed on the toe and along the side.

He raised one foot. A mixture of leaves and dirt was packed solidly in the space between the low heel and the instep.

And J. Arthur's buckskin shoes were white, and the leather sole was barely damp.

"He could have changed'em." Hamilton voiced his own thoughts.

"Them, but he couldn't have changed his whole outfit, Ham. Look at them pants," Asey said. "Cuffs all clean. An' his shirt. An' collar. An' tie. An' then look at me. Hamilton, I wonder if I ain't been pretty much of a plumb out an' out fool!"

J. Arthur coughed. The cough said, plainer than words could have, that Asey had stated the case with admirable exactitude and clarity.

"Brinley," Asey said in a subdued voice, "what was you doing up there? What's your story?"

"Why, after I got home," Brinley said, "Walter Rutledge called and told me that Win Billings had run off, and would I help hunt for him. I'd got my clothes off, and I didn't want to much, but I felt that I ought to, and Bessie was busy around the house—she hasn't had a speck of time to get things done, of course—and she said, why not help for a little while. She thought it was my place to. So I changed my mind and told Walter I'd come—"

"Those your usual clothes for huntin' people on a wet night?" Asey asked.

"Bessie had put out my clean things for tomorrow," Brinley said, "and I never realized it until I got over to Walt's, later. Walt said that Win had probably made for the woods somewhere, and I thought of the ice house—they say Win lived there one winter—so I came up here. I know the way pretty well, because of taking Amos up so often, and I thought I'd just look here and then go, and I wouldn't get dirty. As a matter of fact," he added in a burst of honesty, "I didn't think Win could have got this far from town, and I didn't go all the way to the ice house at all. These are my last clean pants, and the cleaner's man doesn't come till day after tomorrow."

"Huh," Asey said. "An' there are lots of others out huntin' Win Billin's, too?"

"Oh, yes. Weston and Jeff Leach—that's why I thought I'd better go, if they were taking the trouble. There were a dozen or so others. Jeff and Wes had a town map, and were marking off spots where Win might be, and everyone had a spot to go to—"

"Didn't you take any kind of light with you?"

"I had a flash, but I lost it in the woods," Brinley said. "I thought I knew the path pretty well, but I stumbled and lost the light, and rather than get dirty, I just turned around and came back. It must have washed out in the rain, that tree root. I'm sure I don't remember it whenever I've brought Amos up here, and I take that path so often—"

"Who was you with durin' the fireworks tonight?"

"Sara, and Jane, and Jeff, and Bessie," Brinley said, "and a lot of others. The fireworks weren't very good tonight. The dampness, I guess. There's no fog uptown now, and the radio says fair tomorrow, and I do hope it clears off for the tag day—"

"When I stopped you an' held you up," Asey said, "why didn't you tell me this?" Asey knew he was being unreasonable, but now that he knew for sure he had let his man slip through his fingers, he couldn't help being and sounding irritated.

"I tried to," J. Arthur said, "but—well, I was afraid. I've never liked firearms, and there you were, poking me in the stomach with that gun! In the way, that is, while I was at Camp Devens, they made me a clerk because I didn't like guns—"

"Brinley," Asey said, "have you the keys to your car? Give'em to Ham—I know, you don't like strangers drivin' your auto, but do you want to walk back to the car? I thought not. Hamilton, get his car. We'll drive him back to the hollow. An' drive me, too. I don't suppose I was ever so weary in all my born days."

He felt very old and tired as he got out of the car at the Randall house.

Lane ran up to him.

"By George, Asey—you got him! How you did it, I don't know or care, but—"

"I didn't," Asey said. "Brinley was just on a hunt—"

"Who said anything about Brinley? Come into the house and take a look—we found him. One of your shots got him in the shoulder. Not much, but enough to stop him, apparently. He was down by the pond. Come on! And how you could ever hit him on a night like this, with this fog, I don't know! Man, you're wonderful—"

"Lane, are you crazy?" Asey demanded.

"Oh, come on! He even had Kay's beret beside him—he's the one, all right! Come on—"

CHAPTER 14.

WALKING mechanically, as though he had been wound up with a key, Asey followed Lane into the living room of the Randall house.

On the couch lay the haggard figure of a man; he was muddy and dirty, and his clothes were torn and his hair in wild disorder.

Cummings, bending over him, obscured the man's face.

"Who?" Asey asked blankly. "Who is it?"

"Win Billings," Cummings said. "He—why Asey, you look about done up!"

"I am. Win Billings—you mean, Win Billings?"

"The last," Cummings ripped in two a strip of adhesive tape, "the last Billings of Billingsgate. Maybe you can get a word out of him. We can't. Nice clean wound, Asey. You're one of the few men I know who can shoot someone up without making a nasty mess for me. Those fellows at the coast guard were always shooting their rum runners in the damndest places. There. You'll recover, Win. In fact, you got off about as easy as Kay did."

Asey sat down in a chintz-covered arm chair.

"Doc, this is sort of mixed up in my mind. Just what happened here?"

"Ask Win," Cummings said. "Maybe he'll talk for you. He won't for us. You'd think he'd taken a vow, or something. Not a peep out of him."

Asey looked over at Win.

"Lane," he said, "you an' the doc clear out for a few minutes, will you? Maybe I can settle this—"

"I don't trust him," Lane said. "I'm going to stay. He's playing possum. He's not anywhere near as weakly as he looks. And he's sober—"

"Run along," Asey said. "Oh, you didn't get any bullets, did you?"

"He and Kay were both nicked, that's all. Asey, I—"

"Run along."

Hamilton stuck his head in the room. "Can I—"

"All of you, beat it."

They left reluctantly. Asey took out his pipe and then remembered he had no tobacco.

He looked around, forgetting that there would probably be no tins of tobacco lurking about in an exclusively feminine household.

"In m' pocket," Win said. "Coat's on the chair."

"Thanks." Asey fished around in the coat pocket until he found an oiled silk pouch. "Pretty swell, that," he said. "Present, I guess?"

"No damn good," Win said. "Don't taste right."

"Same tobacco I use," Asey remarked.

"Same I use, too, but gimme t'bacco from a tin, I says to them wimmen. I don't want no sashay bag!"

FIGURE AWAY

"Kind of fed up with Old Home Week, are you?" Asey inquired.

Win Billings sat upright on the couch and spit with great accuracy into the fireplace.

He was tall and straight, and remarkably well-preserved for an old fellow, particularly one so rarely sober. His hands were amazingly steady, and his voice firm, and the stubborn jutting of his chin interested Asey. A hawklike nose, a high forehead and a stubborn chin were Billings characteristics, to judge from the Town Hall portraits, but hitherto Asey remembered no trace of such stubbornness or force in Win.

"Huh," Win said, leaning back against the wall. "Damn this shoulder, it's worse'n rheumatiz. Look now, Asey Mayo. Did I ever ask anythin' of 'em? No. House? No. Food? No. R'lief? No. Pension? No. Never asked nothin' of nobody, 'cept maybe t'bacco, an' I done work for that."

"An' they washed an' dressed you up," Asey said, "an' they—"

"An' made a show of me!" Win said violently. "Won't stand for it. Won't stand it no longer. Said so. Mean it." He drew a pipe from his pocket. "Gimme that pouch."

Asey filled his pipe and lighted it for him.

"Win," he said, "what'n time happened tonight?"

"Put me t'bed, they did," Win said bitterly, "seven o'clock. Locked the door. I got out the window. Got out b'fore, if you want to know. Take away a man's drink like that! This time, I was through. Feller give me a ride up here. Nice feller, no nonsense about him. I says, gimme a lift, an' he did."

"Headin' for the ice house, huh?"

Win nodded. "Well, kind of lost m'bearin's in the fog. N'en first thing I know, someone starts shootin'—one, two, three.

Right to me. Says I to m'self then, I says, b'God, I *am* through! Won't stand it no longer. They can shoot me full of holes like a sieve 'f they're a mind to, I says, but no more showin' off for'em. Why? Never asked'em for nothin'. Why sh'd I have to dress up for'em? That's what I says to m'self. Cel'bration! They don't know how to hold no cel'bration, Asey! Take like when the Gen'ral come. Turkey red carpets, urns full of flowers, silk hats an' Prince Alberts, plenty to eat, plenty to drink— Asey, I thought it all over, an' it ain't right. They can shoot me all they're a mind to, but it ain't right. Won't stand for it no more, neither!"

Asey puffed at his pipe. Without any doubt, Billingsgate had vastly underestimated the spirit of the last Billings.

"Damn gov'ment," Win said. "That's the trouble. Reds. Can't do this, can't do that, can't shoot 'thout a license, can't fish 'thout a license, can't dig yourself a quohaug 'thout a paper sayin' so. Can't get a drink—'f my father could see things, he'd shoot himself. 'F gregrampa could see it, he'd rue the day the British was licked. Always said it was a mistake, gregrampa did, lickin' the British an' startin' off a new gov'ment—"

"Win," Asey said, "how old are you?"

"Eighty-nine, ninety—m'god, must be ninety-two! Dunno. Round there. But I know one thing. Won't go back to show off no more, see?"

"Y'know," Asey said, "I don't much see why you should, Win. Look, what happened after you was shot?"

Win turned two watery blue eyes on Asey and stared at him for a moment.

"Won't go back. Made up m'mind." He grinned.

"Okay," Asey said with a chuckle. "I'll see to it."

"Promise?"

"I promise on my word of honor, Win. Now, what's the story?"

"M'shoulder hurt," Win said. "I kep' out of their way, an' got down to the ice house. Awful thirsty, I was. Stopped for water." He made a face. "Know what gregrampa said? He said, water was God's way to grow gardens, but it wasn't nothin' to rust the human body with. Gregrampa was *right!*"

Asey went to the door and called for Cummings.

"Got anythin' to drink, doc? Whiskey? Gimme some."

"Ten minutes with that old tank," the doctor said, "and you yowl for spirits. It's disgraceful. If the Ladies' Aid ever found out—"

Asey took the bottle back to Win.

"Not," he said firmly, "at one gulp. All right. You got some water, an' then what?"

"Why, thanks, Asey, you're a good feller. No nonsense about you. Y'come to the point. Well, y'see, I was kind of tired like, so I sat there by the pond an' then when I rested up, I was goin' to the ice house. An' then they come up b'hind me, an' hit me a crack over the head, an' when I come to, here I was with these p'lice, an' the doctor—all talkin' to once, an' yellin', an' sayin' they was goin' to send me t'jail. How can they? Ain't no lawr, my dressin' up an' bein' made a show of. Can't put me in jail for that. Know m'rights. Gregrampa allus said, know your rights, an' stick to 'em, an'—"

"Why wouldn't you talk to 'em, Win?"

"Why sh'd I? B'sides, they talked about you. I knew you'd come. Waitin' for you. Shoot me some more, 'f they want. Put me in jail. I won't go back."

"Where was you," Asey asked, "the night before last? Monday night."

"Last night," Win said, "I met a nice feller, up to that circus. Nice, sensible feller. No nonsense. I says, gimme a drink, an' he did, an'—"

"The night before that," Asey said.

"Night b'fore." Win rubbed his chin. "Night b'fore. Didn't have no drink, night b'fore. Went to the circus—seen you there. You was shootin'—b'god, you busted every clay sparrer in the place."

"That's right. How long'd you stay there, Win?"

Win chuckled. "Oh, I r'member now. Sure thing. The big wheel got stuck. Damn fool woman—she was on it. Know what?"

"What?" Asey asked obediently.

"Feller—some feller—looked like a Swett to me. Dark, like. Come up to me—not Swett. Higgins. It was when they first took me off. Works to the store, he does."

"Zeb Chase?" Asey made a valiant stab. "His mother was a Higgins."

"That's the one. He gimme some money, when they first took me. Here, pop, he says, an' gimme the money. Twenty dollars in ones, an' two tens, too."

"Good for Zeb," Asey said. "So you had forty bucks?"

"Nice feller. Here, pop, he says, they got you cooped up, see'f you can have some fun with this. Said I d'served it. Forty dollars, all in them little sized bills they got now. God, even money's small! But 'twas forty dollars, for me t'spend."

Asey began to understand how Win might very possibly have mistaken the engineer for General Grant that morning.

"So I give the feller ten," Win said, and chuckled until the pain from his shoulder forced him to stop.

"What feller?" Asey asked. He wouldn't have admitted it

to Cummings, but he was beginning to wonder if the whiskey hadn't been a mistake.

"The wheel one. He caught on." Win winked. "Damn fool woman, tries to make a show out of me. Guess I made a show out of her!"

Asey let out a roar of laughter that brought Cummings and Lane rushing to the door.

"Go off," he said. "Go 'way. Win—you mean that you gave the ferris wheel feller ten bucks to keep the wheel stuck? So Bessie Brinley would—"

"That's her. Damn fool. Pokey. Nosey. Did I ever ask her for anythin'? No. Why sh'd I make a show for her? An'," Win smiled broadly, "she don't know 'twas me that done it, neither! I showed her up!"

Asey laughed until the tears ran down his cheeks.

At last he went to the door and called Hamilton.

"Ham," he said, "drive Win over to my cousin Syl Mayo, will you? Take him right over, an' tell Syl to take him over to my gunnin' shack, an' provide him with enough to drink so as he won't have to rust his innards with no water."

"What's that?" Lane said. "You—but he's the one! The Thayer girl said so! He had her cap, and—"

"Win is over ninety," Asey said. "Bear that in mind."

"But he's sore at the town and everyone for making him dress up, and why—Brinley was just telling me. Brinley says that he—"

"Win," Asey said, "deeply r'sents bein' deprived of his rights, an' he don't feel that bein' dressed up an' stared at is what his great-grandfather won the battle of Breed's Hill for. Lane, Win is over ninety. The feller that I chased an' lost, he outrun me. He outguessed me. He outsmarted me. He outstayed me. Win just happened to get in the way of one of my wild shots, that's all. Someone knocked him out an' planted the beret beside him. An' besides, Win's got a cast iron alibi for Monday night—"

"What sort of alibi?" Brinley demanded. "They say he's skipped out of Mrs. Holt's every single night he's been locked up there—nobody knows how. The old fool's crazy. He's a maniac. Stark raving crazy."

"On the contrariwise," Asey said, "Win is as sane as anyone I know, an' he's one feller that'll stand just so much henpeckin' an' no more. Lane, did Kay tell you for certain that he was the one? Did she see him plain? Can she tell?"

"Well, no. She didn't say it was him exactly, but she agreed with us that it must have been, after we talked it over with her."

"Uh-huh, I see. Is she back at Sara's?"

"Went back with—who's that, Konrad?"

Konrad ushered in Jeff Leach and Weston, both worried and distraught and very much the worse for wear. Jeff's white flannel suit was solidly caked with mud, and Weston was wet and bedraggled.

"We thought—oh, you've got him! Well, thank God," Weston said wearily. "Come on, Win, and—"

"Did I ask you for anythin'? No!" Win said. "Why sh'd I show myself off—"

"Sit down," Asey said as Win got up from the couch. "You, too, Weston. What happened to you?"

"Oh, we chased someone we thought was Win," Jeff said, "in the meadows over by the Mill Road. Wes landed in the creek, and I hit a mud hole. It seems we were chasing a perfectly good tourist. We don't think he recognized us. And what Sara'll say to my clothes, I hate to think."

"Look here, Asey," Weston said, "what's all this? What's the matter with Win?"

"Win's been honorably wounded in the service of the town," Asey said, "an' he's herewith bein' excused from any more paradin' whatsoever."

"That's right," Win said complacently. "Won't go back."

"But he's got to!" Weston said. "Don't you see, tomorrow he's on the radio program! It's town day, and he's going to read a piece about the town when he was a boy. He's the oldest inhabitant, you know. And—"

"Won't," Win said.

"See here, Win Billings," Weston lost his temper, "we have this settled, and you—"

"No," Asey said. "Nope, Weston. Win is through."

"Well then," Weston said, producing a trump, "if he doesn't go on the radio, you'll have to!"

Asey drew a deep breath. "Oh—oh, well. All right. But I'll speak my own piece."

"And Win," Weston continued, "was going to get paid ten dollars. What do you think of that, Win? Ten dollars!"

"Got more'n that'n m'pocket right now," Win returned airily. "Got m'poll tax, an' enough to live six months on. Keep y'ten dollars."

His tone indicated that ten dollars was so much pig feed.

Jeff laughed. "I admire his spunk. Let him off, Weston. Asey's right. Enough is enough. Don't you agree, Brinley?"

"No," Brinley said. "No! He's had more care and attention lately than he's had in years, and what thanks do we get for it all?"

"Y'can put me up in front of that tin pan on a broomstick,"

Win referred to the microphone, "but gregrampa used t'say, you can lead a hoss to water, but even he won't drink the stuff."

Asey and Jeff chuckled.

"Consider," Jeff said, "that angle. Suppose Win decides to give some unexpurgated anecdotes over the air. That is very definitely something to think about."

"I'll tell 'em," Win promised, " 'bout you," he waggled a long forefinger at Brinley, "you an' that girl. I seen you, while y'wife was stuck up in the wheel. I seen the two of ye, out b'hind that tent! I seen what y'was up to. 'N I'll tell."

There was fortunately a chair behind Brinley, and he collapsed into it.

"It's a lie!" He tried to speak out manfully, but his voice turned out to be a hoarse whisper. "It's a lie!"

"Lie nothin'," Win returned. "I seen you, makin' up to her. Seen it all. Girl the feller throws knives at. Furrener. Eye-talian, or somethin'."

"So that," Asey said, "was where you was, durin' the ferris wheel fun? Just frollickin', huh? J. Arthur, it's lucky for you he told. We couldn't seem to get you placed, an' believe me when I say you was goin', sooner or later, to be run through the mill until we did find out where you was."

"I'll resign," Brinley said. "I'll resign. Only—don't tell Bessie! Don't let Bessie know! Bessie wouldn't forgive me, ever! And it was just—just a—only—I mean—"

"Just what?"

"Oh, I'll resign! Bessie said, when I first went into politics, that a slip would mar—I know it means the end of my career. And I did want," Brinley said plaintively, "to go to the state legislature!"

Asey looked at Jeff, who nodded.

"Come, come, Arthur," Jeff said soothingly, "no one knows but us here, and look—come along home. Wes, you come too. You've got to settle about the tags for tomorrow, Brinley, and your accounts. Come on. Forget this. Asey, you take care of Win, will you? We'll explain it officially as a bad cold, and perhaps native pride'll keep the town folks from telling what they'll know has happened."

"And don't you forget," Weston said to Asey, "about the radio!"

Dr. Cummings watched the selectmen leave and then wandered back into the living room.

"Sometimes," he said, "I wonder how governments exist. If a midway girl that gets thrown knives at can cause a flurry like this in town—well, well. What about Win?"

"Syl can take care of him over at my gunnin' shack," Asey said, "until his shoulder's all right. What're your plans for winter, Win?"

"I been spendin' winters lately," Win said, "up to Philbrick's big barn. Got me a stove off the dump, the kind you stick into the e-lectricity, an' I tell you, it's mighty fine up there. Keep good'n warm."

"So that," Cummings said, "is why the General is suing the light company for winter bills! Asey, we'll have to solve some problems for Win."

Asey nodded. "We will. Now, Win, this feller Hamilton's takin' you away, an' you're goin' to stay at my shack with Syl. Know Syl? Nate's grandson. Hang around there till I come, will you? An' don't you wander away, either, 'cause someone might bring you back here. Will you stay there?"

"Wonder," Win said, "can he play Hi-low Jack? Nate could."

"He is probably," Asey said, "the finest player in the country. Now, Win, will you b'have, sort of?"

Win smiled as he got up from the couch. "Gregrampa allus said, do unto others as you're done by, 'less they give you water to drink. Gimme m't'bacco."

He followed Hamilton out to a car.

"Majestic old duffer, isn't he?" Cummings said. "Are you sure, Asey, you're doing right in letting him go?"

"He's not the man I followed. Where'd he get the money for a silencer? Where'd he get the stamina? What about Kay?"

"I'll go over with you," Cummings said, "she'll tell you the story."

Lane walked with them to Asey's roadster.

"I hope," he said, "the next clew or suspect we get, you'll let us have it for more than ten minutes. My God, I don't get a chance to bite into anything before you yank it out of my sight!"

"Chickenbones," Asey said, "but they're gettin' meatier, I think. Keep your fellers here, Lane. 'Night."

"How about sending some into the woods again," Lane said. "We might find your man. Perhaps you hit him, after all."

"You keep your men here," Asey said. "Two casualties tonight is enough. So long."

Asey and the doctor found the entire household except Jeff camped in Kay Thayer's bedroom.

"It wasn't Win, was it?" she asked. "Asey, did you—you didn't find anyone else, did you?"

"I found J. Arthur, but nothin' come of it. Kay, what happened? What was you doin' there? What went on?"

Kay avoided Asey's eye.

"This afternoon," she said, "I found the two paths you told

me about, and then I found another one down to the ice house, and then it cut around the ice house and went off into the woods to a road. I guess it was the road where Brinley said he parked this afternoon."

"Whyn't you tell me?"

"Well, it didn't seem important at the time. And besides, you told me to take the shortest path, or way, and this was circuitous and roundabout. And this evening it suddenly came to me that perhaps it was the path the murderer used. After all, he'd hardly park on the main road, and he had to have a car somewhere. And it sort of fascinated me, the idea did, so I slipped away—"

"She told me," Sara interrupted accusingly, "that she had to see some reporter!"

"I did. And afterwards, I got into the percolator and drove up there— Asey, if you look like that at me, I shall cry, I swear I shall! I know how crazy it was, but I didn't think of it then."

"Go on."

"Well, I had a gun," Kay said. "I shot, too. I shot twice—you don't seem surprised!"

"The fellow had a silencer," Asey said, "but we heard two shots. You pretty much had to have a gun. B'sides, you said once you was a sucker for a shot. Go on."

"Well, I went there, and waited, and after a while I got bored, and scared, and cold—I'm a city person. I don't understand country noises, and I confess they terrify me. So I lighted a cigarette, and about two seconds later—"

"Somethin' whizzed by you, an' you d'scovered what a bright girl an' what a sucker for a shot you really was. Lightin' a cig'rette then! Was—look, couldn't you—oh, go on!"

"I fired back. I don't know why. I couldn't see anything to

fire at. And then something whizzed and stung my head—I didn't know that being shot was like that. And I began to understand that the popping sound was a silencer. At that point," Kay concluded honestly, "you could have poured me into a glass. I wasn't even a pulp, I was liquid. Wow!"

"An' then?"

"I flopped down behind a tree and tried to become an inconspicuous part of Mother Nature, and then I heard someone coming toward me, and not just toward me, but sort of *at* me, if you know what I mean. I got up and started to run, and he grabbed me, and I screamed, and pulled away. And then I tripped headlong—look, d'you know that theory about not being scared of the bear, but being scared because you run from the bear? Well, it's true. After that bit of action I was almost turning from a liquid to a gaseous state—"

"Where was your gun?" Asey demanded.

"I am pained to say," Kay told him, "there were only two bullets in it. Well, I got up as he made for me, and tried to smack him with the gun, and I kept yelling—"

"Why did you yell for me?"

"I was slowly solidifying at that point," Kay said. "I was coming to. I began to realize what I'd let myself in for. So I yelled for you, hoping it might make the gent take to his heels, if he thought you were around. Your name is curiously potent. And my, how I felt when I heard you bellow back! I thought it was a mirage at first. Anyway, I got behind a tree, and the gent was playing tag with me around the trunk—"

"Didn't he shoot?"

"If he did, he didn't hit me. I wouldn't have known, anyway. I dodged and jerked and switched around as though I had St. Vitus dance. He got hold of me just before you came, and I thought he was going to throttle me, but then up you dashed—and you know all I could think of? That ditty about the girl in the saw mill, and the saw coming closer and closer and closer—"

"A more appropriate ditty," Sara said, "being 'Nearer My God To Thee.' Kay, I don't know whether to scold you for being utterly bereft of your senses, or to congratulate you on being alive."

"What I'm most interested in," Asey said expectantly, "is the man."

Kay sighed.

"Kay, you don't mean you can't tell me anythin' about him?"

"He's a good shot. He's an artful dodger. He's strong—he has fingers like pilliwinks."

"Like what?" Cummings demanded.

"Pilliwinks," Kay said. "They were a torture thing for squeezing fingers. I learned the word from a dictionary, and I've waited ten years for a chance to use it, and my, is it apt! He nearly broke my whole right hand, with one squeeze. Every finger—"

"What was he like?" Asey asked. "If he throttled you, you must have been near enough to see somethin'."

"He had on dark clothes, and a handkerchief over his mouth an' chin. I can't tell you if he was short or tall or anything. He seemed mountainous when I was on the ground, but he didn't when I got onto my feet. It was so dark dimensions didn't matter. I never was really near him. He held me off at an arm's length during the throttling process. Death was his aim. Not destruction, as Dr. Cummings was inclined to think at first. No, Asey, I can't help you a bit."

"Didn't he make a sound, or speak, or cuss, or anything?"

"Not a peep out of him, not even an 'Ugh,'" Kay said. "Strong and silent, that was my pal. And a more grimly determined individual I never met. Well, I did what is probably the silliest thing I'll ever do in my life, and from now on, Asey, I'll leave the case to you. Next time I have any hunch that pal's coming, you get told. And I ruined your coat, Jane, to absolutely no avail. I'll buy you another."

"It was awful, perfectly awful!" Eloise was goggle-eyed. "Oh, I think you were brave, I do, really! That awful man—I always say, you can't tell about these reds. No beard, of course, but still red. I'm sorry now I said we'd keep this thing quiet—not that I don't think mother would have preferred it, and of course one must always respect the wishes of the—but just the same, if the people really knew, that man would—why, the papers would have him jailed at once—really, Mr. Mayo, not that I don't think you know best, of course. And I'm always willing to be convinced—but why don't you arrest that man, instantly? It makes my blood boil, to think of that murderer—and I'm sure he was going to kill Kay, too, if not worse—the nick of time, wasn't it, really? I do think perhaps tomorrow you'd best arrest him, before we're all of us murdered in our beds, at the least."

"Are you," Jane's voice was curiously hard, "by any chance talking about Mike Slade?"

"Why of course—who else, I'm sure!" Eloise said nervously. "We know—I mean, we *do* know, don't we—though of course we keep pretending it's all a mystery—but I'm sure I may say here, in the privacy of our own group—why, we know Mike Slade is the one!"

Jane walked over and stood in front of Eloise.

An uncomfortable silence followed. Twice Sara Leach started

to say something and twice she changed her mind. Everyone knew there was going to be a scene, but no one knew exactly how to stop it.

"So strange of you," Eloise got up from the sea chest on which she had been sitting, "really, I always said to mother, so strange of her to like that—my dear, really, don't you think you're going a bit too far? You know—I'm sure mother said often enough—I, myself, often wished she had said more—the man's a scoundrel. So unsporting of you, to take this attitude—so—so *grim* about it, when it's proved to you—"

Jane moved so swiftly that Asey, later, admitted he had not seen the blow that struck Eloise squarely across the mouth. It caught her off balance, and she fell heavily into the corner.

"And the next time you mention Mike Slade," Jane said, "I'll do more than smash your teeth. I'll kill you, d'you hear?"

CHAPTER
15.

THE shock of Jane's words and her accompanying gesture was so intense that it affected even Dr. Cummings' professional instincts.

While his prospective patient groaned and writhed on the floor, he stared at Jane as she coolly walked across the room, opened the door and departed. For fully ten seconds he was speechless.

"By—by George!" he said. "By George, that girl meant it! Now isn't that extraordinary, when you stop and think it out. That, from a nice appearing girl, apparently in the best of health. Emotionally unstable, that's the answer. Emotionally unstable. Sara, what's she been eating lately, d'you happen to know?"

"Doc." Asey pointed to Eloise. "Consider this end of it, will you?"

"Go get my other bag," Cummings said to Zeb, "out in the car. Dear me, more hysterics, I suppose—once she finally assimilates the situation, it will probably be an all night job quieting—by George, what's the matter with her? Look—"

Eloise's mouth was working strangely. She put both hands to her jaw.

FIGURE AWAY

"Broken, I'll wager," Sara said. "That smack—Asey, what do you do in a case like this? Isn't it assault and battery, or something? The poor woman—"

"Doc," Asey said, "Jane said somethin' about smashin' her teeth—say, has she got false teeth? 'Cause if she has, I bet you they're wedged, or busted."

"That's it!" Sara said. "It happened to my mother once. Carry her to—oh, her room, I guess. We'll have to separate Jane and Eloise, under the circumstances, and I'm sure I don't know where we can put Jane, unless it's the trundle bed in the attic— Kay, I know this isn't helping your head any!"

"Kay's all right," Cummings said. "I shouldn't wonder if Eloise weren't the more badly hurt of the two. Kay's got just a superficial— Zeb—help us here. Oh, put the bag anywhere. That's it. Uh!" he grunted as he helped Asey and Zeb lift Eloise. "Sometimes I think this fad for a slim form is a lot of nonsense, and sometimes in a case like this, I wish there were more of it."

They finally managed to pry Eloise's mouth open and remove her broken plate, which had, as Sara and Asey guessed, somehow wedged in such a manner that it locked her jaw.

But once open, Eloise's mouth proceeded to make up for lost time.

She raised such a din that Uncle Jeff and Brinley and Weston, who had been solving town problems down in the living room, came flying up the stairs.

"You can't help." Briefly Asey summed up what had taken place. "You might as well go. Oh, Zeb, see if you can find where Jane went to. In the mood she's in, she's capable of anything at all."

"Asey," Zeb said, "with a great respect for your wishes, the answer is no. The door mat has resigned. This particular worm has turned. Let someone else find Jane and cope with her mood. Not me. She's fooled me once too often. I thought, after yesterday—but that doesn't matter. I'll help you with Eloise, but as for Jane, no."

"I can see how you feel," Asey said. "Wes, you or Brinley, or someone—find Jane for me. Thanks."

"What's the matter with her now?" Brinley nodded his head toward Eloise. "What's happened to her? She sounds as if she was crazy."

"Just lisping," Asey said. "To use an old Cape phrase, she's gummin' it. You all get along and find Jane."

Obediently the selectmen of Billingsgate marched off to find Jane.

After a while Eloise quieted down.

"Thank God," Cummings said. "My, what a nervous system she must have. To be able to take this sort of outburst in your stride, the way she does—by George, you can call women the weaker sex if you want to, but no man would be able to work himself into a frothing state like this, and then snap out of it —what's that you say?"

"Thee theece. In the thace." Eloise pointed to Asey. "Thee theece, thee?"

"She sells sea shells," Cummings recited cheerfully. "By the sea shore. Sea shells she sells, and of that— Eloise, what *do* you want? Say it again."

She said it again, but the results were not any better.

"I got it," Asey said. "The teeth—you got spares, have you?"

Eloise nodded vigorously.

"Where?"

She pointed.

"Oh, the case. The teeth are in the case. Sara, that's your department. Get her teeth."

He tactfully strolled over and stared at a picture of four fat sheep in a field until the process of equipping Eloise with new teeth was completed.

"How fortunate," Eloise said in a moment or two, "I thought to bring them—several times I haven't, and really, it's most embarrassing—but how could one anticipate—after all, falling down, or dropping them, yes. Why, everybody has accidents. But one can't anticipate—er—a blow, I'm sure. But I do think it was fortunate I had them."

With that commentary, Eloise dismissed the situation.

"It was unfortunate," Sara said, "but I know that none of us there will mention it. Jane has been terribly upset, and she's not demonstrative. I suppose everything's seething inside her, and it came out all at once. It's too bad she landed on you and proceeded to make you her safety valve—she's probably crying her eyes out somewhere, and wondering how she can apologize."

"Poor Jane!" Eloise said. "Of course her father—that ruined her life, I know—you couldn't call her mother anything but flighty. Just flighty. Mother warned me—of course mother understood Jane. But I couldn't help wishing—Zeb is such a nice boy. So nice-looking, and of course his family is beyond—but when I saw how things have been going lately, I just couldn't help suggesting—and I'm sure she'd have found it a very wise choice. Mother thought so, and we both hoped—but I suppose she knows her own mind."

"I'm afraid she does," Sara said.

Eloise nodded. "My own fault, I suppose—but I'm sure I didn't mean to plague her so that—really, no! My, no! I've just been trying to point out to her how Zeb—after all, that red man—and particularly *now*."

"I take it," Asey said, "you been suggestin' that there was a lot of sanity in hookin' Zeb, instead of botherin' with Slade, considerin' this situation?"

"Why yes, of course. I'm sure I didn't mean to plague her till she—but one never knows, does one—" her voice trailed off.

"One doesn't, I'm sure—it," Asey said. "It—oh, Sara, if I stay here any longer, I'll talk like that too. See to her, will you? I'll be back."

He could well understand how Jane might have been driven to the breaking point if Eloise had been pumping out a steady if disconnected stream of propaganda in favor of Zeb Chase, and apparently she had been doing just that. That accounted for Jane's spending the previous day with Zeb. Eloise had simply driven her into it.

Weston and Jeff were in the living room, busy over a batch of papers.

"Nice hunters you are," Asey said. "Where's Jane?"

Weston smiled. "Brinley found her. I didn't know he was such a lady killer. He found her out under the trees, and brought her in, and she's crying on his shoulder in the dining room, and he seems to be handling her so well that Jeff and I decided to leave the affair to him. Asey, what's to be done? I'm going crazy and that's a fact!"

Asey shrugged. "About all we can do is wait an' hope, right now."

"I worry about tomorrow," Weston said. "It's town day, and tag day for our new hospital. I want it to go off. Friday is the historical day—that doesn't count much, and Saturday'll take care of itself, with the week-end crowd, and all. But tomorrow has simply got to go smoothly. Oh, I forgot. The state police head wanted you to call him. He didn't come with the governor, he came later and stayed only a few minutes. He said he'd call Lane. Asey, isn't there anything we can do to keep tomorrow from being spoiled?"

Asey sat down. "I don't think you need have any fears about tomorrow. Or tomorrow night. I got as much endurance as the next, but he done me up. He done Kay up. I sort of hope he'll rest tomorrow. B'sides, he's done a number of things he ought to sit down an' take stock of. On our side, we'll take stock, too. I'd say that Friday night, he ought to bounce back, bigger an' better than ever. By that time, maybe we can have doped out what he was after at the hollow tonight. Probably aimin' to plant somethin' else."

"Plant something else?"

"Yes, he's been plantin', but don't ask me to go into it now. Maybe if he'd keep on plantin', we might get some place. Honest, I can't move. I like to think of our friend somewhere, soakin' his feet in Epsom salts. You know, someone's got to cut my shoes off, the way I feel. Tell Brinley to bring Jane in here, will you? An' you two go in the dinin' room."

Jeff sighed as he got up. "You may feel that way, but Wes and I are feeling worse. Our adventures in that meadow— Sara hasn't had a chance to notice this suit yet. That's the real disadvantage of having a wife, they're so fussy about clean clothes. You and Wes, Asey, can hang your suits on the line when you want, and send them to the cleaner's—"

"Is that so?" Sara appeared in the doorway. "Jeff Leach, you march up this minute, and Weston, you run along and change, too. Neither of you can catch cold till after Sunday. Asey, before—I don't care if you do have to talk with Jane. Before you do another thing, you go upstairs and take those things off!"

"Ma'am," Asey said, "I haven't anything to change into."

'Yes, you have!" Sara said. "I phoned Syl's wife this evening, and told her to go to your house and get some clothes and have someone bring them over. Those corduroys and jacket and flannel shirt are all right for local color, but that's no reason why they should grow on you."

"I r'sent that," Asey said. "I been borrowin' Zeb's things, an' I ain't in no condition to grow anything—"

"That's what you think. Don't you laugh, Weston, you're worse. Have you any clean flannels? Well, then, go up with Jeff and take those off, and put on some pants of his. I'll see those get cleaned before tomorrow. All of you, move!"

They protested, but they went. Sara watched them go upstairs, and then marched into the dining room to interview J. Arthur.

"You're dazzlingly clean," she said, "but you go along home, before Bessie takes to worrying and coming after you. Sometimes, I think men have no sense."

She saw him out the front door, and then returned to Jane.

"Now as for you," she said, "you've indulged in enough self-pity. Go up and apologize to Eloise, and answer any questions Asey wants to ask you, and then go to bed. Eloise is irritating, I'll admit. She irritates me profoundly most of the time. But that doesn't in the least justify your actions or your words. In your way, you're quite as irritating, and you'd know it if you weren't so sure that you were the only pebble on the beach."

"Why, Aunt Sara!"

"I mean it. You're so occupied with your problems, and your life, and your misfortunes, and particularly your misfortunes —and your two beaus, and your trials and your tribulations—

for heaven's sakes, if you want Mike Slade, take him. He'll doubtless beat you daily, but he may beat in some sense."

"I—why—no one ever talked to me like that in—"

"That's the trouble with you. Now you've heard the truth, run along."

Sara turned out the lights and walked briskly into the hallway.

"You've been very kind, Dr. Cummings," she said brightly. "But now we're going to bed. Zeb, go to bed. You've got to be at the store early, I heard you say so. Good night, doctor."

"Upon my word, Sara, you're certainly speeding the departing—"

"Good night."

Sara closed the door behind him, turned the key and shot the bolt above, just as Asey came out of his room.

"Jeff will lock the door so I'll be restrained," she said. "Lord knows I've provocation to sleepwalk tonight! And now, good night to you. If you want anyone, they're where they should be, in bed."

Asey was grinning when he went back to his room.

"Aunt Sara," he said, "is on the warpath. She's a great old mopper-upper!"

"She gave Jane hers," Zeb said. "Did my heart good to listen."

"I'm sorry about this Jane business," Asey said. "I s'pose, now, your little flurry with the grocery business is all over an' done with?"

"Funny thing," Zeb said, "but I began because of Jane, really. Wanted a nice excuse to stay here, and dad was sore at his listless heir. And now, d'you know, I've got quite worked up over—well, Jane's one thing, but baked beans are another."

Asey agreed gravely that there was much truth in what he said.

"You know," Zeb went on, "I think I'll buy a half interest in Matt's store. Great possibilities. And besides—well, there's a lot *to* beans. That sounds like dad, but it's true. I'm going to get into this end of the business first, and then I want to see what I can do with dad. You know, the family used to be in the spice business—caravans and things. Now as I see the bean situation—"

He was still running on about the romance of the bean business when Asey fell asleep. Apparently Jane's stand in defense of Mike Slade hadn't begun to touch Zeb anywhere near as much as she or anyone else anticipated.

Tag Day went off smoothly, as Weston had hoped.

Asey spent the morning with Lane, and in the afternoon he dressed himself up according to Sara's rigid specifications and took Win Billings' place on the radio program.

After the broadcast the golden-voiced Vincent Tripp came over and congratulated him.

"And you have another accent, don't you?" he said. "Quite different from your usual—er—speech."

"It's knowin' so many Boston folks," Asey explained. "That does it. An' honest, if a New England native spoke natural on the air, the listeners'd faint. Some day I'm goin' to take time off an' teach some of your broadcast actors how we talk up here in the chill provinces. Through the mouth, not half a nostril. So long."

Madame Meaux waited at the door for him.

"Pretty hot," she said. "Tomorrow you'll get sixty-one offers of marriage and a thousand letters about how to quadruple your capital. Say," she lowered her voice, "if you really want to know where Honeyboy was Monday night—"

"J. Arthur? I do. How'd you find out?"

"Pinky." Madame Meaux pointed to the orchestra leader. "He dated the girl up last night, and boy, did he walk into a jam! The knife thrower got wise and followed 'em, with knives. But before all that happened, Pinky found out from the girl, and he told me today. And say, that dog tag stuff was on the level. The license on his collar is last year's. What happened last night?"

"How do you know anything did?"

"It took Arthur two hours to explain where he'd been," Madame Meaux said. "The partition's thin. I couldn't get to sleep till they finished hashing over old man Billings. What else was there besides him? Arthur gulped a lot."

Asey caught her up with the events of the night. As he finished, outside the Town Hall, Slade came rushing up.

"I got to see you, Asey, right away. Mind if I snatch him, Em? And look. About that money. I'll pay you Saturday."

"Getting religion, Mike?"

"Getting married," Slade said. "Okay, Em. Come on, Asey —got your car here? Well, let's drive somewhere out of the mob and get this settled."

On a hill overlooking the bay, Asey stopped the car.

"Whatever it is you want to settle, let's have it."

"I've just seen Jane," Slade said. "At least, I saw her this noon. She's terribly ashamed of herself, and so am I. She's acted badly, and I've acted badly, and I'm sorry and so is she."

"What's come over you?" Asey asked curiously.

"Well, two things," Slade said. "Jane and I are going to get married, and I—well, I hadn't realized the enormity of this until today. I went off half cocked the other night. I knew that the Randalls wanted Jane to marry Chase, and I suppose from their point of view, you can't blame 'em. Not that I think that money is any—well, they don't know any better. Today, and yesterday, and since I've been working and helping with things, I've just begun to realize what this means to the town. Prosperity, publicity, no debt—I see why you kept the murder quiet. I've just realized what a thing this town undertook—and d'you know, it's going over?"

"I'm glad to know it," Asey said. "I'd forgotten to ask, with everythin' goin' on."

"This week's going over with a bang," Slade said. "I forget how much we had this noon, but we're going to get our hospital. It'll be small, but we can support it, and we can get the local doctors to—honestly, I'm proud of this damned town! We've got enough already this week to pay off our debt, and already we can plan to—"

Asey let him talk on and work off his enthusiasm.

"But there's just one thing that bothers me," Slade said finally. "What'll happen when this story does break?"

"I was sort of hopin' to clean it up by the end of the week," Asey told him, "so's Billingsgate'd have a nice happy climax. But I dunno, Mike."

"I've an idea, Asey. It's crazy, but have you ever thought that someone either in the town, or someone who came from here originally, might be sore at it? Suppose they'd been failures, and blame the town. Perhaps among the tourists or the old settlers, there's one with that type of grudge."

"P'raps," Asey said, "but the feller I chased knew around that region like a book. That lets out tourists—say, that r'minds me.

There's one thing I wanted to ask Jane an' Eloise, about that path Kay found—"

"And hasn't Eloise crashed through, about that sock Jane gave her? She's been swell. Jane says she's working like a Trojan and being an old sport."

Asey nodded. "Sort of person like her does crash through, when you least expect it. Slade, where was you last night, around fireworks time?"

"Didn't you know? I was on the evening radio program," Slade answered with a touch of pride. "When? Oh, it began half an hour before the fireworks, and ended up as the real town fireworks began. They use a record for the program fireworks, did you know? I didn't. Tripp said I was pretty good. And you know, a lot of people must listen to that program."

"Got fan mail, did you?"

"No, but a dealer I used to know came down from Boston. He heard me and he—well, he bought four pictures, and wants more."

"Fine!" Asey said. "So you can pay off your debts an' get married, huh?"

"These white flannels," Slade said bitterly. "These, and that radio talk, that's what got him. He thinks I've been making a pile of money, so he wants a cut. My stuff's no better or worse than it was, but he thinks—what are you laughing about?"

"A crack of Aunt Sara's," Asey told him. "I wonder if you won't die a Republican—don't start anything, I'm jokin'. An' thank goodness you was on that program. It's got you an alibi as well as money."

"You mean you thought I was the man in the woods? Now see here," Slade began angrily.

"Cool off," Asey advised. "An' when you an' Jane get a house,

I'm goin' to get a sampler worked to put over your fireplace. 'God Bless Our Happy Home And Count Ten.' In red. Now, let's go see Jane an' Eloise about that path."

At the hollow they found Lane pretending to weed the lawn. A hospital tag dangled from one of his shirt buttons.

"Eloise," he indicated the tag. "Can't you squelch her? And the tourists, Asey. I don't like it. They've been here in herds. I wish we could shut the place up, but I suppose we can't. I've got two men around, but I don't like this at all—and by God, here come more people!"

"Do your best," Asey said. "I guess we won't bother to ask questions now. Looks like they had their hands full with customers. We'll run along, Slade."

The rest of the day passed off quietly, although as Kay said the next morning, it was rather worse sitting and waiting for something to happen than actually having it.

There was only a small bandage on the side of her head to record her encounter in the woods. She explained it, when she had to, by saying that she had taken a tumble.

"What's today?" she asked at breakfast. "Where's the program?"

"Historical tours," Zeb said. "Very instructive. Sites of the first church, first store, first graveyard, first schoolhouse. Where the Pilgrims didn't land. Where it is thought they did, although I personally think they're all wet. Where the British were repulsed by embattled farmers, once in seventeen-seventy something, and again in eighteen-twelve. Very repulsive folk, these Billingsgaters. Also where Mr. Thoreau stayed, and where Mr. Webster and Mr. Coolidge fished—"

"Now there's a thought," Kay said. "Fishing. My boss is a fisherman. I wonder if—mm. Famous Folk Who Fished in

FIGURE AWAY

Bottomless Pond—got a bottomless pond? There usually is one. Asey, how's for taking me fishing? I can do a fish story and please the boss and work in local color to beat anything."

"I can't," Asey said. "I've got to see Lane, and Weston's rung me in for some judgin' at the hall. What makes him think I know a better tomato or jar of jam than anyone else, I don't know—"

"Your cousin's made you a judge?" Bertha interrupted as she took away his plate. "Oh. You're a judge?"

"Yup, an' I ain't forgot your stuff, either," Asey told her. "Seems it's all numbered an' not named, but don't you worry —I'll know your jelly!"

"I would like to fish," Kay said. "Oh, dear—"

"I'll take you," Zeb said unexpectedly. "It's probably going to rain, but—well, let's go."

Asey and Sara exchanged amused glances.

"Huh," Asey said to her later after Zeb and Kay had gone, and Eloise and Jane had started for the hollow, "huh. So that's what he meant by the romance of baked beans!"

"It's the resiliency of youth," Sara said. "What was that, Jeff?"

"I said, 'Off again, on again, gone again, Finnegan,'" Jeff told her. "Come on, we're late, and our driver's blowing the horn."

It was mid-afternoon before Asey remembered that he had failed to ask Jane and Eloise about the path Kay had found. Turning in his last judge's slip, he drove up to Hell Hollow.

The fine drizzle had not curtailed the tourists' enthusiasm. The Randalls' house and barn were surrounded by customers.

"I wish," Lane said, "all the historical spots weren't on this road. They see those figures, and stop, and—there. There goes one drove, and another. That helps. Jane? She's up to her ears. Eloise just went indoors, into the house. At least I think she did. There's Jane now—yell and ask her."

Asey called to her.

"Eloise?" Jane said. "She went for heavy cord and boxes to pack some stuff in before some man gets back from viewing the wishing well. In the house cellar, she is. I've got to dash—tell her to hurry, will you?"

Asey went into the house and walked out to the kitchen. The cellar steps, steep and protected only by a swinging railing, were in the corner.

"Eloise!" he bent over the rail and called. "Miss Randall! I wonder if—"

At his hand was the electric light switch. He flicked it on and peered down into the tiny circular cellar.

Eloise lay in a heap at the foot of the steps.

As Asey mounted the stairs a few minutes later, Lane hurried into the kitchen.

"Say, Asey," he began, "Jane wants you to tell Eloise she must hurry, that man is back—"

"You go tell Jane," Asey said, "to carry on without Eloise. Say I'm busy with her. Then you lock the doors an' come back here."

"What's the matter?"

"Look down there."

Lane stared down at the figure in the cellar.

"Is she badly hurt? Fell, did she?"

"She's dead," Asey said. "Fell, or was pushed. Probably the last, if you want the bitter truth."

CHAPTER 16.

"I'LL go clear these people out," Lane said, starting for the door.

"You'll do nothin' of the kind," Asey told him. "Look, this business can't be made public any more than the other. You can't send 'em off—you're the gardener. You can't say who you are without givin' everything away. Go find Jane, like I said, an' tell her I'm busy with—no, change it. Say that Eloise has had a sick spell, an' we've called the doc, but not to come in an' excite her. Just to carry on with the customers. Now, hurry. Before she comes in."

He managed, by a miracle, to get Cummings at his office phone.

"Hollow," he said briefly. "Cellar stairs this trip. No, not Jane. Look, can you get someone to help Jane—your wife? Good. Tell her all you have to. I want her."

An hour later, Cummings, Asey, Lane and Hamilton sat in the kitchen. The shades were drawn. On the table were Cummings' open bags, and Lane's camera, and a suitcase with more of his paraphernalia.

"All right," Cummings said, "we've hashed enough. Now, Asey, why not suicide?"

"She fell backwards an' landed on her back. You say her head hit the cement floor, an' she died in a second."

"True, but couldn't she trip up the stairs as well as down'em? When I first got my bifocals, I tripped upstairs for a week."

"She went downstairs," Asey said, "for heavy cord an' boxes. Neither's been touched. Therefore she never got downstairs to get what she was after. Never had a chance to."

"Wait," Lane said. "There was that pair of shears on the floor. Suppose she got halfway down, remembered she'd left the shears, and started back, and then tripped?"

"The shears," Asey pointed out, "was way over by the stove. She come in the dinin' room door. If she'd detoured way around to the stove an' dropped'em there, she certainly would have r'called the fact before she got halfway down the steps. B'sides, what'd she detour for? She was after somethin', an' she was on her way to it. Why cross over to the stove?"

Lane pounded on the table with his fist.

"Then why, will you tell us, are the scissors there? She had them in her hand when she entered the house. I saw them. Now, you explain why they were on the floor by the stove!"

"She threw them at someone." Asey knew perfectly well what Lane's reactions would be, and he was not disappointed.

"Threw them at—" Lane began scornfully. "Asey, you—"

"Now just a moment, Lane," Cummings interrupted. "I wonder if—yes, Asey's right. I know Eloise. Suppose, as she starts down the stairs, she hears someone. Turns around, sees someone. Someone menacing. She recognizes the fact that she is in danger, and hurls at the person her only weapon, the shears she has in her hand."

Lane ridiculed the doctor's story.

"If she had scissors, and recognized someone as a menace,

FIGURE AWAY 227

why didn't she wait and use them to stab with? That's the logical thing for anyone to do," he said. "Why, throwing the scissors at someone would be like throwing a loaded gun instead of shooting it!"

Dr. Cummings sighed. "Of course, Lane, of course! That's just my point! That's what a logical person would do. I agree. So does Asey. But you fail to take into consideration the fact that Eloise is not logical. Never in this world would it have occurred to her to hold her ground and stab her assailant. Never. It's a perfectly characteristic gesture for her to hurl the shears futilely—de mortuis and all that sort of thing, and of course the woman had many good points, but she was none the less a futile woman."

"All right, all right," Lane said. "Be psychological, if you want to, but it's the practical things that interest me. Why, if someone pushed her, is the swinging railing intact? She had either to be pushed through it, or if she was on the top step, on her way down, she'd have been clinging to it—and her grip on it would save her, or the railing would be down there with her. One thing or the other."

"Lane," Cummings said plaintively, "you just simply do not understand the type of woman involved. You claim she pestered you—can't you tell, couldn't you tell, that she was a futile individual? Can't you tell from what you know that she never knew which way to turn a key to unlock a door? She couldn't tune a radio to save her life. She couldn't unscrew a dead electric light bulb and put in a new one. Did you ever see her try to drive that beach wagon? Man, she was a menace to public safety when she drove that vehicle! Your trouble, Lane, is that you're practical. Eloise is not practical. You'd grab the railing. Eloise would not grab the railing. Put Eloise in a shipwreck.

Throw a life preserver to her. Would she put it on? No. She'd try to sit on it. Lane, can't you grasp this?"

"The woman tripped and fell," Lane said doggedly. "That's that."

"The woman," Asey said, "was pushed an' thrown. Lane, walk over to the head of the steps. That's it. Now, what do you do first, starting down, before you touch the rail, even?"

"Put on the light, of course," Lane said impatiently.

"That's what I'd do, too. But the light was off. You can say she started down, turned to put it on, an' fell. But that's the one way she couldn't have fallen, because she'd have to be leanin' more over the rail. She couldn't help but save herself if she started to fall then."

"Whyn't you tell me about the lights?" Lane demanded.

"You never gave me any chance. I think she started down, was reachin' to put on the lights from the top step, an' heard someone. Turned around, there on the top step. Someone comes toward her, from over there by the stove, an' she throws the shears. He rushes over, takes her by the shoulders, an' hurls her down."

"There were the marks of your rubber soles going down and coming up," Lane said. "No marks for her, but then she came across the wooden walk and wasn't in the damp grass. But if someone threw her down, wouldn't you think they'd have gone down to make sure she was dead? And if they came from outdoors, why can't we find some marks? Any marks, here or—"

"Give the feller credit for stockin' feet," Asey said. "B'sides, after hurlin' her straight onto a concrete floor nine feet b'low, he could be reasonably sure he'd achieved his purpose. He could have made sure by snappin' on the light an' lookin' down. Let's go down there again for one more look."

The four of them went gingerly down the almost perpendicular steps.

"Why are so many cellars on the Cape circular, like this?" Hamilton wanted to know.

"In the old days, bricks was scarce an' expensive," Asey said. "A circular cellar took fewer bricks than a square one. Most are semi-circular. Mine at home is."

"But this is new. Those concrete blocks aren't any old time things."

"Prob'ly laid 'em against the old brick," Asey said, "when they made the house over."

To the right of the steps was an electric pump and a water tank, and near them an electric meter. Behind the steps was a neat pile of corrugated paper boxes and another pile of folded sheets of brown paper, all obviously salvaged. Apparently Mary Randall was a thrifty soul.

"Why'd she keep this stuff down here, and not in the barn cellar?" Hamilton asked.

"Rats," Asey explained briefly.

Hamilton wandered around, peering at the old book case whose shelves were filled with preserves and "put-up" jars of vegetables and fruit. He even removed the lid from an old stone crock, and after sniffing at its contents, hastily replaced it. The odor of sauerkraut filled the cellar.

"Let's get back upstairs," Lane said. "I don't see anything here that's doing us any good. If she was killed, she was killed, and we might as well get to the Warren girl and get it over with."

"What?" Asey asked as they climbed back to the kitchen. "What's that?"

"Jane Warren. She came in the house after Eloise did. I saw

her. She was here a couple of minutes. I saw her come and I saw her go."

"You didn't tell us about that."

"You didn't," Lane said tartly, "give *me* any chance to. Don't you want to amend your ideas, and say she fell or tripped, instead of was pushed?"

Asey shook his head. "Nope. Doc, how did Jane take it, when you told her Eloise was sick?"

"She said Eloise had eaten any quantity of lobster salad and peach shortcake with whipped cream for lunch," Cummings replied, "and had been taking soda mints by the pound ever since. I should say that Jane was philosophical, and more or less unmoved about it all. Eloise's stomach and its eccentricities are hardly a closed book to anyone who ever slept under the same roof with her, you know."

"Didn't seem to see anythin' strange about your comin', or your wife's comin'?"

"She said it was thoughtful, and that she couldn't possibly have managed the tourists alone."

"Brazening it out," Lane said. "Remember what she threatened, Asey! One more word from Eloise about Mike Slade—"

"You're so obvious, Lane." Cummings began to put things back into his bag. "I knew you'd say that. I've been waiting for you to say it. Tell me, what sort of things do you eat, usually?"

"I eat what I can get." Lane was annoyed. "What do you think?"

"Specifically, what?"

"Oh, meat and fish and vegetables—"

"Obvious foods," Cummings said cheerfully. "See how it works out, Asey? Eloise eats futile things—you get the idea."

"You tell me," Asey said, "what the feller we want feeds on, an' I'll pay your grocery bills for a year. Hamilton, bring Jane in, will you?" He lifted the curtain and peered outside. "The tourists seem to have let up."

He led Jane into the dining room and motioned her to a seat from which she could not possibly see the blanket-covered figure on the living room couch.

"How's Eloise? Was it indigestion again? And Asey, wasn't she sporting about that sock? I've felt a beast. Sara laid me out in lavender, in a few well-chosen words. Oh, I'm so tired!"

"Jane," Asey said, "what'd you come indoors for, just after Eloise?"

"Cards. Shop cards, you know. Business cards. Those tourists were yelling for 'em, and the ones in the barn had all been taken off."

"Where were they?"

"The cards? In the corner cupboard here. See, I spilled some on the floor, I was in such a rush. D'you know what Eloise said? She said if I could sell that oak chest, I could have the money for myself, and I did! To a friend of General Philbrick's. Now I have a dowry, isn't that swell? Mike told you about the man who bought his pictures—"

"Did you go into the kitchen when you came in?"

"No, I just got the cards and went out. Asey—" she looked at him, "whatever's the matter now? Does Eloise think she has appendicitis again? Because she did have her appendix out, and Mary has a thing signed by the doctor saying so. She had to get it, because Eloise has fits of thinking that they just opened her up and peered at her appendix, and left it there. Why, I can't imagine. I should think it would be one of those things you'd just naturally sense, whether you had an appendix or not, no matter how much you mistrusted doctors. Asey, we're going to be married next week, did Mike tell you?"

"Jane," Asey said, "Eloise has had an accident."

"A—what? What happened?"

"On the cellar stairs. She—"

"Oh, I thought you meant she was killed, like Mary—you nearly took my breath away! Is she badly hurt? I hope not. You know, she's terrified of those stairs. The three of us always worry about them. We used to have a sign tacked up, saying 'Stop, Look, Grab.' Is she badly hurt?"

Involuntarily Asey looked toward the living room. Jane followed his gaze and saw the figure on the couch.

"Oh," she said. "Oh!"

She got up and went into the other room. In a moment she came back.

"You did your best to tell me, didn't you?" she said in a flat voice. "Well, tell me. Everything. I suppose she just didn't fall."

"No. Jane, did any of you—you, or Mary or Eloise, ever really fall down those stairs?"

"Never. We were so afraid we took particular care, all of us."

"What about that bruise on your shoulder?"

Jane flushed. "Oh. Kay told you? You want to know the truth? Eloise struck me."

Asey paused in the process of lighting his pipe.

"That's the truth," Jane said. "Monday. She was mad with me. She often was. She was jealous, because she thought Mary cared more for me than for her. Mary didn't, of course, but—well—can't you see how hard it would be to be affectionate about Eloise? She—she cluttered so. Everything she did or said

FIGURE AWAY

was cluttery. Then she'd be perfectly swell, like she was about my socking her the other night. And just as you thought how swell she really was, she'd tip the ink bottle over your knees, or something, and be more cluttery than ever. And Mary wasn't cluttery, and it was hard for her—"

"Tell me about those paths to the ice house," Asey said.

"I don't know anything about them," Jane told him. "I was scared to death to set foot off the place here, if you want to know. I—I can't explain, but there always seemed to be something so evil about those swamps, and the mists, and everything. It's a queer place."

"You got that gun license 'cause you was scared?"

Jane nodded. "Mike said it was foolishness and there was nothing to be afraid of, and then he realized how I felt, and he said he'd get me a gun, and it would make me feel better, even if I couldn't use it so well." She sighed. "After I learned more about shooting, he was going to get me a gun—"

"Where'd you meet Mike, Jane, down by the ice house?"

"Truly, Asey, I never went near the place but once. I'm scared around here. Like Kay, I'm a city person. The country quiet and noises simply terrify me. I usually met Mike at the beach. He couldn't come here because Eloise raised such a rumpus. It was all open enough."

"I wonder," Asey said, "who did go down there by the pond from this house?"

"I don't know, but it always seemed to me I heard droves of people around. Mary laughed at me and said it was my imagination, but she wouldn't stay here alone at night! There was a noise that drove me crazy—a sort of laugh. It was the most uncanny thing, but I found out what it was."

"You found out—what?"

"A whistle sort of arrangement, only it looks more like an ocarina than a whistle. I found it out by the barn, weeks ago. I decided what I'd been hearing was local boys and girls, parking around—those back roads are simply stopped up with cars, sometimes. I've heard the sound since, but it hasn't bothered me so much now that I know what it was. I thought at first it was an escaped lunatic. It sounded that way. Probably some kids, signalling."

"Haven't got the thing now?" Asey asked. "Or do you know where it is?"

"I stuck it in the fire. I think it came from candy, or popcorn, or something like that. You know, one of those gadgets they put in packages— Asey, what'll we do about Eloise?"

"We'll have to explain it as we did about Mary. Jane, did you kill Eloise?"

She looked him squarely in the eye. "No, on my word of honor, I didn't. I thought I could have, the other night. Things were all mixed up. Once I'd really taken a stand about Mike, they all cleared up. I—I think you believe me, but what about Lane and the others?"

"We've proved you couldn't have killed Mary," Asey said. "You was with Sara an' Jeff an' the rest when Kay an' I had our meetin's with the feller. We can't prove a thing about Eloise today, but I b'lieve you. I'll see to Lane."

It was no easy task to convince Lane that Jane Warren had not killed Eloise, but Asey and Dr. Cummings kept at him until he gave in.

"All right, have it your own way! She didn't. Let this go, let that go, let the other thing go! Neither of my men saw anything outside. Not a soul come into the house but Jane. I'm sick and tired of hanging around this house, and so are my men. And what's the use, if you won't—"

Still grumbling, he strode out of the kitchen.

"He's just sore," Hamilton said. "He'll get over it. Doc an' I'll take care of things, Asey. You take the girl and Mrs. Cummings back, and then you and I can settle about someone staying here, because you still want a guard, don't you? Come up later, after Lane's cooled off."

Asey drove Mrs. Cummings home and then took Jane back to Aunt Sara's.

"I suppose," she said, "we've got to tell them the truth, here. Oh, Asey—what's someone trying to do?"

"I wish I could tell you," Asey said. "Come along in, an' we'll get it over with."

Around nine that night he returned to the hollow.

"Everything's all settled about Eloise," Lane said. "Cummings fixed it up. He saw your cousin Weston, and he said Weston nearly collapsed at this. So did Brinley. Brinley was there at the office, too. Asey, you want a guard here tonight, don't you?"

"No, I'm goin' to stay here myself," Asey said. "One of your fellers might drop in every so often. Maybe if we could fox this feller into thinkin' the place was empty an' unguarded, he might get to what he's after. He wasn't after Eloise the other night, 'cause she was uptown. I've left my car up the road, hidden away. Fireworks time seems to be his pet time for action. 'Bout then, you might be in the neighborhood. Anyway, we'll see what we can see."

"Asey," Lane said earnestly, "I'm sorry I was such a fool this afternoon, but as Cummings said, killing Eloise was simply adding insult to injury. And under my eyes! I can't understand it—oh, if you say Jane's innocent, all right. But I still don't understand it. And listen, I don't like to leave you here alone. We ought to have some signal."

"If I run into that feller," Asey said, "you won't need signals to know it. I'll be okay."

He took up his stand on the porch, in the shadows of the bushes near the house; but as the minutes passed, the drizzle that had begun in the afternoon turned into a heavy rain. Asey unlocked the door and let himself into the house.

As he closed the door, someone ran up on the porch after him.

Asey wheeled around. "Who—"

"Don't shoot," Kay said. "I've been opposite, across the road, for half an hour, trying to make out if it was you lurking here, or my imagination, or my friend of the other night."

"Haven't you had enough?" Asey demanded. "For heaven's sakes, do you want any more of what you got Wednesday? Go 'way. Go home. Go off—"

"The Thayers," Kay said, "have a nasty stubborn streak, Mother says. Father claims it's the Harding blood. Both are pretty stubborn. Rugged individualists. Horses and buggies—"

"Sulkies, if you ask me," Asey said. "Who told you I was here?"

"I guessed. You've got a score to settle with that fellow. And when you come right down to it, so have I. You can have your eye and your tooth, but why shouldn't I have mine?"

"Oh, come in!" Asey said. "Come in. You take the window an' I'll take this. Anyone fool enough to prowl around in this rain d'serves to lose both eyes anyway."

The minutes ticked on.

"I guess the fireworks are thwarted tonight," Kay said at

FIGURE AWAY

last. "It's long past the time. Philbrick should have something in the fireworks line that coped with rain. Waterproof fireworks. Probably a lot of money in it. You might dally with the idea in your spare time. Why was Eloise killed?"

"In general," Asey said, "there are two main an' leadin' motives for murder, one of which is love an' its variations, an' the other is money an' its variations. Eloise had forty-one dollars in the bank, an' ten shares of Tel. an' Tel. She kept'em in her right-hand bureau drawer, in case you're int'rested. She owed Doc Cummings nine dollars an' twenty-five cents, an' she owed Quimby for four chocolate sodas. Said so on her mem'randum pad. Under the circumstances, I don't feel she was killed for money or its variations. Mary Randall's antique stock is good, but it ain't worth more'n five thousand dollars. The land an' house is worth four or five, but it's got a thumpin' mortgage on it."

Kay rubbed at the window pane with her handkerchief.

"Who," she said, "loved or hated Eloise? How *could* you love or hate Eloise? How could you do anything more than accept her for what she was?"

"As Madame Meaux might say," Asey remarked, "you can't love a woman whose teeth click."

"But you couldn't hate her," Kay said, "because her teeth clicked, either. I have a grandmother whose teeth click, but I love her dearly. Can I smoke?"

"If you keep the end hidden."

Twelve o'clock passed.

"I place my son John in this room," Kay said suddenly, "and the first thing he saw was a big F and a little f."

"Big fool an' little fool," Asey returned promptly. "What is the one an' only word you can make out of the word 'scythe'?"

"Chesty," Kay said. "I read it in a psych book in Psych sixty-two. Mental Growth and Mental Decline. I never knew which part it belonged in."

Another half hour went by.

"I must say," Kay sounded tired, "that for one so teeming with action Wednesday, this man is curiously lassitudinous—is that the word I want? Asey, don't you suppose he's shot his bolt for the day? After all, he's killed someone. Benvenuto Cellini would have considered that ample. It wasn't before breakfast, but it ought to count."

"Uh-huh."

"What do you brood about?"

"Bertha."

"Bertha—oh. What for? Do you cherish a secret passion for Bertha, Asey? Do you long for the touch of her hand, or what?"

"I was wonderin'," Asey said, "if I'd picked her beachplum jelly this afternoon durin' the judgin'. I sort of gypped on that."

"For shame, how?"

"I went out to Sara's preserve closet an' looked at what was there, an' what kind of jar, an' then I picked the one most like it later. After all, Bertha's a good cook, an' why not? You get cups an' things, an' why shouldn't Bertha get 'em as well as Mrs. J. Arthur Brinley?"

"Why not?" Kay said. "Ask Mike Slade."

"An' b'sides, I r'sent what I call unfair agitation on the part of J. Arthur. He told me in fourteen ways, an' all underhanded, just exactly what Bessie's jelly looked like, an' how she'd won prizes for years an' years. Told me everythin' but the number, an' with a little encouragement on my part, he'd have told me that— Kay, there's a car slowin' up. Wonder if it's Lane—move over, will you?"

"It went on," Kay said. "Just a lot of merrymakers, didn't you hear the radio going? Probably they stopped to look at the figures—they're simply hideous from the other side of the road. By the way, oughtn't we to bring them in from the rain? They're haggard and weatherbeaten enough—"

"They're already soaked through," Asey pointed out, "an' so'd we be if we tried any rescue work. Kay, look again. Are you sure that car went? Seems to me I can hear the radio."

"I thought I did, too," Kay said, "but I can't see a tail light, or any light at all. Parkers, I guess. What a night to park in, and what a ghastly place— Asey, aren't we being silly, watching the front of the house this way? If anyone's going to come, they're not going to come and pound on the front door knocker. They'll creep up from the woods in the rear, shouldn't you think?"

"I was thinkin' that, in a way," Asey said. "S'pose you keep your eyes on the parkers while I wander out back an' take a look around."

Kay had moved to another window when he returned.

"The radio's still going," she said. "I think the car's just beyond the house, off the side of the road. Much ribaldry, or else they're listening to a ribald orchestra— Asey, I thought there were four of those figures."

"There are."

"Only three that I can see," Kay said.

"One's probably fallen down again. One of the gents has a sort of dropsy. Lane tried to fix it, 'cause he claimed it was unnervin' to watch it fall. I guess too many tourists pawed it over—"

"There are so only three," Kay said, "and there's none on the lawn. Now that's funny—I wonder if—let me look out of that window. No, I can't see any on the ground here. Where do you suppose—"

Outside, a car engine raced.

"Tourists!" Asey sprang for the door. "I bet those birds pinched one—"

Kay raced along after him.

"There goes the car—Asey! Oh, the pigs! Can't we do something—"

Asey's Colt barked.

"Scare 'em, maybe— Kay, let's give that bunch a chase. Come on. My car's yonder."

As Kay fell breathlessly into the roadster's seat, Asey pulled at her arm.

"Get out—quick—"

"Why?"

"Get out!"

"What for?"

"Is your car here? Where? Hustle! Come on, show me. Quick!"

"But it's—what's the matter with yours?"

"Tires slashed," Asey said as they ran down the road. "Those weren't any tourist snatchers—that's our man!"

CHAPTER 17.

ASEY jumped in behind the wheel of Kay's battered coupe, and grabbed at the key she stretched out to him.

"Asey, he's out of sight!" she said. "I can't see any tail light —come to think of it, there never *was* any tail light. Here, I'll pull the choke—"

The little car bounced off as though someone had given it a swift kick from the rear.

"Asey," Kay said, "you couldn't catch a bicycle in this thing! It won't go over forty. The tires—don't mind that door, it just seems open. It's really closed. It's sprung or warped or— Asey, can you see him?"

"Yup," Asey said unexpectedly. "See there, way ahead by the school?"

"How'd you know it's the right car?"

"Headlights, no tail light, an' the rate he's goin'. Yessiree, that's our man!"

"Maybe he is our man, but you'd better give up any idea of catching him, right this minute," Kay said. "You can't!"

"Give up nothin'," Asey said. "At least we can trail him. He's clever, Kay. Keeps his radio goin' to mislead us—in fact, he might's well have brought a brass band, for all I caught on.

An' slashin' my tires—yes, this's our man. Now, hang on tight. I got to catch up enough to see which way he turns up at the forks."

He pressed his foot down on the accelerator, and Kay began to understand that Asey meant exactly what he said when he told her to hang on. The little coupe was hurling itself forward in a series of leaps and bounds, and it quivered tremulously, as though it were frightened to death.

In a daze, Kay watched the speedometer tape jiggle, and then she looked around at the ragged upholstery and at her leather jacket stuffed up behind the seat, and at the paper bag of jelly doughnuts Zeb Chase had bought that afternoon from the food sale. It all reassured her. This was indeed her car, going at this clip.

"Right," Asey said. "So he thinks he can fool me, does he? Huh. Keep hangin' on. We're goin' to have fun—"

The speedometer jiggled past the last figure, kept on jiggling past the zero, and arrived triumphantly at ten on its second trip around. Serenely and rather proudly, it stuck there.

"Hey!" Kay had to howl to make herself heard above all the noises of the car, "hey—Asey! This—this thing! This car! It was six years old when I inherited it at the office. Six years if a day. And the tires—"

"Just keep hangin' on," Asey howled back. "I helped put the first Porter car together, an' I drove it afterwards. Four weeks from Boston to New York. This has a few improvements on that model—"

"But the tires! Ugh—ow!"

Her knees hit against the dash, and she braced herself to meet the bumps.

They were on some side road or other. To her left was the center of Billingsgate; she could see the yellow star on top of the mast at the midway, and as she watched, it blinked once and went out.

"We ain't ridin'," Asey said. "We're flyin'—whee! Look out for your head!"

"Red lanterns!" she howled accusingly at him. "Red lanterns! The sign said 'Road Closed!'"

"We ain't on the road."

They weren't. They were billowing nonchalantly, but at a slightly slower pace, along the edge of a corn field.

After several moments the car lurched back up on the road again. A bayberry twig slatted against the windshield.

"That was just a little bad strip there," Asey said soothingly. "I knew about it. Honest, I did."

"Sure," Kay said. "Of course. Mayo the omniscient. Asey, I hate to bring it up, it withers me, but are you just driving for fun, or do you know where our friend is? I haven't seen the slightest trace of any car ahead."

"He ain't ahead," Asey told her as he cut around a puddle. "He's to one side."

"Indeed!"

"Yup, he's takin' the high road, an' we got the low road, but we'll get there b'fore him—"

"We'll get to heaven before him," Kay said, "if that's what you mean!"

"Wonder how he missed your car."

"Probably just had yours in mind," Kay said. "Jack the Ripper, thinking only of you. Asey, you must understand about the tires—my God!"

They skidded in a puddle, and the coupe turned completely around twice.

"Now there," Asey said, continuing his unabashed way, "is where this thing beats even my roadster. The Porter'd only of skidded half around, leavin' us facin' the wrong d'rection. Kay, your windshield wiper appears to of died. Help, will you?"

"How?" Kay demanded. "Want me to crawl out and sit on the hood with a handkerchief? What do you think I am, I'd—"

"Hold the wheel," Asey said, "an' I'll fix it."

Somehow with a sudden lurch he managed to clean enough of a space to see through.

A few hundred yards on, he slowed the car down and snapped off the headlights.

"Ahead," he informed Kay, "is the main road to Boston. An' just b'low us here to the left is the road where that feller's got to come out. It's two miles longer than the thing we come over, bein' a work r'lief road, an' it's kind of windin'—"

"And what are you going to do with this fellow, providing he turns up? Shoot him?"

"I got no d'sire to kill him, I want to find out who he is—aha—there—"

A sedan raced out of the new road and sped past them at a terrific clip.

"That's it," Asey swung the coupe over and followed. "License number's covered up—now, let's see what he does, an' where he thinks he'll go. Ah. There—there he turns off. That's nice. We'll string along."

"Where's he headed?" Kay asked as they left the main road. "Where are we headed?"

"Toward my home town," Asey said, "an' I'd like real well

FIGURE AWAY 245

to play tag with him on some of them back roads there. I know them roads."

"You seem to know these."

"Today, while judgin'," Asey said, "I read through the whole blessed Old Home Week program, includin' a map of roads, past an' present. Looked like a close-up of a perm'nent wave, but I got a lot out of it. Fellow's slowing down. I don't like that—"

"Why not?" Kay demanded. "Catch up—find out who he is—it's your chance to—oh, dear, there he goes again! What are you slowing down for now?"

"Want to see if I can peer through this windshield an' see—no, I guess he didn't."

"Didn't what?" Kay asked as Asey's foot again went down hard on the accelerator.

"I thought he might have tossed a bottle or somethin' for us to run over—the road narrows here, Kay. Hang on."

The speedometer tape jiggled again, but this time the effort was too much. It jumped wildly around and then came to rest at the figure eight, and there it stayed.

"Asey," Kay shouted in his ear, "give this up! He's out of sight—I can't even see a trace of his headlights on—"

"Goin' to try one more thing," Asey said, "an' this time, brace yourself an' watch that wound of yours. We're goin' to bounce considerable."

He turned the car off the tarred road, apparently into the middle of the woods. Kay thought at first that the coupe was completely out of control.

"Old wagon road," Asey explained casually. "If I can get through, we got him."

Kay peered out the side window and automatically ducked.

But the tree didn't break the glass, it ground hard against it, and then scratched noisily against the body as the car bounced along.

She looked at Asey in amazement. The branches were actually coming in the car on his side, where the window wouldn't close. Bushes and trees were scraping the coupe's underpinning and running boards.

She leaned forward and found a spot on the windshield through which she miraculously could look ahead.

"Road? My God, Asey, it's a forest! Look at that tree! We can't—what—what happened to it? It was right there in the middle of the road—"

"We went over it. Couldn't do this in my car," Asey said. "Too low slung."

Twice he stopped to wipe the rain off the windshield, and once he got out to pull a fallen tree out of their way.

"This," Asey said, "used to be the main road to Boston, in the old days. The stage coaches used it. This part we're goin' through now, it used to be a big settlement. Tavern an' store an' church an' blacksmith shop. I s'pose the clothes on them figures often visited around here. Maybe b'longed here—"

"Asey, what about that figure? What's the idea in swiping that, if any?"

"Wait'll I get out of this mess," Asey said. "I think—Kay, in about two seconds, we'll be back on the main road once more. If God's good to us, we'll be ahead of that feller. An' anyways, we can't be very far b'hind him—"

But the last forty feet of the old road turned out to be the worst part of the entire ride.

Asey swore under his breath as he shifted and gingerly began to pick a way for the little car through the heaps of tin cans and trash which suddenly loomed ahead.

"Some lazy bums," he said bitterly, " 've been usin' this for a dump. Back in, dump their junk, an' drive out—"

The coupe bounced through it bravely.

"My hat's off to this vehicle," Asey said. "She can take it. Now, I'll stop here, an' we'll leave our lights on, an' see—"

"Why not drive the coupe out into the middle of the road," Kay suggested, "and we'll get out, and then wait for—"

"For some honest burgher to get killed? Nope. If he goes by, we'll follow. We ain't got a chance of catchin' him, but we can trail to the bitter end. If I can just get the chance of seein' what he does at the next forks, then I can weave around him like a spider, an' get him no matter how fast he goes. If—Kay—"

"It's coming hell bent!" Kay said. "I bet—"

The car flashed by them.

"That's it—hurry, Asey! Hurry, that's it—why, what's the matter? Start—"

"The percolator," Asey said, "is through perkin'."

"Tires? I don't wonder, after what we've been through. I've been trying to tell you, even your friends the state cops have been suggesting that new tires would be nice. Asey, why couldn't they have held out a little longer?"

"Not tires, but rear axle," Asey said, leaning back and folding his arms. "Kay, did you see anythin', or recognize the man?"

"It went by so fast, and the windows were wet and drippy. No, I don't know what kind of car it was, even. I didn't see anyone. Did you?"

"I know the car. It's Lane's. His own car, not his official one. Brownish, with a dented front fender."

"You don't mean it was Lane!"

"His car, I said. Not him. It's got a radio, I know. Huh. The nearest house is about a mile up the road. Feel like walkin' it?"

"Sure," Kay said. "Get my brief case, will you? That's all that's worth taking. And my leather coat. The doors won't lock, but it won't matter, someone'll just figure it's an integral part of the dump. And oh, the doughnuts—they're mussed, but would you like one?"

"We'll eat'em en route," Asey said. "I got a great desire to get to a phone. Maybe we can hitch a ride back to town—"

The first two cars he hailed merely swerved out and continued on their way.

"Sensible people," Kay said. "I wouldn't dream of giving us a ride, myself."

The next car slowed up, and a woman's voice came through two inches of open window.

"Asey Mayo, you'd ought to be ashamed of yourself! At your age, too!"

Before Asey could answer, the car departed.

Kay chuckled. "What you've got to live down, what with me, and Madame Meaux! Who was that?"

"Miss Nickleby," Asey said. "She believes in sin. I'd like to know what she's doin' out, this time of night, herself!"

The next car was a truck, and the driver pulled up for them.

"Now," Asey said ten minutes later, as they stood by the four corners in Billingsgate, "now we'll go to the drug store an' phone. So long, feller, an' thanks!"

Before they had a chance to cross the street, a car swerved around the corner and pulled up beside them.

FIGURE AWAY

"Asey, where have you been?" Lane demanded. "Hamilton and I got there, and couldn't find you, and your car tires were slashed—we've been nearly crazy! Where have you been?"

"We've left Konrad and two others at the hollow," Hamilton said, "and Jeff Leach and Sara are going crazy about the girl, and Zeb Chase has organized a one man posse, and he's ripping around, and Weston's been after us—what a time! Where—"

"You two," Asey said, "have been together for the last hour or so?"

"Together? Of course we have! We—"

"Where's your car, Lane? Your own car, chump! I see this one here!"

"At the filling station, up the street."

"Get in, Kay," Asey said. "Drive over, will you, Lane?"

"What *is* this?" Lane demanded.

"Nothin', except I'm bettin' you it ain't there."

"Bet away," Lane said, "there she is."

He pointed to the sedan parked a little apart from a row of other cars.

"What's your mileage? How much gas in her?" Asey wanted to know as he jumped out and walked over to the brown sedan.

"Thirty odd thousand, and the tank's half or three-quarters full—what's the idea, do you want to buy a good used car? I'll trade even for your roadster," Lane said, "and considering your tire bill—who slashed those tires, by the way?"

"Same fellow that's been driving your car," Asey told him. "Say, do you always keep your key in the car, like this?"

"Who steals cops' cars?"

"Does your tail light work?" Asey asked.

"Always has. I guess so." He switched on the lights. "Sure. See?"

Asey looked in the front seat. Both side windows were open and the upholstery and floor and wheel were soaking wet.

"Always leave your windows like this, too?"

Lane frowned. "Say, I did wind 'em up. And—Asey, look at the water gauge—say, it's *hot!* Someone has been—say, let's go find the boy. There's usually a kid here at night."

They finally found the boy in the drug store, chatting with the night clerk.

"You want gas?" he asked with a yawn. "I—what?"

"Did anyone take my car tonight?"

"One of your cops had it, didn't he?" the boy looked at Lane and yawned again. "I don't know. I been so busy today, I'm all in. Maybe it was Konrad with the other car. I haven't sat down for a month, and the parking space's been full all day, with people wandering around, in an' out, in an' out, in an'—"

"Listen," Asey said, "how long you been here?"

"Oh, since twelve. I can see if anyone comes for gas, or they blow their horn," the boy yawned again. "Or—"

"Come on," Asey said to Lane. "This isn't goin' to get us any place. The fact r'mains, we seen your car, Kay an' I, an' we got some reason to b'lieve your car was the one we been chasin', if you could call it that."

Kay reminded him of the tail light.

"You could twist that," Asey said. "Brown sedan, bashed fender, radio—"

"Brinley!" Lane said. "Brinley!"

"What about him?"

"Brinley's got a brown sedan," Lane said. "Bashed fender— Mrs. B. bashed it this afternoon against a phone pole! Fellow

FIGURE AWAY 251

in a trailer crowded her off the road. And their tail light doesn't work, because she was so upset after hitting the phone pole that she backed too far, and smashed the tail light to smithereens. I was there."

"Let's," Asey said, "call on Brinley."

Just as their car pulled up to the walk in front of the Brinleys' house, a brown sedan with a bashed fender turned into the driveway.

J. Arthur, rather sketchily clad, greeted the group with amazement.

"Is anything new the matter?" he inquired anxiously. "The cups—the prize cups for tomorrow—if it's those, we have them. Did Weston tell you? I'm so sorry he got worried—he knows now. You see, Bessie got anxious about them, with all this going on, so I brought them all home and put them under our bed to be safe from—"

"Asey!" Kay's shriek made Asey's hair stand on end. "Look in this back seat! Look! Look!"

Sprawled grotesquely across the back seat of Brinley's sedan was the top-hatted, tail-coated dummy.

"Oh, that?" Brinley laughed. "Isn't that one of Mary Randall's figures? I thought so. Look, there's Bessie at the door—she's worried about Amos. I must go in and—"

"Rain or no rain," Asey said, "dog or no dog, you stay right here an' tell me about that figure!"

"Why, it was in the road," Brinley said. "At first I thought there'd been an accident. It did look like someone injured lying there. Then I saw what it was, so I picked it up and brought it back. I guess some boy stole it, and then dropped it off to fool someone."

"Where have you been?"

"Amos," Brinley shook his head. "Poor Amos, our little—"

"Black dog," Asey said. "I know. What of him now?"

"Why, Bessie had guests this afternoon, and one of them fed Amos a whole solid box of chocolate creams—of course we didn't know it till now. Amos loves chocolate creams, but oh, how *sick* they make him! He was so sick, and Bessie was so worried, I thought I'd better take him to Dr. Graves, just on the outskirts of town, you know. Dr. Graves is wonderful with Amos, and he knows all about him, and Bessie couldn't remember if it was two pills or four pills, so I went. Er—do you want to come in? I think my wife—it *is* rather wet, and she wants to know about Amos, she's so upset over him—"

With Mrs. Brinley in the hall were Madame Meaux and Weston.

"What're you doin' here?" Asey asked the latter.

"They phoned me from the Town Hall that the cups were gone, and I came over here to see Arthur," Weston said. "I offered to go with Arthur, but he seemed to think—"

"Protection," Mrs. Brinley said. "I always think you feel so much safer, somehow, with a man around. And with everything that has happened, naturally I'm uneasy, and I know that Madame Meaux is, too, though she's been just as brave as anything, so I made Arthur go alone with Amos, and Weston stayed with us. And it was more than twelve minutes, dear. It took you seventeen minutes, to the time you came in the drive. We timed you. You see," she explained to Asey, "Arthur bet he could go to Dr. Graves' and back in twelve minutes, and he said it wasn't worth while for Weston to stay, but as I told him, things do come up, don't they—why, just see, here *you* are, Mr. Mayo, with your policemen! Why, where are you going, Mr. Mayo! Always in such a horrid rush!"

FIGURE AWAY

Lane, Hamilton and Kay followed Asey outdoors.

"I still," Lane was thoroughly bewildered, "I still would like to know what in hell you have been doing, and what about this figure, and your car and the slashed tires, and what about my car, and brown cars, and Brinley—"

"J. Arthur," Asey said, striding down the walk, "has managed to ease himself out of something else. That dog! I s'pose if it wasn't a dog, it'd be a cat, or white mice, or a parrot or goldfish—maybe guppies. Seventeen minutes lets him out, with people to check on either end."

"Why was the figure dropped out, Asey?" Kay asked. "Honestly, do you suppose it was boys, or tourists, all the time? Do you? After all, remember Sammy and his girl friend up at the pond. They were plenty sore. I wouldn't put it beyond them to slash your tires— Asey, where are you rushing to now?"

Asey went to Brinley's sedan and lifted the dummy out of the back seat and carried it over to the trooper's car.

"Come 'long," he said, getting in behind the wheel.

The other three managed to pile in a split second before he started off.

She should have known, Kay told herself, as they careened off on the road to the hollow. She should have known that it would be like this if Asey happened to be in a good car while he was in a hurry.

Hamilton, beside her in back, was unperturbed. He grinned at her as they got out in front of the Randall house.

"You'll get used to him," he said kindly. "I have. And when he takes to driving like that, he's got somewhere—"

"Take that figure in, Ham," Asey said. "I'll take the other."

He walked over to the other beaver hatted dummy, lugged

it into the living room, and stood it beside the one he had taken from Brinley's car.

"Now, Lane," he said, "which was the one that you said had dropsy, the one that toppled over all the time?"

"That one," Lane said, "with the scarf around his neck. The one you just brought in from the lawn. That was the one that dropped, but I fixed it."

"An' this one from Brinley's car, with the stock an' fancy vest?"

"That's the one that's just acquired dropsy," Lane said, "just today. I was going to fix it tomorrow. What in the name— what are you doing?"

Asey set to work disrobing the dummy he had just brought in from the lawn.

"But it's the *other* one," Kay said. "It's the o*ther* one he took, Asey! You're working on the one that was *here*, the one he didn't take, the—"

"I know it."

But he continued to rummage around in the pockets and the lining of the tail coat belonging to the figure he had just taken from the lawn.

"There!" he said triumphantly at last. "There! Catch, Lane. Catch'em and' hold onto'em. There's your clews."

Lane and Hamilton stared blankly at the two shells Asey had brought out of the lining of the figure's coat.

CHAPTER
18.

HAMILTON turned to Kay.

"See what I mean?" he asked. "I knew he was after something."

"Asey," Lane said, "how did you guess that?"

"On Monday night," Asey said, "I went to the fire at Slade's shack. N'en I cut across lots to this place. Them dummies scared me to the point of drawin' my gun. But get this, Lane. I saw only three figures. Two women, an' a man. Next day I said somethin' about it, an' you told me that one man kept fallin' down. So I thought of course that the fourth figure'd been on the ground when I first saw 'em. But it's been botherin' me, all this time, just the samey. Because I was certain of there bein' three then, an' only three later when Zeb an' I drove up. An' I couldn't remember one on the ground either time."

"But there really are four figures," Kay said. "Two men and two women, what do you mean, only three—" Lane's look silenced her.

"Put it this way," Asey said. "When I came here first on Monday night, there was three figures standin' outside, but the fourth wasn't on the ground. It was in the woods. An' somebody was busy peelin' off his coat an' things, an' puttin' on the dummy's clothes. Then—the land slopes there, remember. Then he rolls down easy an' cautious, dressed in the dummy's clothes, with his shotgun. After a while he gets to his feet. To any car goin' by, or anyone passin', he's just a dummy. An' he can wait there for his chance to shoot Mary. An' he's also, Lane, in the proper place to fire accordin' to your line."

Lane nodded slowly. "I begin to—that's why I placed him over by the garden, where the figures wouldn't have been in his way. I never thought about—go on."

"The fireworks begin," Asey continued. "Mary Randall leans across the window to get a cigarette box. Fellow shoots twice at her head outlined on the shade, all under the cover of the fireworks noise. He don't have to run. Because if anyone hears, or catches on, he's the dummy on the ground again. But no one comes. Jane's listening to the concerts on the short wave, with static galore, an' the fireworks is boomin'. He waits till he feels he's safe, an' then cuts back to the woods to put on his own clothes. An' then, I'd say, to his great annoyance an' alarm, Zeb an' I come back durin' the process."

"But the shells," Lane said. "How do you account for—"

"Wait. He's stuck 'em in his pocket—he must have reloaded, an' he knew better than to leave the shells. So he sticks 'em in his—that is to say the figure's—pocket. Then Zeb an' I come. We rattle him. He changes in a flurry, puts the dummy's clothes back on it, an'—"

"But now wait," Lane said. "There were four dummies there when I came with the doctor. I know that. The fourth was on the ground then."

"Sure it was. Zeb an' I go in, see? Fellow gets on his things, dresses the dummy, puts the hat on—it's held on with safety

FIGURE AWAY

pins, see? Anyway, after dressin' up the dummy, he rolls it down the slope an' goes. The dummy lands back where it should. An' I'm willin' to wager that about halfway home, the feller remembers the shells in that pocket."

"Then why didn't he come right back?" Hamilton asked. "I would have. Pronto."

"Maybe he did. But Lane's here, and the doctor, and Weston, and Zeb and Jane and I. An' mind you from that time on, there's not a minute someone hasn't been around this house. He hasn't any chance to get to the dummy. See, he's got to take the coat off, an' hunt around in the linin', because there's a hole in the pocket. It's easier for him to plant shells, an' he does it, prob'ly while Prettyman is here. It's a lot better to give us fake shells that'll lead us to Jane an' her gun she gave Slade, than to get caught findin' the real shells, or have anyone catch on where they are."

"All he really needed to do," Lane said, "was to pose as a tourist. The tourists nearly picked those figures apart the last two days."

"Prob'ly would have, if he could have posed as one. But someone's on guard here all the time. Anyone tryin' to find anythin' is suspect. If he could be sure of gettin' the shells right off, that'd have been fine. But I had to grope for'em. That's a stiff interlinin'. He knew he might have to grope, an' that'd have given him away."

"What was he after the night I met up with him?" Kay asked.

"Got to guess at that," Asey told her. "He had a silencer. I shouldn't wonder if he didn't intend to silence the cop an' take his shells then. Maybe he was just waitin' for some chance when he could get to'em. But he runs into you, an' into me.

Perhaps he was on a peaceful foragin' expedition, an' had the gun just in case."

"Now, what about Eloise?"

"Let's settle this first. Tonight our friend comes right out in the open, apparently havin' d'cided he ain't gettin' places with his skulkin'. Barges up in his car—"

"My car," Lane said.

"Your car, that he's previously borrowed from the fillin' station. I should think that kid there might lose a lot of cars, if that's the way he looks after'em. Anyway, fellow comes with his radio goin' full blast, to make us think it's a bunch of kids or parkers or tourists, or all three in one. R'verses his ord'nary methods. Grabs the figure that's down, thinkin' of course it's the same one that was down the other night. Only Lane's mended the one he wants, an' this is the other. But not bein' a fool, when he's through his searchin', he dumps it out on the road for someone to find, so's we'll think that it was just kids havin' fun."

"Wouldn't he have done the same," Kay said, "if he'd got the right figure?"

"Sure. He'd have dumped that after he got the shells. But it come over me sudden about Lane fixin'em, an' I just wondered if there wasn't a chance the feller got fooled. If a pranky soul was after'em, they'd take the one nearest the road, not this that was farthest away. Wouldn't have gone at my tires so careful, so's not to be followed in case of a slip. There was a risk involved in stealin' that figure, but it was important enough to him to take it. Well, Lane, there you are. That's how Mary Randall was killed. There's your shells."

"Isn't there a chance that he might come back for the other figure?" Kay asked.

"He might. Stick'em back, Hamilton, an' have someone watch. But I don't think he'll be back. He ought to be disposin' of his shotgun. If you hadn't talked so about that figure fallin', Lane, I'd have passed this off as kids. After all, we can't prove your car was taken, even though we know it. Maybe Kay an' I followed two other cars. Maybe Sammy slashed the tires. But—well, we found the shells. Now all you got to do is to find a gun that fits."

"That's all." Lane's laugh was hollow. "That's all. But one thing I know, those shells didn't come from Jane's gun. Altogether different mark. We'll play with'em for prints. Why do you suppose, Asey, after stealing Jane's—that is, Slade's—gun, another was used?"

"P'raps he preferred his own to a mail order one," Asey said. "P'raps it was just his idea to plant all he could on Jane, in passin'."

"What I'd like to know," Kay said, "how did he manage to get back so quickly, if he took Lane's car?"

"After he whizzed by us," Asey said, "after the axle broke, he might have turned right around. Might have been the first car that passed by us. Can't tell. Prob'ly he'd already thrown the figure out by then— Lane, I hear any number of cars outside."

Zeb Chase dashed in, followed by Jeff Leach and Weston and Brinley.

"Are you all right, Kay?" Zeb demanded. "There's something—your head's bleeding! Look at your neck—"

"That's jelly, from jelly doughnuts," Asey said. "What's got into all of you?"

"Weston and I," Brinley said, "want to know what's going on. I got Phillips to stay with Bessie—oh. Dr. Graves phoned. He said Amos would be all right tomorrow, that is, if—"

"I've been tearing around," Zeb said, "trying to find some trace of you, and when I just went back to Aunt Sara's, Jeff said he'd called Brinley, and Brinley said you'd been there—what's happened?"

"Kay an' I," Asey informed him, "are a little late on our historical tours. We covered most of'em, though. She needed some local color—'course it was a mite dark an' wet, but Billingsgate local color is bright enough to shine forth at night. Come on, Kay. Zeb's takin' us home with Jeff."

"What about your roadster?" Kay asked.

"Like your percolator, no one'll steal it in that condition. I'll phone Al to fix it. He'll have it re-tired 'fore mornin'. Come on."

"Aren't you going to tell us anything?" Brinley sounded annoyed. "Anything—what's happened?"

"Good night," Asey said.

"What happened? What are you going to do?"

"Figure," Asey said, "away. That's all the story there is, an' what I'm goin' to do. Now Wes, don't you start! Come on, Kay."

Back at Aunt Sara's, Asey exclaimed at the terrific litter of papers in the living room.

"That's Jeff Leach," Sara said, "trying to balance his accounts. He'll spend the winter with'em, by the looks. For once I don't blame him. What can you do, with old settlers and new tourists and everyone giving you odd sums and saying it's for those taxes in 1929, and for this and that and the other thing. Weston had some fancy slips, but we ran out of'em day before yesterday. You all go to bed. I've got to help Jeff figure. He counts on his fingers, and with his arthritis his fingers are none too reliable."

"Where's Jane?" Asey asked.

"Upstairs in bed, long ago. Mike's been here most of the evening. I told him about Eloise. How'd he take it? He was perfunctorily sorry, and brought out the budget he started today. The two of them argued themselves hoarse. It did Jane good. She hasn't been anywhere near so lugubrious since he left. He told her to trust you, Asey, and I guess she is. Oh, this is all such a horrible thing! Asey, what are you going to do now?"

"Figure," Asey told her. " 'Night."

Around four-thirty that morning Zeb woke with a start and the uneasy feeling that someone was moving around in the room. He snapped on the light to find Asey, fully dressed, pacing around the outer edge of the big braided rug.

"What are—haven't you been to bed yet?"

"Go to sleep," Asey said, and continued his monotonous pacing.

He was eating breakfast when Zeb got down to the dining room in the morning.

"Marvelous day," Sara said. "Thank goodness, it'll end in a blaze of glory, this week will, and all I've got to do today is hand out silver cups at the Town Hall with Bessie Brinley and Mrs. Philbrick. I'm going to watch the yacht races, and tonight is the grand ball; that will doubtless sap the last ounce of strength I have. I look forward to Church Day and the end of it all. Not for a Billingsgate wallowing in gold would I go through a week like this again!"

"When," Bertha asked anxiously, "when is the jelly? I mean, the prizes?"

"Three o'clock," Sara said, "and I want to give warning to you all, this is the last meal Bertha and Sally bother with till

Monday. Jeff and I will have lunch with the notables, and the rest of you will have to fend for yourselves. There's a buffet supper at the golf club, and you can come there with us, or not. Tomorrow being the Lord's day, I suppose the Lord will somehow provide. Jane, you certainly aren't going to the hollow, are you?"

"No!" Asey said.

"No, Mike said not, either. I'm going to spend the day with Mike."

"Very wise of her, isn't it, Asey? Come to Jeff or me if you get bored with Mike. Zeb, you'll be at the store all day, I suppose? It's Saturday, and you'll have—"

"It *is* Saturday," Zeb said. "Isn't it? That's the hardest part of business, remembering Saturday as the day you work on instead of just part of a week-end. I can't get used to it. I suppose I'll have to go to the store. Matt gave me hell for taking off so much time yesterday. I did want to grab time for— Kay, what are you doing?"

"Me? I've got to get my stuff ready for Shorty. Asey, Win's picture was in last night's paper. I cut it out for you to give him, if you want to. And what are you doing?"

"I figure," Asey said rather gloomily. "I just figure and figure. On an' on."

His figuring led him first to the ball field, where the sports program was already in progress. He allowed himself to be dragged into the horse shoe pitching, and won the event, to his own amazement, from Weston and Mike Slade.

"Snappy work." Zeb Chase, dressed in running trunks and a sweater, appeared at Asey's elbow. "Now come and mile run with me, Tarzan."

"Yah," Asey jeered. "What the hard-workin' business man

wears for Saturday! The vig'rous Chase boy, who thinks so much about beans. Yah. Slacker!"

"It's for the honor of the firm." Zeb pulled up his faded crimson sweater and displayed the six-inch letters on his shirt. "See, Chase's Baked Beans. That's me. Isn't it tasty? Old Matt had to let me off when I showed him this jersey. Just couldn't resist it. And Kay said if I won—"

"You know you will."

"It's no cinch. Purdy's here, with ex-Senator Puddleface. Purdy's going to marry Puddleface's daughter—at least she hopes so, and that's why the cup's so big. Puddleface gave it, and I owe Purdy a bit, and—oh, Kay said, if I won, she'd give us any amount of space, and that'll charm father. At school he always wanted me to say I trained on beans—number forty-one? Hey, I'm forty-one—wait!"

Mike Slade rushed up.

"Come on, we need you for the tug of war, natives versus visitors, and Wes wants you to pitch the soft ball game—"

"Dream on," Asey said. "I shot my bolt with the hoss shoes. I done my bit."

"Is that cooperation? Is that—"

"No," Asey said, "it's common sense. I got to—"

"Asey!" Weston raced up. "Did Mike tell you—"

"He did, an' I'm not. Wes, I never seen such vigor! Rushin' around—"

"Someone's got to!" Weston said. "You really won't? Hey, Carruthers! Slade, go get Carruthers and tell Zeb Chase he's got to pitch—"

Weston rushed off after Mike.

Asey grinned and strolled over to the Town Hall. In the exhibition rooms, Mrs. Brinley and Aunt Sara and half a dozen other town women were matching up contestants' names with the prize-winning numbers on the various entries.

"Here's one!" Mrs. Brinley said excitedly. "Here—oh, look, girls! Look at this jar of jelly! It's won—why, gracious sakes! It's the best in the show, best in all the jellies, and best beach-plum jelly! What do you know about that! Three prizes! That means three cups and the big prize money—"

"What's the number?" Sara asked. "Thirty. Let's see. Oh, isn't that simply splendid, now! That's Bertha. My Bertha. Bertha Cook from over by the point. She'll be simply tickled to pieces, and she deserves it. She's a marvelous cook and a splendid jelly—"

Mrs. Brinley sniffed. "Well, I don't think that jelly looks like much, if you should ask *me!* Those judges— I told Arthur, I said, Arthur, you couldn't have picked worse judges! And when I see one of them, I'm going to tell him what I think! Him, or her. Not that I intend to make any trouble—dear me, no! I always say, what's the use of entering anything if you haven't the spirit to lose as well as the spirit to win. I mean, if you can't be a good loser, what's the use. And I entered the very same batch of jelly that won at the Grange, and the church fair, and the county—not that I dispute for one instant what the judges think, but I always say—"

"We understand, dear." Sara tried to soothe her.

"But the first one of those judges I see," Bessie said ominously, "the very first I see, I'm going to *tell* him—"

Asey quietly withdrew.

He viewed the tug of war, and watched Zeb beat out Purdy by an eyelash for the mile run, and then got into his roadster and drove slowly over to his shack on the outer beach, where his cousin Syl Mayo greeted him cheerily.

FIGURE AWAY

"Hi, Asey. Want Win?"

"How is he? Been troublesome?"

"He ain't a mite of trouble," Syl said. "Good's gold. Nice old feller. He just sleeps an' sleeps—"

"Drunk, huh?"

"No," Syl said. "You know what I think, Asey? I think the old feller's been starvin'. He eats a meal, an' then he sleeps, an' after a while he bobs up to see if I'm here, an' he gets some more to eat, an' then he sleeps again. I always heard tell he was an awful old souse, but he don't drink much. An' you know, it don't seem to affect him none, what he does drink. Seems to think a heap of you, he does. I'll go fetch him. The doc's been here reg'lar to look at his shoulder," he added. "Doc says he understands Billin'sgate if the first Billin's was as rugged as the last."

Win pumped Asey's hand. "Nice feller, Syl," he said. "No nonsense to him. When you want t'eat, he feeds you. What you got there?"

"Picture of you, cut from the Boston paper."

Win peered at it and then held it off at a distance.

"That me? You sure?"

"Certain sure. See what it says underneath?"

"By gorry," Win said. "Whaddye know. Huh. That thing goin' on yet?"

"You don't want to go back, do you?"

"Didn't know I looked so good," Win said. "Look pretty good, don't I? Don't look such a fool's I thought."

"Looked pretty swell," Asey said. "Say, want to be in on the finish? Syl, take my car an' go get him some clothes from my house. Mine'll fit him. Got one of them white suits. I'll wait here."

He sat down with Win on the rough wooden settee outside the shack.

"Win," he said finally, "how much do you know about Billingsgate, anyway?"

"Keep posted." Win puffed at his pipe. "Hear a lot. See a lot. Folks think I'm an ole fool, say a lot of things they wouldn't say t'others. What you want to know?"

Asey scratched his head. "Honest, Win, I don't know how to put it. S'pose there's trouble in town. Trouble with the runnin' of the town. Who's to blame?"

"Sairey Leach," Win said after due deliberation. "An' Bessie Brinley, the nosey thing."

"What do you know about Mary Randall?"

"Up to Hell Holler? Nice woman, no nonsense. Knows when a man's hungry. I grub in the dump for her often. Gives me dollar for an ole butter firkin, fifty cents for knife boxes—"

"Who didn't like her, Win? I mean, who don't like her?"

Win caught his slip into the past tense. "Oho. Didn't, huh? Thought they was trouble. Daughter hates her. Hellcat. Hated the other girl, too. Seen 'em fight."

"Who?" Asey was confused.

"Daughter'd fight Mary Randall an' the girl. Throw things. Hellcat. Seen a lot while I was to the ice house. Know what? Daughter went off at night. Often."

"Win," Asey said, "what do you mean? You talkin' about Mary Randall's daughter Eloise? Let's get this straight."

"Fat woman," Win said. "Jerky talker. Used t'go off nights. Some feller. Don't know who. He'd laugh funny, an' she'd walk 'round the pond to the east road an' drive off." He used half a dozen vigorous Anglo-Saxon nouns to sum up his opinion of Eloise. "Know Brinley, fat feller? Seen her with him on

FIGURE AWAY

the beach once." Win gave it as his opinion that J. Arthur was little better than Eloise.

"So that," Asey said, "is the answer to the other path, is it? That's Eloise's own. By—by the Almighty! An' that laugh is her boy friend, signallin'—no wonder Jane thought there was folks around! Win, tell me more about Sara an' Bessie."

"Brinley woman hates Sairey," Win said. "Jealous. Know what? She made Brinley switch Jeff Leach's books. Made mistakes. Jeff's no good at books. Brinley is."

"Win! How do you know?"

"Cold spell this spring," Win said. "Had t'leave Philbrick's place. He was comin'. Slipped into Town Hall. Lived there week or so. Heard a lot. Brinley's fixin' to get Jeff out. Wants t'be head of the board, n'en go t'the legislature. Wants t'go t'Congress. Fixed Weston's books, too."

Asey blinked. "Win, whyn't you tell someone?"

"Gregrampa always said, more rope y'give a feller, the nicer knot he hung himself with. No one'd b'lieved me, anyways. What's the use?"

"Win, I can't hardly believe this!"

"Didn't b'lieve it m'self at first," Win said. "Sly one. I know. Gregrampa said, look out for potbellied fellers with sharp eyes, an' if they got a naggin' wife, look out twice. I'm thirsty."

Before Syl returned, Asey began at the beginning and questioned Win all over again. But he couldn't shake the old man's story.

With Syl's help, he dressed the last Billings up in a white linen suit, combed his hair and shaved him.

"There!" Asey gave a pat of approval to Win's blue tie. "You look like J. P. Morgan, Win. I'll see that Kay's friend takes another picture of you. Syl, I'm droppin' you at your house. You dress up, an' then take Win over to Billingsgate in your car, an' find Mike Slade, an' see Win finishes out the program in style. Win, I wouldn't want you to rust your innards, but go easy, won't you?"

"Asey, you nicked m'chin!" Win was peering into the mirror. "Think it'll show in the picture?"

"Vanity," Asey said, "vanity! Syl, take care of him for me, won't you? I'll be seein' you."

"Where you bound?" Syl asked.

"In a manner of speakin'," Asey said, "I give up figurin', an' I'm goin' to get another figurer. I'm goin' up to Boston, but I'll be back in four-five hours. So long."

Around supper time he returned to the Leach house, not remembering until he reached the front door Sara's warning that Bertha was to have the week-end off.

But Bertha herself called to him from an upstairs window as he returned to his car.

"Asey! Asey Mayo! If you want supper, come 'round to the kitchen door!"

Asey grinned, and returned.

"There's plenty to eat," Bertha said, "if you don't mind cold things—look at my cups! Three!" she pointed proudly to the silver cups on the kitchen table. "And fifty dollars, cash money! I give it to my mother, the money. She was so happy she cried. Oh, I was hopin'—but I thought Mrs. Brinley would get it. She always does! An' I know it was you that did it!"

"I was one," Asey reminded her, "of four women, an' four men."

He didn't feel it was necessary to add that he had manœuvred things so that he made his decisions first, and that the others

FIGURE AWAY

had used the same blank afterwards, or that he had commented rather outspokenly on his ability as a Cape Codder to know good jelly when he saw it in front of his eyes. At least five of the judges had been returned settlers, and they were very anxious to prove themselves good Cape Codders.

"You fixed it, somehow," Bertha said. "And I want you to have the jelly. I told mother, and she said you should have it—"

"I can't," Asey said. "Why, you ought to put that on the mantelpiece an' show it to all your beaus. Get you a husband if you ain't got one picked out."

"No," Bertha said obstinately. "I want you to have it. Say, did they do anything to the jelly, like cookin' it? This looks dif'rent from when I took it up."

"Not while I was there, an' not that jar," Asey said. "Look, I can't take—"

"You will. You'll have it for supper, right now," Bertha said, "with cold roast beef. There." She removed the paraffin, and turned the jelly out into a dish. "It certainly looks different," she said. "They must have done *some*thing to it after they got through the judging."

"It's a crime to open that, Bertha," Asey said, "but I want you to know I appreciate it."

While he waited for her to cut his beef, he spread some of the jelly on a piece of bread.

"How is it?" Bertha asked. "How—what's—what's the matter?"

Asey, with his hand to his mouth, rushed from the room.

Bertha's eyes filled with tears, and then she grabbed a teaspoon and tasted the jelly. She was rushing from the kitchen as Asey returned.

"Well," Asey said when she came back, "well? I mean, I'm awful sorry to act like that, but seein' as how you done the same—"

"Asey Mayo!" Bertha said, "Asey, that's not *my* jelly! I never made anything like that awful burned smelly stuff! Why, I should think someone swept out a coal bin and boiled the sweepings with burned sugar! I didn't think, this afternoon, that it was mine. It looked dif'rent. But the number was right on it, and it was my number, and it was the same jar, and all— Asey, how do you suppose—how did it happen?"

"I don't know."

"But you tasted it—didn't the judges taste it?"

Asey nodded. "You c'ntestants put in two jars, an' they had the same numbers. An' the judges used one to taste from, an' then stuck the duplicate under the light an' stared at it, an' peered around. Bertha, this ain't the same jelly of yours we tasted this afternoon! Now, that's curious. Flip it back into the jar an' let me stare at it again."

He held it up to the light. "No, it's not. Bertha, let me see that paraffin. Huh. Now, get me one of your glasses of beach-plum from the preserve closet."

"Same jars," Bertha said.

"Nope. This here's a bluer glass."

"They all come from the same set of jars!"

"Paraffin's dif'rent," Asey said. "Not as white. Bertha, let me think."

"Well," Bertha said after fifteen minutes, "where'd that awful stuff come from? What's the matter, Asey, couldn't you spit it out in time? You look awful funny—"

"I think I know," Asey said slowly, "I think I know where

it come from. I can't be sure. I looked at so many jars of jelly yesterday. Bertha, gimme this—"

"That stuff? I should say not! It goes right out to the garbage hole!"

"Nope," Asey said. "Bertha, I want you to do somethin' for me. I'm goin' to take this awful tastin' stuff, an' you're not goin' to tell a soul I got it. Take the labels an' put 'em on another jar. Whatever you do, don't you tell a soul!"

"You—you kind of scare me," Bertha said. "Why—what're you so solemn about? What's the good of that nasty stuff?"

"You know what's been goin' on, don't you? About Mary Randall an' Eloise?"

Bertha nodded. "Aunt Sara told us, but we haven't told. What's that got to do with it?"

"I figured one thing," Asey said, "I figured another, an' now, with luck, this nasty stuff's goin' to solve them two murders, an' it's goin' to solve 'em before I go to bed tonight!"

CHAPTER
19.

HAMILTON stood just inside the Town Hall ball room and hummed under his breath the tune that Upjohn's Merrymakers were swinging to the skies.

He had hoped to attend the final grand ball in an entirely unofficial capacity, but he had reckoned without Asey Mayo.

He finally located Kay Thayer, dancing with Zeb. He winked at her and jerked his head toward the corridor, and then leaned back against the wall as though his only problem in life was to prop up the rafters.

The girl got it. Asey said she would.

At the end of the dance Kay wandered over to him.

"Hi, trooper," she looked at the interested watchers and satisfied their curiosity. "Found my brief case yet?"

"Yes, ma'am," Hamilton said. "Will you come look at it?"

He led her out the back way. "Look," he said, "here's a note from Asey. Read it, and then take this to Zeb Chase. I'll wait for you here. Go grab a coat."

"Not leaving, are you?" Brinley asked Kay a few minutes later. "What about that other dance you promised me?"

"Call from my editor," Kay told him brightly. "Just a wage

FIGURE AWAY

slave, that's what. It's a simply marvelous party, Mr. Brinley, and you deserve tons of credit for the way you planned it." She smiled. "I must dash, but we'll dance again when I come back—I don't think!" she added to herself as she hurried down the corridor. One dance with J. Arthur was, she felt, sufficient punishment for anyone.

Zeb watched her departure with increasing irritation. But Asey's note, in his pocket, had been firm and definite. When Asey wanted him, Asey would tell him, and in the interval he was to mind his own business.

"Has Asey really got anything?" Kay demanded as Hamilton turned the car toward the Leaches' house.

"I wouldn't say this to everyone," he told her, "but the guy's losing his grip. He lands up at the hollow this afternoon late with a jar of beachplum jelly—"

"With a what?"

"You heard. And with that, he goes into action. And when Asey—"

"Goes into action," Kay said feelingly, "he goes into action. I know. I had some brief experience with it last night. What have you—what's he been doing?"

Hamilton smiled. "Go change your clothes. I'll tell you later."

"I haven't the key. Aunt Sara has—"

"Oh, I forgot. I got one. We busted in here tonight, among other places."

"You what?"

"Got in a window and took the spare key. Hustle. Asey's waiting."

The darkness and quiet of the old house made Kay glad that the trooper was within call. She changed in a hurry and rushed back to the car.

"Tell me more!"

"Oh, we busted into Brinleys'—damn dog, it bit Lane. He's mad as hell. We been here twice. Asey, he's burglarized the town offices, with all that gang of you below. He—"

"But there were new locks on the offices, he told me so. After Prettyman got in. And say, what's become of Tertius?"

"Oh, he's okay. Asey phoned him tonight. I don't know why. No, locks don't bother Asey. He went to sea with a burglar mate once, and he learned all the tricks. And the fellow he had with him helped—"

"What fellow?"

Hamilton shrugged. "Asey brought him from Boston—"

"From Boston?"

"Yeah. He's been there today, didn't you know? I don't know the man and nobody told me who he is. While Asey was doing that, we combed around the hollow—oh, I almost forgot. We held up your photographer and we kidnapped General Philbrick."

"Buck—what for? And the General—" Kay shook her head. "Hamilton, this is pure Munchausening!"

"No, sir," Hamilton protested. "The General didn't mind coming. He seemed to like it. Lane and I did the hold-up. We stole his rain coat and his pictures of the exhibition—"

"I know it's a lie," Kay said. "Buck only has negatives, not pictures—"

"Pictures," Hamilton said firmly. "Local man developed 'em. For the winners. Pictures taken yesterday. Lane and I put on long coats and tied handkerchiefs around our faces, and held him up in his car, just outside where he rooms. We tied him up. Little later we came along as police and undid him and gave him everything back. Asey'd already found out what he wanted. He was waiting in the bushes. Anyway, Buck thinks we're swell. But what Asey wanted a lot of pictures of jelly and string beans for, nobody knows!"

"Jelly!" Kay said. "It's insane—hurry up. I can't stand this suspense!"

Inside the Randall house, Asey greeted her absentmindedly.

"You, huh? 'Bout time. Wait outside, Ham. Sit down, Kay. Listen an' don't interrupt. You got a job."

She was white-faced when she came out on the porch a short while afterwards.

"Did he tell you?" Hamilton asked eagerly. "Did he—hey—you're lighting the cork end! Did he tell—"

"Hamilton!" Asey's voice had the quarterdeck ring to it.

"Yes, sir!" Hamilton raced indoors.

"Go to the Town Hall," Asey said. "Just before the last dance, give these notes to Mr. an' Mrs. Leach, Weston, Brinley, his wife, Win Billings, Madame Meaux, an' Jane an' Slade. Give this one to Zeb an' see he starts right along. Corral the others an' take'em to Aunt Sara's, an' see they go, an' stay. Lane or someone'll tell you what to do from there. Get'em all, an' keep'em all, see? Beat it!"

Of all the group assembled finally in Aunt Sara's living room, no one was more bewildered than Hamilton himself.

Lane came at last.

"All here? Come along, please."

He marshalled them into their cars, whispered orders to Hamilton, and acted as a rear guard to the procession up to the hollow.

"Now," he said, "if you'll come indoors—"

"Why?" Sara demanded with asperity. "What is this nonsense? Why—"

"Asey's orders, ma'am," Lane said with finality.

Asey himself came out in a moment.

"Sorry to keep you waitin'," he said, "but on the whole, I thought it might be a good thing to have you all here together. Some things has got to be cleared up—"

Another figure appeared behind him.

"My God!" Brinley said in a choked voice. "Paterson!"

"The auditor!" Sara's voice was even more choked.

"If you'll all come in," Asey said blandly, "maybe we can settle some things."

He was tremendously solicitous about finding seats for them all in the living room. Sara couldn't help thinking how her grey cat had the same manner while he waited at a mouse hole—bland, casual, and apparently not a bit eager.

"Now," Asey said, "do let's get this shortage fixed up first."

Sara and Jeff exchanged glances.

"My fault," Jeff said promptly. "I know. I'm getting too old—I—I might as well face it, I suppose. Whatever the amount is, I'll make it good, Paterson. And then I'll resign and let someone else take my place. On my word of honor, Sara and I have slaved over those figures—what's that, Bessie?"

Mrs. Brinley was muttering reproachful things under her breath.

"I wouldn't," Asey said, "look quite so smug, Mrs. Brinley. Paterson's found you an' J. Arthur out."

J. Arthur's shoulders sagged. He seemed to shrink.

"Asey," Weston said, "which of'em is it? For my part, I've worked over the books, and worked over'em, and—"

"All Brinley," Asey said. "He didn't dare play with your figures as much as with Jeff's. You wrote that note to Slade, didn't you, Brinley?"

FIGURE AWAY

"I—yes, I did! But what about Jeff and Sara? Where were they on Monday night?" Brinley said. "Where were they when Mary Randall was killed? What—"

"Think they're so much!" Bessie said darkly. "Think they're so much—where were they, and why should Arthur and I be persecuted by—"

"Bessie," Sara's voice was like an icicle, "I'd stop, right there!"

"Jeff Leach's too old to try and run things!" Bessie said. "Blaming his dotage on Arthur! The old—"

Aunt Sara stood up, and in a few brief words, she told Bessie Brinley what she had been aching to tell her for years. Not to be outdone, Bessie got up. Her voice rose and drowned Aunt Sara out.

Asey silenced her.

"We're not gettin' ahead, here. Let's consider this shortage, an' let's consider the problem of motive— Bessie Brinley, shut up! First things seemed to be against the town, an' then against Mary Randall, an' then Jane—with so much planted on her, an' then Eloise. As a matter of fact, we got just two motives. One's money—the town's money. The other's pure hate. The money come first, an' the hate come in later. The money come in because someone got ambitious, an' the hate part's mostly on account of Jane Warren—what'n time's the matter, out there, Hamilton?"

"I didn't hear anything," Hamilton said truthfully.

"Go see—"

Hamilton went outdoors. When he returned his face was drained of color.

"Asey—that figure! Asey, look—look out the window!"

The whole group rushed to the front door, and every head

turned toward the four figures, more grotesque than ever under the moonlight.

"What figure?" Sara said. "They—it's moving!"

"Nonsense," Jeff said.

But one of the figures *was* moving.

It fell down, righted itself, and stood up again. The face was a glob of chalky white, apparently without any features at all. Suddenly it wheeled and ran with a peculiar swaying stride around to the back of the house.

"The kitchen, Lane!" Asey yelled. "Cut it off, outside there! We'll go through the house—"

He avoided the skeptical eyes of Madame Meaux as he rushed out to the kitchen, with the rest following pell mell behind him.

"Snap on the lights, Hamilton!" Asey ordered. "They—well, light that candle if they don't work, then—my God!"

There was no sight or trace of the beaver-hatted dummy, but at the head of the cellar stairs appeared an odd glaring light, and a smell that Mike Slade vaguely associated with fireworks.

"What'n time," Asey began, "is—"

"Jane!" It was Eloise Randall's voice that sounded from the cellar. "I really think—that is, of course—"

Mike Slade blinked. He almost seemed to see Eloise before him, in that old checked skirt with the uneven hem and the baggy cardigan with the hole in the sleeve.

"Eloise!" he said, and put out a hand to prop up Mrs. Brinley.

"Of course if Jane really wants—I mean, one can't really tell, can one? Can one, Weston? Weston thought, at least, I think he thought, that he killed me yesterday, but Weston—where are you, Weston—"

FIGURE AWAY

Sara Leach swung around. Weston had been standing behind her and Jeff.

"Weston!" Sara said. "He's gone! He—he's gone! He was right here, but he's slipped away—"

"Okay," Asey said. "Lights, Hamilton. No, Mike, don't follow. Come up from the cellar, Kay. Zeb, come out of the closet—"

"Asey," Sara said, "what—you don't mean that it was Weston, do you? You—are you letting him get away?"

A series of shots outside answered her question.

In a moment, Lane came in.

"I got as far as 'I arrest,'" he said. "He said, we'd never get him alive, and we didn't. There's his gun. The silencer's in his car. Here. He said to give it to you—"

Asey turned away. It came over Madame Meaux that Weston was his cousin. After a second he turned back, as calm as ever. There, the soprano thought, was New England for you.

"Look after things, Lane," Asey said. "Kay, that was fine. You d'serve prizes for your imitatin'. Wash the dough off Zeb's face. It drives me crazy. I'm sorry, the rest of you. We had to do it. We give him a chance to admit it, but we had to keep on an' try his imagination—what is it, Sara?"

"A chair," Sara said. "And a glass of water. Asey, I don't—I can't believe it!"

She stared at Kay as the girl washed thick dough from Zeb's face. The dummy's clothes hung limply from his body. General Philbrick came up from the cellar.

"How was the effect?" he inquired. "I think it worked, don't you? Down there it was fine."

He took two pans to the sink and nonchalantly began to

wash them. Already in his mind he saw the headlines. "Fireworks Magnate Aids Capture of Murderer. Philbrick's Fireworks Help Detective."

"Asey," Sara said, "I shall go mad—hurry and tell us, and get Jeff a chair. He's shaking—"

"Was it Weston's accounts?" Jeff asked in a forced voice. "Weston's?"

"I don't wonder," Asey said, "you thought you was gettin' old. Brinley's been gyppin' in a small way, to make you seem dumb, but Weston knew, an' was doin' a much better job on top of that. We got all the books tonight, from everywhere—town offices, your house, Weston's, Brinley's. Win Billings said it didn't seem a town like this could be so much in the red, an' for fun I went to Boston an' got Paterson today. Didn't know then which of you three selectmen it was. It'll take Paterson weeks to straighten things out, but Weston's plucked a hundred odd thousand, an' judgin' from his calculations, he—"

"What?" Jeff said. "A hundred thousand?"

"Over a period of years. He aimed to get as much more this week. He also had two steamship tickets for tomorrow night."

"No wonder," Slade said grimly, "no wonder he wanted to make Old Home Week a success!"

"What do you mean, two tickets?" Sara asked. "Why two?"

"For him, an' Eloise."

"For him and—and Eloise?" Sara said. "And Eloise? I—I never thought. But everyone thought that was off."

"It wasn't. Jane, Eloise hated you, didn't she? And she hated Mary, too. Get Cummings to tell you the name for it, but it's a sort of general thwartedness. Eloise was ineffectual, an' her mother wasn't. It riled Eloise. She was also gettin' along in years, an' the state of single blessedness sort of went to her head."

"Then it was Eloise, and Weston, at night!" Jane said. "She told Mary it was me, meeting Mike!"

"Eloise wormed out Weston's plans to take his money an' grab a boat," Asey said. "She prob'ly said, me too. They planned to clean up an' beat it, tomorrow. As time goes on, Eloise thinks how nice it'd be to make a clean sweep. An' then Saturday, Tertius Prettyman brings over this policy of Mary's. I called him, and he said Eloise seen it. Seen it was for Jane. It—"

"For me?" Jane said. "Oh! I saw the policy around, but I never looked, or asked. I didn't know that!"

"That was the last straw," Asey said, "for Eloise. She called Weston, and told him Mary Randall had found out. They'd have to kill her. I'm sure her murder was no part of their plannin' before. So Weston calls me in—"

"What on earth for?" Sara demanded. "And what about the shootings, and the fires, and all the sabotage?"

"Why does a magician have a pretty girl in his troupe?" Asey asked. "Why's he tell funny stories? Just so you'll be twice as amazed when the bird goes into the cage an' melts away. Of course he called me. You don't arrest the feller who calls the cop for help. Now he begun this sabotage with an idea of takin' folks' minds off the town accounts an' such durin' a crucial time. In case you get suspicious, here's this menace to hang your suspicions on. That's how it begun. Then Eloise tells Wes that her mother's found out—Mary's got to be killed."

"*Did* she know?" Sara asked.

"I thought so at first, because Jane said she wanted to see me. I think now, she wanted to have me find out what was goin' on up here nights. But it was Eloise's opportunity, an' she had someone else to do the dirty work. All the sabotage could pave the way for a murder, just as nice. They planned on the fireworks noise. An' Weston went through with it for Eloise—"

"Lady Macbeth," Kay said.

"Sort of. Now Weston come here from the fire, an' he got back uptown in time to r'turn with Lane an' the doc. General Philbrick's told me how Wes popped in' an' out b'fore the fire, an' after, sayin' he had 'Town Stuff' to attend to. After the fire—which he set—at Slade's, he cut over here, posed in the dummy, shoots Mary, an' rips uptown. He stole Jane's gun she give Slade, to have if he needed to plant clews. Used his own gun, though. Know where we found it?"

"I know," Jeff said. "At least, I guess. At the town offices, hanging over his desk."

"Exactly," Asey said. "Nicest place to hide a gun, in full sight of all. That's why Weston was so jittery when Tertius broke in there. After he found out all was well, he calmed down. It matches up with the shells we found in the dummy, his gun does. Oh, he had to plant things, Slade, because you didn't react right. You went off the handle an' forced his hand. He planted that note in your studio, even though Brinley wrote it."

"That laugh," Zeb said. "What about that?"

Lane passed over a small, oddly shaped metal object.

"This," Asey said, "this thing here. It was a signal for Eloise—an' partly just to mock us, later. Where'd you get it, Ham?"

"Weston's pocket. It's like the one you found in Eloise's things."

"Nice signal," Asey said. "Not somethin' that'd attract a crowd. All right, to get back. Weston plants shells an' Jane's

FIGURE AWAY 283

gun. We don't fall for'em. He comes here to try an' get his own shells from the dummy's pocket. He gets thwarted by Kay an' me an' the troopers. He's gettin' scared, an' I think he's beginnin' to figure Eloise double-crossed him an' that Mary Randall didn't know a thing. That chase let you out, Jeff, an' Brinley, just from the physical end of it. Now, we get to day before yest'day."

"Historical Day," Brinley said automatically.

"Also judgin' day," Asey said, "for the exhibitions an' contests in the hall. Historical tours. Weston slipped off on one of the tours, an' sneaked in here. Came to see Eloise, found her goin' down cellar, an' realized that he had his opportunity, the opportunity of his life, to get rid of her. He did. That night he made one last attempt to get the shells he'd left in the figure's pocket—sure, it was him we chased in Lane's car, Kay. He left the car an' beat it for Brinleys, an' got a swell alibi out of Amos. He strung me up there, though. Jeff an' Lane an' Brinley said he called'em, but we looked into the calls. He made'em enroute, not from his house. And there you are."

"Maybe," Kay said, "but the jelly—the beachplum jelly? What about that?"

Asey smiled. "After the judgin', that photographer took all the prize stuff, the veg'tables an' preserves an' all, to another room to make pictures of'em. Bertha's prize jelly was among the stuff. He an' Weston carted the stuff there, so as to take the pictures with the background of the big banner an' the cups— Weston wouldn't let the cups be moved. The photographer, General Philbrick remembers, had on his rain coat. Later, he took it off. He left Bertha's jelly in his rain coat pocket."

"What of it?" Kay said.

"Weston, in a hurry to see Eloise, grabs the photographer's rain coat for his own. They're most duplicates. In the kitchen here, Eloise, at the head of the stairs, throws the shears at him when she realizes somethin's happenin'. They strike the rain coat pocket. Pop goes the jelly. We got Buck's coat, where Weston cleaned it up. Buck didn't notice it, but Lane found enough to prove our point. Weston has to have prize jelly. So he goes down cellar, grabs a jar of jelly from the preserve closet—well, it's a book case that acts as one—an' later puts the labels from Bertha's jar on it. Takes it back to the show. Been all right, if Bertha hadn't given me the jelly as a present."

"How'd you know the jelly came from here?" Kay asked.

"I thought an' thought," Asey said honestly, "an' the only person I could think of who could make as bad jelly as that was Eloise. I r'membered the preserves in the cellar, an' hotfooted it up here, an' found what was supposed to be Bertha's was a mate to the stuff in this cellar. Took a little connectin', but it proved someone who had to do with the judgin', or the town, had been here. Wasn't the photographer. He spent the rest of the afternoon at the hall. I could place Brinley, an' Jeff. 'Bout that time, Paterson was sure of one or the other of you. But I could place you—that's the advantage of havin' wives. Weston started out to guide one of the historical tours, but he eased out on account of 'Town Stuff.' He came here, an' then rejoined his tour. An' r'member one more thing about Weston's bein' a bachelor. He wouldn't see the error of switchin' jelly, like Brinley or you, Jeff."

"I still don't see," Jeff said. "But—yes, I do too. The more he protested that this trouble would have to come to light, and ruin the week, and the town, the more it spurred you on, Asey,

FIGURE AWAY

and the rest, to keep it quiet. And then he had Eloise to play the trump card, and say that her mother would have wanted it kept undercover, to help the town. He bullied us into silence with his dolefulness. And he was the last person *you'd* suspect, Asey, too. By the time things got out, he would have been gone. He's a planner. Mathematical minded—why did he plant so much against Jane?"

Asey smiled. "Jane," he said, "when Weston first come here, did he specifically announce that he come to call on Eloise?"

"Why, no, but—"

"You thought so, but he come to see you," Asey said. "Yes, that's so. Up to his house, we found four pictures of you. He come to see you, but he got Eloise. Does that clear some of that up? You naturally turned him over to Eloise, an' she done the rest. She hated you, an' I guess by then he did, too. An' then you want to r'member, on them chases we had, on foot an' by car, he—he thought like a Mayo, pretty much. An' today, when I seen him up to the ball park, runnin' around, an' winnin' the tug of war, an' all, I—well, there you are. Weston b'gun it an' Eloise finished it, an' him. Town money, an' a lot of hate."

Sunday night's fireworks wound up Billingsgate's Old Home Week.

Asey, a little apart from the crowd, watched the big cross with all the little crosses around it melt out of sight. Upjohn's band struck up "Billingsgate Beautiful," and Madame Meaux, with the expression of one tried beyond endurance but none the less determined to endure still more, began the song. She sang it with infinite care, and for the first time, Asey heard most of the words.

> *"Where e'er the wandering foot may roam,*
> *On foreign land or sea,*
> *Our thoughts turn ever more to Home,*
> *Oh Billingsgate to thee."*

He saw Kay and Zeb sneak away from the crowd to Zeb's car. Jeff and Sara and the Brinleys stood by the grandstand spotlight, and something about their fixed smiles made Asey think of the stars at the final curtain on a Saturday matinee.

Upjohn's band arose, and crashed into the "Star Spangled Banner." They played it through twice before, rather belatedly, there burst across the end of the ball park Philbrick's finest special, an enormous American flag. Mike Slade, Asey noticed, was the only person present who knew the third verse of the national anthem. Everyone else was humming self-consciously.

"Billingsgate," Asey said, "Boom!" and walked to his car.

Today's papers had no story of Mary Randall and all the rest, but tomorrow's would. It was time for him to get along.

Half an hour later, the "Rock and Roll" set out from his wharf.

Asey, at the wheel, spoke to his cousin Syl.

"Take Win b'low an' get him into his bunk."

"D'want to go t'bed," Win said. "Want t'stay an' watch. Ain't been out this harbor in years."

"You won't get no bluefish," Asey warned him, "if you don't get some sleep!"

"Huh," Win said. "Anyone can catch a bluefish!"

Available from Foul Play Press

The perennially popular Phoebe Atwood Taylor whose droll "Codfish Sherlock," Asey Mayo, and "Shakespeare lookalike," Leonidas Witherall, have been eliciting guffaws from proper Bostonian Brahmins for over half a century.

Asey Mayo Cape Cod Mysteries

The Annulet of Gilt	*288 pages*	*$5.95*
The Asey Mayo Trio	*256 pages*	*$5.95*
Banbury Bog	*176 pages*	*$4.95*
The Cape Cod Mystery	*192 pages*	*$5.95*
The Criminal C.O.D.	*288 pages*	*$5.95*
The Crimson Patch	*240 pages*	*$5.95*
The Deadly Sunshade	*297 pages*	*$5.95*
Death Lights a Candle	*304 pages*	*$5.95*
Diplomatic Corpse	*256 pages*	*$5.95*
Figure Away	*288 pages*	*$5.95*
Going, Going, Gone	*218 pages*	*$5.95*
The Mystery of the Cape Cod Players	*272 pages*	*$5.95*
The Mystery of the Cape Cod Tavern	*283 pages*	*$5.95*
Octagon House	*304 pages*	*$5.95*
Out of Order	*280 pages*	*$5.95*
The Perennial Boarder	*288 pages*	*$5.95*
Proof of the Pudding	*192 pages*	*$5.95*
Sandbar Sinister	*296 pages*	*$5.95*
Spring Harrowing	*288 pages*	*$5.95*
Three Plots for Asey Mayo	*320 pages*	*$6.95*

"Surely, under whichever pseudonym, Mrs. Taylor is the mystery equivalent of Buster Keaton." —Dilys Winn

Leonidas Witherall Mysteries (by "Alice Tilton")

Beginning with a Bash	*284 pages*	*$5.95*
File for Record	*287 pages*	*$5.95*
Hollow Chest	*284 pages*	*$5.95*
The Left Leg	*275 pages*	*$5.95*

Available from bookshops, or by mail from the publisher: The Countryman Press, Box 175, Woodstock, Vermont 05091-0175. Please include $2.50 for shipping your order. Visa or Mastercard orders ($20.00 minimum), call 802-457-1049, 9-5 EST, Monday–Friday.

Now Back in Print

Margot Arnold

The complete adventures of Margot Arnold's beloved pair of peripatetic sleuths, Penny Spring and Sir Toby Glendower:

The Cape Cod Caper	*192 pages*	*$ 4.95*
The Catacomb Conspiracy	*260 pages*	*$18.95*
Death of a Voodoo Doll	*220 pages*	*$ 4.95*
Death on the Dragon's Tongue	*224 pages*	*$ 4.95*
Exit Actors, Dying	*176 pages*	*$ 4.95*
Lament for a Lady Laird	*221 pages*	*$ 5.95*
The Menehune Murders	*272 pages*	*$ 5.95*
Toby's Folly (hardcover)	*256 pages*	*$18.95*
Zadock's Treasure	*192 pages*	*$ 4.95*

Joyce Porter

American readers, having faced several lean years deprived of the company of Chief Inspector Wilfred Dover, will rejoice (so to speak) in the reappearance of "the most idle and avaricious policeman in the United Kingdom (and, possibly, the world)." Here is the series that introduced the bane of Scotland Yard and his hapless assistant, Sgt. MacGregor, to international acclaim.

Dover One	*192 pages*	*$ 5.95*
Dover Two	*222 pages*	*$ 4.95*
Dover Three	*192 pages*	*$ 4.95*
Dead Easy for Dover	*176 pages*	*$ 5.95*
Dover and the Unkindest Cut of All	*188 pages*	*$ 5.95*
Dover Beats the Band (hardcover)	*176 pages*	*$ 17.95*
Dover Goes to Pott	*192 pages*	*$ 5.95*
Dover Strikes Again	*202 pages*	*$ 5.95*

"Meet Detective Chief Inspector Wilfred Dover. He's fat, lazy, a scrounger and the worst detective at Scotland Yard. But you will love him." —*Manchester Evening News*

Available from bookshops, or by mail from the publisher: The Countryman Press, Box 175, Woodstock, Vermont 05091-0175. Please include $2.50 for shipping your order. Visa or Mastercard orders ($20.00 minimum), call 802-457-1049, 9-5 EST, Monday–Friday.

Prices and availability subject to change.